RD046728

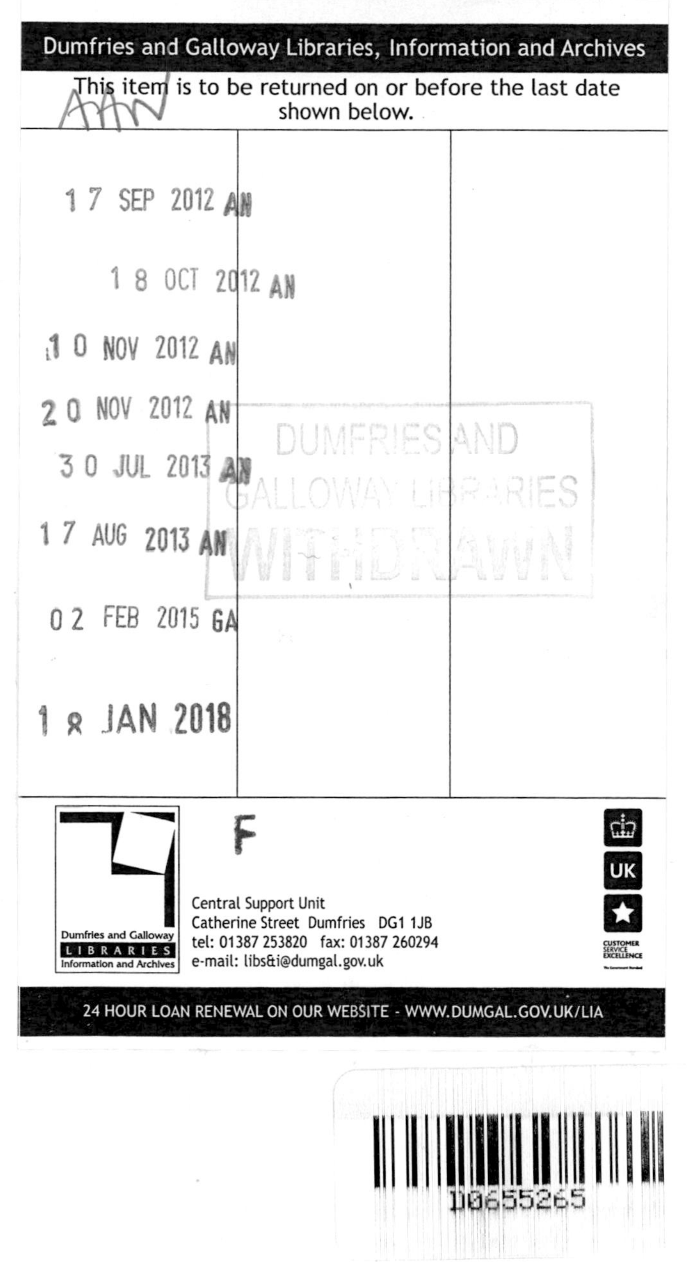
Dumfries and Galloway Libraries, Information and Archives

This item is to be returned on or before the last date shown below.

17 SEP 2012 AN
18 OCT 2012 AN
10 NOV 2012 AN
20 NOV 2012 AN
30 JUL 2013 AN
17 AUG 2013 AN
02 FEB 2015 GA
18 JAN 2018

DUMFRIES AND GALLOWAY LIBRARIES WITHDRAWN

F

Dumfries and Galloway LIBRARIES Information and Archives

Central Support Unit
Catherine Street Dumfries DG1 1JB
tel: 01387 253820 fax: 01387 260294
e-mail: libs&i@dumgal.gov.uk

UK CUSTOMER SERVICE EXCELLENCE

24 HOUR LOAN RENEWAL ON OUR WEBSITE - WWW.DUMGAL.GOV.UK/LIA

10655265

PHILIP HENSHER'S novels include *Kitchen Venom*, which won the Somerset Maugham Award, *Other Lulus* and *The Mulberry Empire*, which was longlisted for the Man Booker Prize, shortlisted for the WH Smith 'People's Choice' Award and highlighted by no fewer than twelve reviewers as their 'book of the year'. Chosen by Granta to appear on their prestigious, once-a-decade list of the twenty best young British novelists, Philip Hensher is also a columnist for the *Independent* and chief book reviewer for the *Spectator*. He lives in south London.

From the reviews for *The Bedroom of the Mister's Wife*

'Enlivened by sharpness of detail and phrasing . . . ranging from Brussels to Prague, from Germany to an unnamed outpost of empire, and, above all, London and its suburbs, Hensher's tales are cleverly intriguing, willed but entertainingly stylish.' *Sunday Times*

'If novels are relationships, then short stories are one-night stands. They're tempting, but do they amount to anything? Well, Hensher proves they can. Like the truly great short story writers, he spins brief, strange, exciting tales that seem as satisfying as novels . . . If the stories weren't funny – laugh-out-loud funny in places – this might seem a tense, introverted collection. But it's not. Hensher's humour makes it just about warm and sweet enough – sometimes really beautiful . . . astonishing.'

JULIE MYERSON, *Mail on Sunday*

'[A] cool, unsettling collection' *Spectator*

'One of the arresting foreground figures in any prospect of contemporary British fiction' *Observer*

'An ominous and skilful collection' *Guardian*

'[A] nastiness that keeps you reading and giggling'
Evening Standard

'From a nice young married couple buying their first flat to a strange erotic nightmare set in Istanbul; an eccentric Russian landlady who sweetens her tea with cheap strawberry jam and wages war on a friend who may or may not be Stalin's daughter. Particularly recommended is a tale called To Feed the Night – a brilliant modern horror story about an estate agent who is not what he seems . . . The thread that draws them all together is Hensher's clever, deceptively plain writing style, which illuminates a tremendous amount but keeps parts of the stories unexplained, so that you feel compelled to read them again to tease out a solution.' *Daily Mail*

By the same author

OTHER LULUS
KITCHEN VENOM
PLEASURED
THE MULBERRY EMPIRE
THE FIT

THE BEDROOM OF THE MISTER'S WIFE

Philip Hensher

HARPER PERENNIAL

Harper Perennial
An imprint of HarperCollins*Publishers*
77–85 Fulham Palace Road
Hammersmith
London W6 8JB

www.harpercollins.co.uk/ha

This edition published by H

1

First published by Chatto &

Copyright © Philip Henshe

Philip Hensher asserts the m
be identified as the author o

DUMFRIES &
GALLOWAY
LIBRARIES
046728
Askews & Holts
M-9

A catalogue record for this
available from the British Li

ISBN 0-00-718019-5

Typeset in Stempel Garamond and Diotima by
Palimpsest Book Production Limited, Polmont, Stirlingshire

Printed and bound in Great Britain by
Clays Ltd, St Ives plc.

All rights reserved. No part of this publication may be reproduced, stored in a retrieval system, or transmitted, in any form or by any means, electronic, mechanical, photocopying, recording or otherwise, without the prior permission of the publishers.

This book is sold subject to the condition that it shall not, by way of trade or otherwise, be lent, re-sold, hired out or otherwise circulated without the publisher's prior consent in any form of binding or cover other than that in which it is published and without a similar condition including this condition being imposed on the subsequent purchaser.

For Alan Hollinghurst

They say such different things at school.

— CONTENTS —

WHITE GOODS

So Vera said to me, 'Oh, oh, oh. You English. You have no idea. You young. You have everything. You have no idea. No notion' – she often produced these English words she was so proud of knowing – 'no notion of what it is to fly your country with terrible fear of death, with nothing. I have nothing, still, and you young, you have everything. You have no notion.'

I looked around me at Vera's red and purple drawing room, with its teapots and seven little tables, each draped with three table cloths, and the china dogs elbowing each other out of the way on the mantelpiece, and the curtain, and the under-curtain, and the net curtain, pulled across, and the second net curtain underneath it, for privacy. It was a room impossible to walk across. It was a room a Tsar could have lived in, if he had had to live in a two-bedroomed house on the outskirts of Cambridge. There was one beautiful thing in it, a tiny portrait of a fierce bearded man propped up like a Christmas card, and everything else was plush and velvet and unspeakable but somehow nice. 'No,' I said. 'I don't suppose I have.'

'Ha,' she said. 'You English.'

For Vera, all foreigners were English. But I was English, actually.

I suppose I ought to say how I ended up in Vera's house. I don't know. I was a painter once, although this seems to surprise most people. I don't paint any more; I stopped after I left Cambridge. I started because I thought for a while I was good at it. My teachers at school told me I should carry on after I got an A level, and I did. Like most painters, I had no money, but like most people, I needed a place to live. My parents were poor, or poor by the standards I now have; although they did not seem especially poor to me then, they certainly could not have supported me in my romantic ideas. One of my romantic ideas was that I would live in someone's house for nothing, someone who adored the way I painted, and felt privileged I was their lodger. Or – a still more romantic idea – that I would live in someone's house and, instead of rent, paint a picture each month for them. After a year, they would be no richer, but they would have twelve marvellous paintings, and they'd be glad of it. Where I got the notion – as Vera would say – that there were such patient people in the world I do not know. But there are not.

Instead, there was Vera; and I would say how she ended up in her house; except that I have no idea. She did not tell me her autobiography as she interviewed me for her room. I supposed, wrongly, that once I had moved in she would tell me how she fled from the Communist hordes clutching a suitcase and leaving her diamonds behind. I was wrong to think that she would tell me all this, and she certainly did not tell me as I sat in her over-filled, overred drawing room.

'Twenty pounds only,' she said, instead, stirring the teapot. 'Very cheap, very clean.'

'I am clean myself,' I said, sitting on the edge of my chair in a clean shirt and a pair of trousers.

'I did not suggest you were not. I have to think about it.'

She poured herself a cup of tea. On the tray in front of her was a pot of raspberry jam – not a very delicious sort, but a sort that was pink with chemicals and not fruit. She took a spoonful of the jam, and stirred it into her tea. She did not offer me anything, and I was to come to learn that the raspberry jam was kept by Vera for Vera's sole use.

'Very well,' she said after a time. 'You may live here. Would you witness my will and testament, please?'

'Your will?' I said.

'Yes,' Vera said. 'I have just changed it, and my signature needs to be witnessed, if you please.'

She pushed the piece of paper over the table to me. It was written in an improbably beautiful copperplate hand.

'You may write this address as your address after your signature,' she said. 'I do not think it matters a great deal. I will tell you where you can find the will, once I have decided on a safe hiding place.'

Over the next year, I witnessed Vera's signature half a dozen times. She was very well up on the law about wills – which she always called 'will and testament' – and was forever changing her tiny legacies. When I got to know her better, I understood that what she fantasised about was everyone turning up after the funeral, to claim their prize, old friends and lovers and enemies, all in an embarrassing huddle. I don't think she quite understood she wouldn't be there. Her great obsession – what she was constantly concerned with – was the idea that her last will might be lost and a previous, discredited one adhered to.

It was quite a nice room, Vera's spare room, although the bed sagged in a hammocky way, and the violently flowery wallpaper, crawling over the ceiling and even the panels of the door was immediately oppressive, and there was no view of anything whatsoever. Which suited me. The only problem, in fact, was Vera, who was incapable of having someone in her house without having them in her life.

'Young man,' she said a day or two after I moved in. 'When I die, you will find my last will and testament under the bed. The most recent will, the one you witnessed so kindly for me. Do not forget. Or Stalin's daughter will come to take the lot.'

'Stalin's daughter?' I said, laughing. 'Who is Stalin's daughter?'

'Stalin's daughter? Stalin's daughter?' Vera said. 'Have you never heard of Stalin?'

'Yes, of course,' I said.

'Well, Stalin's daughter is the daughter of Stalin,' Vera said. 'I am glad you think it funny. You have strange notions of amusingness, young man.'

'Do you know her?' I said, marginally astounded.

'Yes,' Vera said. She immediately got up and left the room, dramatically.

The next day, curiously, Stalin's daughter came to the house.

'I am Svetlana,' the very firmly dressed woman on the doorstep said. 'I wish to see Vera.'

'I am not here,' a muffled shout came from upstairs.

'I wish to see Vera,' Svetlana said pointedly.

'She isn't here,' I said, hopelessly.

Svetlana turned and went.

'She gave me a refrigerator, you see,' Vera said, coming downstairs. 'She thinks I am poor. And I am poor, and I took the refrigerator. But that does not mean she can insult me and expect me to go on being grateful to her.'

It was characteristic of Vera that she had taken to referring to the refrigerator itself as 'Stalin's Daughter'. It was an enormous white humming affair, into which she put, without discrimination, every item of food she ever bought. I wonder now what I put into the fridge; and, indeed, what I ate then. When I compare how I shop now, our immense trips to the immense supermarkets we drive to, tossing tiny expensive bottles and curious breakfast cereals into the wheeled cage until we have spent enough money, to the way I tried to buy food then, I wonder. I remember going to the supermarket after five in order to buy bread which had been reduced in price, because it was stale; I know that I ate so much tinned tuna and so many tinned chick-peas that for years afterwards I felt sick at the smell of them. I think I was effectively a vegetarian, because meat was expensive. I only ate meat if it was very poor offal, or if Vera took pity on me and cooked something for me. Which, now I think of it, she did not.

A week after I had first done so, I asked Vera again how she knew Stalin's daughter. She corrected me.

'I did know her once,' she said, her eyes closed as if to envisage her. 'I do not know her any more. This is the letter I have written to her.' She whisked out a piece of blue lined paper from underneath the cushions on the sofa.

'Stalin's daughter,' the letter began, 'you are a brute, a murderer and a KGB agent.' Above KGB, in pencil, giving way to the flood of her inspiration, Vera had written 'Triple' with three exclamation marks after it.

'You cannot know,' Vera said chuckling, 'what Stalin's daughter has done to me.'

Taken some jam without asking, probably, I thought, but said nothing.

'I detested her when I first saw her, when we were both children, and I was right to detest her. I was mad to agree to meet her in Cambridge. She is here to destroy my life. She has always worked and planned against me in her money-making schemes.'

'I didn't know you knew her before you came here,' I said. 'Odd that you should end up in the same place.'

'Ha ha ha,' Vera said mirthlessly. 'Odd, he says, that Stalin's daughter should follow me here. Strange, he thinks, that Stalin should send his daughter to follow me. The strange thing is – you want to know the strangest thing, young man? You want to know? The strange thing is that I, Vera, am here, and have nothing, and accept the gifts of a daughter of a man like Stalin.'

'Extraordinary,' I said, since I didn't know what she meant.

'I whose lands once stretched to the horizon and beyond,' Vera started. I concentrated on my tea. Once Vera hit on a White Russian vein in her monologue, there was no point in listening.

'And a woman like that,' she wound up, 'a woman with the blood of nobody in her body, gives me a refrigerator. Bloody, bloody thing.'

She went into the kitchen and kicked Stalin's Daughter. I could hear it whinnying slightly.

Vera's campaigns against Svetlana once got as far as her standing, stout-booted, in the market square with a petition against Svetlana, Daughter of Stalin, and Her Deeds. Too angry and shy to accost anyone, her petition went unsigned until the lady with the CND petition and the gentleman with the anti-apartheid petition took her for a cup of tea in the cellar coffee shop in the market-place and wrote their names on the crumpled sheet. Vera, who grew quickly merry with tea and toast, found the signatures of two petitioners against Svetlana, Daughter of Stalin, too much of a temptation, and forged a third signature in a cunningly backward-slanting hand. She never quite got the hang of English names, and what she wrote was Miss Susan Michael Selection, out of what Russian name I could not guess. Absentmindedly, however, or not trusting to her powers of invention, the address she added was her own.

'You see?' she said. 'Three people feel the same as I do. And,' she added mysteriously, 'I did not ask everyone.'

'Oh good,' I said.

The next day Svetlana came to tea, and after that it was quite all right. What I had thought of as a serious breach turned out to be a tiny annual feud, which needed almost no reason to set it off. I dare say Svetlana – a woman I was allowed to answer the door to, but almost never allowed to talk to – herself needed a break from Vera from time to time. I thought of her, though I did not get to know her, as a woman of quite unStalin-like patience. I used sometimes to pass the red crowded sitting room when they were there together, and listen to the effortful English they strangely used to talk to each other.

I had few friends in Cambridge, and, while I lived at Vera's house, I relished the few a great deal. I have never had the knack of making friends, which I heard once defined as the art of being a good listener. I ought to be a good listener, since I am not talkative, and people sometimes think me shy. That does not seem to be the answer. I knew three boys in Cambridge who I had known at school, but I liked them no better in Cambridge than I had at school, and after two or three months they had amassed enough friends, from their faculties and their colleges and their weekly inter-collegiate societies, not to trouble me any more.

The only people I thought I knew were the people I shared a studio with at the art school. The art school had too many students in it, and too few rooms, so I shared a studio with two other painters and a sculptor. There were two girls who came in very early, who both had black bobs and wore black thick tights and black mini-skirts and lived on black coffee and no lunch. They both painted enormous blank or scribbled canvases in little time, and they were both short and pale. I told them apart because one smoked and the other didn't, but that was all the difference I could see. They looked at my little pointlessly detailed canvases, and did not bother to criticise my foolish attempts to make a bit of cloth look like something it wasn't. Perhaps they were right not to say anything.

The sculptor was a pink-faced boy with a shock of blond hair called James, who came in late in the morning or early in the afternoon. By then, his piles of scrap metal and bits of rubber and packing cases which he found on the street and turned into huge sculptures, of a sort, had often been pushed into a corner by one of the diligent painters. This was a great cause for complaint, and, though I did not exactly like him, we often went out for a drink together in the early evening so that he could complain about the two girls in the studio. Once, I told him about a play of

Sartre I had once seen called *Les Putains Respectueuses*. I immediately regretted it, since he laughed thoroughly for almost five minutes in an insufficiently empty pub, and afterwards would never stop referring to the two perfectly nice, hard-working girls as the *putains respectueuses*, and getting up lurid fantasies of their sex lives for my entertainment, and, worse, seeming to regard the matter as a joke between the two of us. If he ever said, 'Come out for a drink and meet this girl I know,' on the other hand, I usually would. I only remember one girl I met like this, because I married her.

'Where do you come from?' my wife said.

She was not my wife then. She was a girl I had met five minutes before, and we were sitting in a pub over a glass of beer each while James went to buy some cigarettes.

'I come from Nottingham,' I said.

'Nottingham?' she said. 'The Nottingham painter.'

'I am a painter, and I do come from Nottingham,' I said. 'Yes.'

'Are you always going to paint?' she said. 'Or are you going to get a job?'

'Don't say that,' James said, coming back. 'He's a bloody good painter. A bloody genius. Can draw anything. Ask him.'

'Do your paintings sell?' she said.

'I bought one,' James said. 'And I'd buy it again. Bloody brilliant. Not like those old *putains* with their bloody old wank.'

'Draw me, then,' she said.

'All right,' I said. I liked the way she had of looking at me as if she were making a joke out of me; I liked the way she was supposed to be a friend of James, and paid no attention to him, which of course was the way to treat him.

There was an old envelope in the plastic bag I carried things around in. I fished it out and began to draw her.

'Who are the old *putains*?' she said to me. 'Anyway.'

'These horrible old tarts we have to share a bloody studio with, who get in at six o'clock every morning and are sour as bloody old lemons,' James said. 'I was telling you about them. This old bugger calls them the *putains respectueuses*.'

I handed over what I had done. My wife looked at it for a while.

'Is that me?' she said.

'Yes,' I said.

'I don't think I look like that at all,' she said. 'My nose isn't as big as that and my eyes aren't like that. Look, he's made my eyes too close together.'

'Just a sketch,' I said.

'Come on,' James said loyally, 'it looks just like you.'

'I don't think so,' she said.

'I've drawn,' I said, 'what you look like inside. I've drawn your character.'

She looked at the little sketch for a while, and then up at me, her mouth slightly open, and then, without warning, she began to laugh violently. It seemed involuntary and solitary as a fit of hiccoughs, and James and I neither ignored it nor joined in with it. We simply sat and looked at her until she had finished.

'You're wonderful, you are,' she said. 'Has my character got a big nose?'

'I think so,' I said.

'Where did you find this one?' she said to James.

'Behind the shopping centre,' he said. 'I rescue him once a day from the foul clutches of his landlady, who used to be a Russian Grand Duchess and has a million pounds' worth of roubles inside the stuffed corpse of a serf in the attic.'

'Oh yes,' she said, not laughing. 'I ought to be off.'

Svetlana asked Vera to supper at her house.

'I shall not be home a week on Tuesday,' Vera said, casually bustling through the kitchen like a small rhinoceros.

'Why not?' I said.

'None of your business, young man,' she said, making a show of her astonishment. But the news that she had been invited out was too much to keep quiet, and on her way back through the kitchen, she paused. 'I have been invited to a dinner.'

'A dinner party?' I said.

'That is what I said,' Vera said. 'A week on Tuesday.' She refused to tell me who had invited her. Perhaps she felt the fact it was only Svetlana – and it could hardly be anyone else, since Vera knew no one else – would somehow diminish the glamour.

A week on Sunday, Vera called me into her room.

'I should like your advice,' she said. 'I wondered which dress you thought I should wear.'

On the bed she had laid out five dresses. It was impossible to imagine Vera in any of them. Four were chiffon flowery numbers – intimidatingly flowery, actually – and sweetly dated. One was ribboned and boned and lacy and stood up on its own; the sort of cream dress I think Evelyn Waugh describes as manufactured solely for the younger daughters of duchesses. It could only have been Vera's mother's.

'That's rather nice,' I said. 'Isn't it a bit grand?'

'Grand?' Vera said, as if she didn't know the meaning of the word – hadn't invented it, indeed.

'In any case,' I said, poking a bit at it, 'it looks as if the moths have been at it.'

'I see no holes,' Vera said, like Nelson. 'Which do you prefer, of my dresses?'

I chose the least flowery of the chiffon dresses.

'I knew it,' Vera said triumphantly. 'You have no taste whatsoever. You, a painter? That is a dress I could never wear.'

Well, the others are dresses you should never wear, I thought.

On Tuesday I dreaded telling Vera how nice she looked in her cream and lace dress. I would have gone to my studio, but I couldn't face that either. Instead, I went out very early and went to the town library, where I sat all day, looking at the tall books of the works of the great painters. I read not a word. I just looked at the pictures, until I had looked at every painting in every book about painting. I thought about how bad the reproductions of the colours were, and how nice it would be to paint a picture in precisely those muddy reds and muddy blues which merged into each other. This is what I called work. Much of the day I spent going down to the little cafe underground in the market-place for cups of tea.

At seven, the library closed, and I trudged out into the rain, hoping that Vera would have gone out. Hoping against hope. I was passing her room when a dim wail came out of it.

'Oh, young man,' her voice cried.

I ignored her, since I was dripping with rain, the soles of my shoes sucking at the soles of my feet.

Ten minutes later she called me again, more querulously, and this time I went in. As I foresaw, she had put on the cream dress, which, frayed here and there by moths nibbling at it, looked like a slow-motion photograph of an explosion in a dairy. She had succeeded in half-hooking herself into it, but the middle hooks were just too much for her stiff old arms; I don't suppose the makers of the dress thought that anyone would ever wear it who didn't have a maid to stitch them into it.

'I am so sorry, young man,' she said, and in fact she sounded sorry, her voice not just apologetic, but trembling, and perhaps even tearful. 'I wish there was someone else I could ask.'

'Well, all right,' I said meanly. 'I don't like doing it, but I will.'

I noted clinically that she wasn't wearing a bra or a corset, and her brown old flesh squeezed out as I tugged at the dress. It was monstrously tight – she couldn't have worn it for ten years – and when it was done she could not lower her arms from the horizontal.

'How is it?' she asked when I had finished.

'What is that on the bed?' I asked. There was a small plastic bag with what looked like a piece of bloody meat inside it.

'It's a present for Stalin's daughter,' Vera said. 'I was always brought up to take a present, a small one, to dinner parties. I am taking her a very nice joint of pork I saw in the butcher's this morning, who the butcher recommended to me very much.'

'Which the butcher recommended to you,' I said absently. 'I think some flowers would have done.'

'Ha,' Vera said. 'You young people, what do you know?'

'You look quite nice,' I said, in the end.

She had that knack, of wearing you down. When she had gone out, in a rare and significant taxi, I telephoned my wife, on a whim, to ask her out for a drink.

'Where do you live?' I said.

'Where do you live?' she said.

'In a house just over the bridge,' I said, 'I've got an eccentric Russian landlady called Vera. She's got a fridge called Stalin's Daughter.'

'Oh yes,' she said. 'Why is it called Stalin's Daughter?'

'Because Stalin's daughter gave it to her,' I said. 'She lives here, you know, Stalin's daughter.'

'In Cambridge?'

'Yes,' I said. 'They are always having some kind of feud.'

'How interesting,' she said. 'Are you really a painter?'

'Yes,' I said.

'Did you keep that drawing you did of me?'

'No,' I said. 'I could always do another one, a better one, not on the back of an envelope or anything.'

'That would be nice,' she said. 'I'm afraid I was a bit horrible to you that time. It's James really. He just annoys me so much.'

'Me too,' I said. Sometimes people say fateful things, and this was one of those times. If she hadn't said she was annoyed by James, I wonder if I would have seen her again.

'Are you going to carry on being a painter?'

'I don't know,' I said. 'I'll probably get a job.'

'Isn't that a bit sad?' she said.

'Not really,' I said. 'There are worse things. Like being a painter whose paintings nobody wants to buy.'

'Don't your paintings sell? I thought someone bought one?'

'James bought one,' I said. 'Other than that. I would try to give my landlady one instead of a month's rent, if I had the nerve.'

She seemed quite different, and I liked her again, and in a different way.

All afternoon the next day, Vera sat in the drawing room with a great pile of photographs on the sofa, out of shoe boxes, sorting them. I went in around tea-time and sat down. She said nothing.

'How was Svetlana's dinner?' I said.

'Good,' she said.

'What did she cook?'

Vera carried on sorting. She clearly did not want to talk about it.

'Who was there?'

'Oh, oh, Svetlana was there, and I was there, and there were other people there as well. You want some tea, young man?'

She got up and left the room. I sat there for a moment in the dark room, alone. I do not pretend to be able to explain what I now did. On the table next to me there was the portrait I had often admired, of a middle-aged man, or perhaps only seeming middle-aged because of his beard, perhaps quite young. It was not a large portrait; five inches by three and a half. But the work was exquisitely fine, with an untouched hard sheen of glaze which seemed almost enamelled, as if no brush had ever touched the surface. The artist in this tiny space had included so much of the man, the slight slyness of his gaze, the gingery beard which was not thick, but a lacy veil over his starched uncomfortable shirt front. I often wore baggy corduroy trousers with big pockets. It went in easily.

Vera came back with the tea and the pot of raspberry jam, and we chatted for a while about nothing in particular, before I went up to my room to write a letter and read a book I had read before. I put the picture in a drawer; I did not especially want to look at it. It wasn't, in fact, until the day after the day after that that Vera asked me for the picture back, and then asked me to find somewhere else to live after the end of the month. Sometimes I think that it was because of my wife I gave up painting and became a lawyer, but I know I am just indulging myself. It was nothing to do with her. I always knew I would have to stop sooner or later, just as I knew that sooner or later I would have to find somewhere else to live. But we need people to blame for the way our lives go. Vera knew that. And it is nobody's fault but our own, and the things that happen to us are because of how we are.

When I left Vera's house, I felt that her feud with me wouldn't last long. After all, I'd watched her feuds with Svetlana run their course and exhaust themselves. It was easy to anticipate turning up at Vera's house with a large bunch of flowers and letting myself be embraced by her. Or perhaps with a joint of pork. Anyway, it didn't happen. I don't know why. Once I did go and see her, six months or a year after I had moved out. When I rang the doorbell, she inspected me from the window, pulling aside the net curtain. I pretended not to have seen her. I heard her shuffling to the door and peering at me, first through the little fish-eye lens, and then, strangely, through the letterbox. I stood there ringing the doorbell a little longer, but she never answered. And three years after I left Cambridge for a different sort of life, I decided on a whim to go back there.

This time she did answer the door, in her old floral dress. But she didn't know me, or said she didn't, and wouldn't let me in. 'Go away,' she said. 'I am too old.' She didn't say for what. 'You remember me, Vera,' I said, humouring her. I wasn't at all sure that she did. 'I have my own life,' she said. 'I'm not here to entertain you.' In the end I produced my business card, with my address on it, and pressed it on her. She looked at it for a while, but took it, shutting the door without saying goodbye.

Years later, in December, I had to be in Cambridge one day. The business I was there for finished early, and I was on my own. I could have gone back to the office, or home, but instead I went for a walk among the tall colleges with their backs to the narrow streets. I used to see the same faces in the streets every day, and some of them were still here, still walking the streets, a little greyer, a little more crumpled. I walked about like a tourist until it was too cold and beginning to be too dark, and then went into a teashop I used sometimes to go into. There she was.

'Ah,' Stalin's daughter said. 'The shy lodger.' She was sitting at a small table on her own, with a formidable pile of cakes in front of her. I looked at her, as I did before, for signs of a resemblance to her father – a walrus moustache, perhaps, or a murderous glint in the eye. There was none. She was entirely unchanged.

'I didn't know I was shy,' I said, meaning that I didn't know they had a name for me.

'There were three,' she said. 'The shy one, the drunken one and the short one. I can't remember what order they came in. Come and sit by me, young man.'

'She never mentioned any of the others,' I said, sitting down.

'Well, she was never very interested in them,' she said. 'At least she said she wasn't. She often seemed to end up talking about you, and your doings.'

'She talked to me about you,' I said. 'And Russia.'

'I imagine so,' she said. She took a cake – one of those knotted glazed doughy ones which break off in soft strips – and began to tear it absently. 'And her husband, I suppose.'

'No,' I said. 'I never knew she was married.'

'It was after he left her for the last time she took in lodgers.'

'She never mentioned it.'

'Now I see why you were shy. How you were shy. You never talked to her if she never mentioned anything.' She laughed raucously, head back. 'Ask that man for some more cakes.'

I did so, slightly admiring her servanted ease.

'I suppose she left you something in her will,' Svetlana said. 'Strange, that she remembered almost everyone she'd ever known. What was it?'

'Five hundred pounds,' I said. I was surprised, too, and had wondered why when the solicitor got in touch. Perhaps she had changed her mind about me; perhaps she had been changing her will and testament one day, and the card I had left had been to hand, and she had temporarily forgotten who I was. Or, as Svetlana said, she just left something to everyone she had ever known. My wife had speculated in a slightly tiresome way about what Vera might have left me. I think, in our little house conveniently close to the centre of London, and inconveniently full of rooms ten feet by twelve, my wife might have imagined Vera leaving me half of Georgia.

'Five hundred pounds,' Svetlana said. 'Useful, but boring.'

'Yes, rather boring,' I said. 'Not very characteristic, somehow. Was she rich?'

'Oh, no,' Svetlana said. 'Not very.'

'Still,' I said. 'It will be useful. My wife's just had a baby, and we've got to redecorate the spare bedroom. I'm a lawyer now.' I wondered why I had said that.

'The chocolate one,' Svetlana said to the waiter, 'and the other chocolate one, thank you. I thought you were a painter, not a lawyer.'

'I was,' I said. 'I gave it up.'

'Mmm,' Svetlana said. 'A good profession, law. People will always need lawyers.'

'I know,' I said, since this was always what everyone had said to me, and I needed no reminding that what people needed was more lawyers. 'What did she leave you?'

'A little picture,' she said, bundling the cakes into her bag. 'Very pretty, a man with a beard. I never saw it before. Perhaps it was in her room. Perhaps it is you who has painted it?'

'No,' I said. 'Not me.'

'Well, this has been nice,' Svetlana said, getting up. I suddenly saw that I had been sitting with Stalin's daughter for half an hour, and I would never see her again, and in a second I would miss my chance.

'Tell me something about your father,' I said, taking her arm.

She hardly blinked, and I realised this must happen to her twice a day.

'This has been nice,' she said, with a great flash of charm. 'Buy something special with Vera's money, to remember her with. Now, what will you buy?'

We bought an electrical appliance with it – a fridge, of

course. We had an immense argument about it in the white goods department, in the well-lit Saturday basement of the department store, about whether we had room for a double-doored one, and if we did, whether we needed one. Among all the white boxes, among all the other young marrieds arguing about their needs. I can't remember which of us wanted a double-doored fridge now, or why. Sometimes I look at my single-doored fridge and think what I would call it, if it had a name. Sometimes people, when they come to dinner, ask me to draw them, and sometimes I do, and sometimes they recognise themselves in what I have drawn. Not often. I was a painter once, although this seems to surprise most people. Not any more. I am a lawyer now. I stopped painting after I had left Vera's house. That's everything I remember. I thought it was important to write it down before it was all forgotten.

TO FEED THE NIGHT

THEY LIVED IN London at the end of the nineteen eighties. His wife was twenty-four. He was twenty-six. In her job, she earned eleven thousand pounds a year, and he earned thirteen thousand pounds a year.

'It's mad,' he said. He and his wife were entertaining two other couples to dinner. One couple consisted of a man she had known in the past, and his girlfriend. The other consisted of an old girlfriend of his, and her new husband. The purpose of the dinner party was to show these four people the flat the man and his wife had moved into the month before.

'What's mad?' the man's wife said.

'The price of property,' he said. 'It's quite scary.'

'I think we got on to the ladder just in time,' she said, for the benefit of their guests. 'I think in another six months, we wouldn't have been able to afford even this.'

'You want to get on to the property ladder,' the man said, as if advising their guests. 'If you leave it too long, you won't be able to afford to buy anything, you'll be left behind, and you'll never be able to buy anything at all.'

'It scares me,' his wife said.

'You were lucky,' one of the girls said. 'This is a nice flat. It really is. You were lucky.'

'It's smaller than we wanted, really,' the wife said. 'But it's good for now.'

'It's nice,' another man said. 'It's cosy, really.'

The man did not stop eating as his wife's old friend said that his flat was cosy, but a feeling of wrongness fell over him. He continued to eat the tidy food which his wife had cooked seven times before in the certainty that nothing had ever gone wrong with it, and, saying nothing, felt the narrowness of the flat he lived in. His mind roamed quickly over the sitting room and bedroom and galley kitchen. It did not take long. He said nothing.

'I thought that went well,' his wife said when they had all gone.

'Yes,' he said. There was nothing much to say. His wife earned eleven thousand pounds a year. He earned thirteen thousand pounds a year. The amount of money they had borrowed to buy this narrow and depressing place was as much as any firm would lend them. This was all they deserved.

He had drunk too much at dinner, and woke late the next morning. As he walked through the shopping arcade on the way to the underground station, some of the shops were already opening up. They drew his attention. He thought he knew them all. But between the baker's and the newsagent's there was a glossy interior, thick-carpeted and empty. It sold, one might have thought, nothing but photographs. In the window, there were pictures of the insides of houses, and next to them, against the dark-painted wood, a sum of money. He paused, although he was late. His eye was drawn upwards and into the interior. He had never noticed this estate agent's before. Inside, there was one man, at an empty desk, running a pen along his lips like a harmonica, and watching.

The man, outside the window, dropped his eyes and they fell against a photograph; a photograph of a quiet empty room, painted white, sunlight against a window; a white room, edged with green tartan, a calm good peaceful room. The man stood there and looked at the photograph for a while. He was late for his job. He looked at the sum of money. It was barely more than he and his wife had paid for the constrained flat in which they lived. He went in.

'How do you do,' the agent said, rising from his desk. He was narrowly built, hungrily mid-twenties, with the beginnings of a smile underneath the startling blue eyes, a brisk smile of wet white teeth.

'Hello,' the man said.

'I am Mr Bell,' the agent said. 'I saw you, looking at our properties. We have some good properties in, at the moment.'

'Yes,' the man said. 'I don't know –'

'Yes?' Mr Bell said.

'I mean,' the man said, 'I've only just bought a flat.'

'But you saw a flat of ours,' Mr Bell said.

'It looked so nice,' the man said, helplessly.

'The Elgin Avenue flat,' Mr Bell said. 'Or so I imagine. A very nice property. You are in luck. It only came on to the market late yesterday. A feeling I had, to put it into the window immediately. You are the first person to notice it, and I imagine it will not be in the window for very long. I wonder if you would like to see it?'

'I've only just bought a flat,' the man said.

'So you will not have settled, not quite yet.'

'No,' the man said. It was as if he had been defeated, in some way.

He went with Mr Bell to the flat which had been illustrated in the window of the shop he had never seen before. The road was so thickly wooded it seemed a bridge, suspended under a low green firmament, and heavy with quiet. The empty flat was on the first floor. He followed the agent in and was struck by the pleasant and clean air it had. The rooms were larger than the flat he had bought with his wife, and he followed the agent, with hopeless pleasure, from the central hallway into the kitchen, sitting room, bedroom, bathroom. Mr Bell paused, and with a smile opened the last door. It was a second bedroom.

'It's a very nice flat,' the man said to Mr Bell on the way back to the shop, 'but we've only just moved.'

'That needn't be a problem,' Mr Bell said.

'And it is more than we paid for ours,' he said. 'And that was really at our limit.'

'I see,' Mr Bell said, 'but house prices are shooting up all the time. You may even make a profit.'

'And it is bigger than our flat,' the man said. 'We might need more space.'

He told his wife about it. She listened, her lips closed. When he had finished, she said nothing for a while.

'Why not,' he said. 'It's very nice. And we could do with more space.'

'What for?' his wife said.

'If we had a child,' he said, 'for instance. It's very nice. It's a real bargain.'

'If you think it's a good idea,' she said, in the end.

The purchase of the flat was not a problematic one. Mr

Bell was very helpful, and found a buyer for theirs, whose offer matched the price of the new flat. On the day they moved in, the man and his wife followed each other round, running their fingers round the walls of each room.

'I'm amazed we can afford this,' his wife said. 'We made a mistake, really, paying more than we needed for the other flat.'

'It was what was on the market at the time.'

'It's so nice. And the spare bedroom.'

'It won't be spare for long,' he said. He stood there with his hand on the door of the second bedroom. The expansion of their lives had begun. The touch of the cool-painted door against his hand, her impressed gaze, the moment, the lacuna, as they stood in the acquired silence, was like an embrace. He earned thirteen thousand pounds a year; she earned eleven thousand pounds a year, in London in the late twentieth century. Things were possible.

They had another dinner party, and asked the same people to come.

'I can't believe you moved again so soon,' one of their guests said.

'We saw this,' the man said, 'and it seemed too good to pass up. It was an amazing bargain.'

'We keep expecting the walls to collapse, or the Hell's Angels next door to come back from holiday,' his wife said.

'But it hasn't happened,' the man said quickly.

'How did you find it?' his old girlfriend asked.

'It was in the window of an estate agent's,' the man said. 'I don't know if you know the one. It's in the arcade by the tube station. I just saw the photograph.'

'And we had to see it,' his wife said. She made a new gesture with her hands, a fountaining upward wave.

'And once we'd seen it, we had to buy it,' the man said. 'The last place had gone up fifteen thousand in three months, and this was so underpriced we actually made money on the deal.'

'I don't know it,' one of the male guests said.

'Sorry?' the wife said.

'I don't know the estate agent's,' he said. 'I thought I knew that row of shops, but I don't remember the estate agent's.'

'They're very good,' the man said. 'Ask for a Mr Bell.'

'Mr Bell,' the guest said, nodding in thought.

It was eighteen months later when the man saw Mr Bell again. The estate agent was in the street, standing, stroking his chin, as if waiting for someone. He recognised Mr Bell immediately – the azure flash of the eyes, the abrupt smile – and Mr Bell, it seemed, recognised him. Mr Bell took a couple of steps forward, his arm outstretched to shake hands; a gesture from an office, but unfamiliar and peculiar when executed in the street.

'Your flat,' Mr Bell said. 'I remember your flat, how nice it was. And happy there, are you?'

'Yes,' the man said, vaguely. Eighteen months after buying the place, it had become merely the place where they lived, and he and his wife walked through the flat without admiring it, without expending appreciation on the walls, no longer feeling joy as they contemplated each doorknob, each cupboard, contemplated their ownership of everything they could see. 'Yes, very much so.'

'Still,' Mr Bell said. 'I expect you'll be thinking before long of finding somewhere with a garden?'

'I'm sorry?' the man said, but immediately he knew that this was what he wanted; that whatever the agent's reason for saying this, he was right; that a garden was what they wanted now.

'For your children,' Mr Bell elucidated.

'We don't have any children, I'm afraid,' the man said.

'I'm so sorry,' Mr Bell said. 'I thought you were moving into your present flat for the child.'

The man shrugged. They had no children; he had no plans to talk about having children.

'Forgive me,' Mr Bell said. 'My mind was wandering, I expect. Perhaps it was just that I was thinking about this property we've just seen. It's not often that you see a property as interesting as this one.' Swiftly he extracted a file from inside his coat. 'Do you see what I mean?' he said.

The man looked at the photograph. It was as if a dream he had always had but never quite recalled on waking had now been presented to him, in image; a quiet empty room, great double doors opening on to a garden and light streaming in, golden light electric with dust.

'It looks lovely,' the man said.

'And a bargain,' Mr Bell said. 'The old lady died, and her family live in America. The instruction was to price it low and sell it quickly. They came up with a price and – well, frankly, I think they can't have any idea what it would fetch, but they were insistent on a particular figure. Very odd. I've never heard anything quite like it.'

'How much are they asking?' the man said. He steeled himself, but he was still unprepared for the shock when Mr Bell said the figure. He almost gulped.

'Would you like to see it?' Mr Bell said. The man nodded.

'We don't need to move,' the man's wife said, that evening, over dinner.

'I still think,' the man said carefully, 'you might like to have a look at it. It really is extraordinary. All that space.'

'We don't need any more space,' the wife said.

'But it's an amazing bargain,' he said. 'And think of the investment. Don't you want to live in a house bigger than you could possibly need?'

She got up, and scraped the remains on his plate, the brown and sordid ends, on to the remains on hers. She had no particular response, he could see that.

'At least come and see it,' he said.

'What would you do with it?' she said.

'It would be wonderful to have a piano,' he said. 'I always wanted a piano. And the children. I mean, we don't have to talk about this, but –'

'At some point,' she said. 'When we stop worrying about it, I expect. And in the meantime –'

'I always wanted a piano,' he said.

'I never knew you played,' she said. 'You're full of surprises.'

'I don't,' he admitted. 'I always wanted to learn.'

The garden; the spare bedroom; the room for the piano; a room for – what? – for the kitchen machines, for a study, for a dining room, for some purpose. To have so many rooms, to have more rooms than ready purposes. Mr Bell stood at the door, and waited, kindly, for them to get through the empty rooms, remarking only that the house's furniture had been removed two days before, and sold. When they were home, they shut the door behind them, and, in the suddenly little sitting room, looked at each other, and in her shining eyes, he could see his eyes, shining, with possibility, with space, with greed.

'What do you need all this space for?' the man's old

girlfriend said. It was their first dinner party in the new house.

'Nothing,' his wife retorted. 'Nothing at all. That's the beauty of it.'

He felt her rudeness. 'We're going to fill it, of course,' he said. 'And it was such a bargain. It would have been a crime to let it go.'

'I just don't see,' the other girl said, 'what the two of you need with all these rooms.'

The man and his wife barely glanced at each other, and with their cleverness did not say what was the case, that no one they knew had amounted to what they, in their acuteness, had amounted to. He earned thirteen thousand pounds; she earned eleven thousand pounds, in England at the end of the twentieth century, and they lived, somehow, in a house bigger than the house any of their friends lived in.

'Nor do I, sometimes,' the man said in the end.

'Mr Bell,' the wife said. 'The estate agent. He's a sort of genius.'

'I couldn't find it,' another man said. 'I went down there but I couldn't see it.'

'You should look harder,' the man said. 'He's well worth it.'

'I was in a bit of a hurry,' the other man conceded.

A year passed in their new house. Outside, the seasons came and went. She sat in her new kitchen and, out of the window, the wet green garden made her still inside. There were rooms upstairs she never went into; the air-bright yellow room at the back, lovely but unusable, convincing her that her lovely house had more possibilities than she did, or her husband. There was no piano; they could not afford one; but her husband played records of piano music in their house, and the house sounded of music made by other people. It was almost frightening, the half-empty house they filled with what furniture they had, but here, in England, at the end of the twentieth century, with everything changing, with every square inch of carpet, every tiny room doubling in value by the day, there was nothing they could do, nothing but rejoice, self-consciously, in the house, so much bigger, so much more than they, with their puny small movements, could ever think of filling. And the seasons came and went, and in the end there was a day which, in its weather, was precisely like the half-happy day on which she and her husband had moved into their house.

'I went to see Mr Bell,' the man said, as if beginning a conversation he had rehearsed.

'He was amazing, that man,' the wife said, not committing herself.

'Yes,' the man said. 'Yes. I wondered if he could be amazing again.'

She got up and went towards the shelf over the fireplace. On it was a small wooden deer, a solitary ornament, and she turned it, without saying anything, to the wall, as if thinking.

'I thought I would just ask him what was on the market,' he went on. 'He was so amazing last time, and the time before. You never know.'

'And were you in luck?' she asked, dully.

'We might be,' he said. From his pocket he produced a list of particulars. She read them in amazement; the measurement of each room, brazen as a misprint; the legendary street; the radiant adjectives.

'That can't be right,' she said, pointing at the price.

'It is,' he said. 'I can't understand it, and Mr Bell can't either. Let's face it. Maybe we're just lucky people.'

'We've only just moved,' the wife said.

'A year ago,' he said. 'I heard somebody saying the other day that the market's on the turn. It can't carry on going up. It really can't. And the point to be at when the market turns is selling something at a profit. This is an amazing possibility.'

'Can't we –', she said. But it was hopeless; not because she saw what he wanted bullying her into submission, but because as she spoke, she felt her own want move inside her like a child.

'You're getting to be my favourite clients,' Mr Bell said breezily, driving them away from the miracle house, the house they, the city, the decade had always dreamed of. 'I like lucky people.'

'No one we know can believe our luck,' the man said. His wife was sitting in the back seat, and he could not see her expression. He dried the palms of his hands on his trousers, smoothing them down confidently. 'That was an amazing house. And you really think we can stretch to that?'

'It's not much of a stretch,' Mr Bell said. 'The house you're in at the moment, you'll have no problem selling that for double what you paid for it. And that more or less covers the asking price for this one. I know it seems extraordinary, but you know what they say about gift horses. Of course, you will have the gift horse surveyed, but I promise you, there's no problem here.'

'None at all?' the wife said, leaning forward between the seats.

'As far as I know,' Mr Bell said. 'Apart from one.'

They sat; the husband could feel his wife hugging the back of the seat he sat in.

'Yes,' Mr Bell said. He seemed a little distracted. 'A small one, though, I think. There is another buyer, very interested.'

'Has he put in an offer?'

'He has.'

'We'll match it,' the wife said.

'He's offered the asking price,' Mr Bell said.

'We'll match it,' the wife said. 'And add five thousand.'

'My understanding is,' Mr Bell said, 'that he will match any subsequent offer. Can I drop you near your house at all?'

It proved to be the case. The man made a formal offer of five thousand pounds over the asking price, and the other buyer made a second offer, of ten thousand pounds over the asking price. The man and his wife talked, and they walked in the now small and sullen rooms of the house they lived in through a whole night; there was not talk enough to fill a whole night, and still they talked, again and again and again, saying the same things, not arguing, not disagreeing, but still, somehow, talking, and behind their talk, the mad recurrence of an invisible man's noise at a piano, repeating the same notes in different order, trapped within the caged monochrome limits of the invisible keyboard. And the next day the man made an offer of what he could not afford, of twelve thousand five hundred pounds in excess of the asking price. And the day after that Mr Bell telephoned to say that the other buyer had, without hesitation, made a third offer, of a full fifteen thousand pounds over the price the seller had set.

'I don't see what we can do,' the man said. He was in the empty agency. He faced Mr Bell across his desk. There was nothing on it except a single brown folder, the fabulous desired address written neatly on it. Outside, the noises of the street were muffled, and he fixed Mr Bell with a look of what he knew must closely resemble desperation.

'It depends,' Mr Bell said, 'on how much you really want this house.'

'It is beautiful,' the man said.

'It is beautiful,' Mr Bell said, as if conceding a point in argument, 'and it is unlikely a house of this quality would ever come on the market at this price again. As I say, it depends how much you really want this house.'

'I don't see what else we can do,' the man said. 'We can't offer any more.'

'Do you need the house?' Mr Bell said. 'Do you really need to move? Do you need that much space? Those are the sort of questions that, perhaps, you should be asking yourselves.'

It was a surprising thing for Mr Bell to say, and the man was startled. It was only a moment, however, before he saw, with certainty, that Mr Bell was playing devil's advocate, and he replied with confidence.

'But we want it,' he said. 'And now is the right time to buy.'

Mr Bell nodded, as if satisfied at the right response in the catechism from a fast-learning pupil. 'There is something you could do,' he said. 'But it depends how much you really want this house.'

'More than anything,' the man said.

'Then,' Mr Bell said, and with a small gesture he knocked

the manila folder to the floor. Beneath it was what, somehow, the man had always known would be beneath it, a small, needle-neat and shining pistol. He stared at it. It was not a surprise. There was a silence between them.

'The other buyer,' Mr Bell continued, in the same even tone of voice, 'has asked to see the house on his own, at four o'clock precisely this afternoon. I have lent him the key to the house, since I will be too busy this afternoon to go with him. He will be there, and alone. If the doorbell rings, his assumption will be that it is the estate agent who, after all, was able to turn up and answer any questions. He will be alone.'

'There will be other buyers, surely?' the man said.

'There will be no other buyers,' Mr Bell said. 'I think I can promise you that.'

He looked at the man levelly, his quiet eyes blue in the shaded face. The man stretched out his hand, and found that the tiny pistol cupped into his damp palm. He stood up, without shaking, and left the shop, Mr Bell's gaze hot on his back; it was only on leaving that it came that he had not said goodbye, and now, without returning, he knew it was too late to trouble.

He should go to work. It was a Tuesday. But he did not. He left the estate agent's, and walked to the underground. In his pocket was something he had never held before. Its weight in his suit was like heat. He let the station for his office swing past, thinking all the time, thirteen thousand pounds, thirteen thousand pounds, from one year to the next, no more, unpromoted, than that. He went on, at ten o'clock in the morning, barely worrying whether he had been seen, hardly knowing who he should hide from. And after a time he looked up, feeling almost breathless, and saw that he had come to the centre of the city. He got off, and walked through the mid-morning quiet halls of the underground railway until he reached the surface, and, for no reason, turned right, down the hill, his right hand across his chest, feeling the weight of the weapon in his inside coat pocket. There was a museum there, at the north side of the famous square, and, hardly knowing why, or what else to do, he went into it.

The revolving doors were a momentary shock, and he felt hot in an instant, as if he was passing into some airport, through some detecting device. But the attendants barely shifted at the sight of him, who had no bag, and he carried on, not knowing where he was going. The rooms were not crowded, and at first, he walked through them, unseeing.

He stopped for no reason, and in front of him was a painting. Naked people, striking poses, against cloth and a scrap of country and a scrap of sky. Big and hairless and smooth they were, and the whole painting seemed to know how clean it was, how gold and green and blue and fresh. He supposed it was a famous picture. He did not know it, but in some way it was familiar to him. He stood and looked at it, wondering not exactly what it meant, but why it was here; why anyone had troubled; why they could be so sure of what it would amount to in the end. He stood and looked, more conscious of how he must seem to the people walking round him than of what he was looking at, and soon a terrible thought came to him. His eye went up the left side of the painting; along the top, down the right side; along the bottom; and again, around it, measuring it with his eye. It would fit – he was certain of it – on the narrow wall of the sitting room in the new house, the one to the right of the door as you entered.

Cities are big, and cities are empty, lying open to the skies, and to fill them takes time. He had all day, and it was a long day, from ten in the morning until four o'clock in the afternoon. He walked, with his gun heavy in the inside pocket, and stopped, and drank a coffee, and had a cheap sandwich. It did not occur to him to go to the office. He thought, only, of what he was going to do. And finally it was ten past four and the man was in the street where the house was.

He walked up to the front door of the house, unthinking, almost despairing, and before he rang the doorbell, he saw that his luck was holding; the other buyer had left the borrowed key, idiotically, in the lock of the door. It was confirmation; no one so negligent deserved such a house. He turned the lock, with smooth professional silence, and went into the house.

He stood for a moment in the hallway as the door slid shut behind him. The house was perfectly quiet. On the right, the door to the drawing room stood open. And behind that, the vast purple dining room. To the left, a small bathroom, and at the end of the long hallway, the glass-windowed door to the back garden. There was no sign of anyone, nor in the cellar, converted into a terracotta-lined kitchen of cool and massive extent. He turned round, his little gun in his hand.

The colour of the house became paler as he went upwards, like blood draining from the head; the dark terracotta of the cellar became a rich hallway amber, primrose for the first floor, fading imperceptibly, he remembered, into white by the top of the house. The first floor was just as empty; he looked, almost casually, into a study, a library, two bedrooms and a bathroom. And then he heard a creak, above his head, a muffled footstep. There he was; the man to whom nothing could connect him. It was with an unfamiliar resolution that he turned, and walked swiftly up the stairs, not troubling to mute his noise, wanting, rather, to attract the startled buyer, to fix a look of nervous terror on his face, the look of someone disturbing a burglar. But the figure at the end of the landing did not turn, but remained as it was, gazing out of the window, his back to the advancing man. The man made a noise; the noise of one attracting attention, but his voice failed him, unused all day, and he had to try again, more confidently, his voice, this time, not breaking. And this time the figure – the other buyer – seemed to hear, and to turn with a movement devoid of surprise, a gesture almost mournful in its slow certainty.

And it seemed to the man, before he shot – because he did not shoot – that the face of the buyer who now turned to him, his wet teeth bared, was not that of a stranger, but that of the familiar and guiding Mr Bell, taking him towards an inevitable conclusion with the same security and benevolence as he had taken them through so many houses, so many unnecessary rooms; and now, seeing that Mr Bell was holding, so surprisingly, the same gun in his hand as the man held in his own, the impossible vision of Mr Bell's face made the man close his eyes to wipe away the error, knowing that when he opened them, the impossible face would no longer be there, knowing the simple fact with perfect trust.

Afterwards, the man's wife returned, not to the house she had shared with her husband, but to the house she had been born in, where her parents lived, where they had always lived. Because she had nowhere else, in the end, to go to. In her hand she held a grey cardboard box. And inside the grey cardboard box was an alabaster urn, nine inches high. And inside the alabaster urn, there were the ashes of her husband. She held the grey cardboard box, and sat on the end of the bed in the room she had grown up in, and thought nothing. Presently, she stood up, still wearing her coat, listening for the noises, downstairs, of people moving around, conducting their daily tasks in unnatural quiet, so as not to disturb the widow, and she leaned forward and opened the top drawer of the chest of drawers, and put the box inside, and pushed the drawer shut. And the urn was nine inches high. And the box was twelve inches by six inches by eight inches. And the drawer was three feet wide and two feet deep, and the wife shut it. And for him that was space enough.

A HOUSEKEEPER

When my father came home, I hardly knew him and he was a capitalist. My grandmother pushed me forward in the dark hall of her flat towards the man I could not see.

'Look,' she said accusingly. 'It's your daughter.'

He stretched out his hand, a strange gesture to offer a ten-year-old girl, but I took it and we shook hands. I had been trussed up in party wear by my grandmother, who was always ready to transform an occasion into a celebration, always ready to transform a celebration into an exchange of recriminations. The elastic and ribbons cutting into my skin made me accept formality.

'What a man,' my grandmother said, turning and going back into the kitchen. My father looked at me gravely.

'Do you know where I've been?' he asked.

'You've just come out of prison,' I said. The official line perpetrated by my grandmother, which we were supposed to retell to anyone who asked, was that my father was in America. I didn't know if we were supposed to lie to my father about where he had been.

'Good,' he said. 'Is that Bedřich?'

My brother was crouching behind the back of a chair, as if he were still a child. He was seventeen, but understood and remembered too little. He remembered nothing about my father, and if my father went away again, he would probably forget him again.

'I didn't think he would be as bad as that,' my father said.

'He's just a bit shy,' I said. I made excuses for my brother, but it was true that a seventeen-year-old who behaved and thought like someone no more than four years old was a difficult person to deal with. My friends had stopped coming to the house, scared off by Bedřich's loping presence and his unpredictable, frightening naughtiness.

'Why is he sniffing?' my father said. 'Is he ill?'

'Not really,' I said. 'He's always sniffing.'

'Does he know who I am?' he said.

'Yes,' I said. 'I've told him about you.' This was true.

'Bedřich,' my father said, crouching down by him. 'Do you know who I am?'

Bedřich didn't say anything. 'Not a clue,' my father said.

When we were alone, Bedřich would talk. He used to ask me if I remembered our mother, and I used to say no. Then he would ask me if I remembered my father, and I would say yes.

'Tell me,' he said.

'He's very tall,' I said. 'He went away. He went to America.'

'How?' he said, thinking as hard as he could.

'He flew there,' I said. Bedřich accepted that.

'Does he come back?' Bedřich said.

'Yes,' I said.

'Soon,' he said.

'Yes, he'll come back soon,' I said. 'He told me he would. He promised.'

'When?' he said.

'Soon,' I would say. If we were talking on our own, then this would carry on for a while longer. My grandmother used to like to listen to these conversations between us. I think she was saving them up to use against my father when he got out.

But if she wasn't there, Bedřich would generally say, 'What presents?'

Sometimes I would tell him that he wouldn't bring any, or that he would only be bringing presents for me, and faced Bedřich's doleful acceptance of what little he deserved, or ran from his terrifying tantrum, an infant's fit with a man's strength. Generally, I said that he was going to come back with lots of presents, with sweets and chocolate and chewing gum, and maybe an American car. I saw all these bright parcels for us, and Bedřich accepted them, silently.

'Shut your mouth, Bedřich,' my grandmother would say, walking by.

Bedřich was crouching behind the chair and not looking at anything. He was wiping his nose on the sleeve of his sweater, a habit no one could cure him of. My father poked at him with the sole of his foot, like someone trying to get a nocturnal animal to come out into the daylight. Bedřich said something.

'What did he say?' father said.

I got down beside him. 'It's father,' I said.

'What presents?' Bedřich said.

'What did he say?' father said.

'He wanted to know if you'd brought any presents,' I said. 'He thinks you've been to America.'

'And so I have,' my father said. He winked at me; a gesture of complicity, perhaps, but one which filled me with an awful dread, an awful panic and fear at being unable to join in with a game.

He didn't have a car from America – at least, he didn't have a car then from America. We went back to the flat we'd all been born in by taxi, sitting in a squashed line on the back seat like children. Bedřich looked at him with his mouth open, not saying anything. My father ignored Bedřich; I think that, from beginning to end, he found it easier not to worry about Bedřich's existence at all. He talked to me, instead.

'How old are you now?' he said.

'Ten,' I said.

'Do you go to school?'

'Yes,' I said.

'Of course you do,' he said. 'You like school, don't you?'

'Yes,' I said, though I had never considered whether I liked it or not; it was just somewhere I went.

'What do you like the best?' he said.

'I like geography,' I said, thoughtfully. 'That's what I like best, but I'm better at maths, and maybe sometimes at history, though I can't remember dates always. I don't like games, though. We have games on a Thursday afternoon.'

'Oh yes,' my father said. 'Hey. How much are you going to give me for fifty American dollars?'

The taxi driver didn't respond; his neck only tightened a little. Father said it again.

'How much will you give me for fifty American dollars?'

The taxi driver looked at him warily in the mirror.

'What fifty American dollars would that be?' he said.

'The fifty American dollars I just happen to have in my pocket,' father said. The taxi driver looked at him silently for a second, then named an enormous sum. Bedřich took father's hand, and began to tug it, beseechingly. Perhaps he thought he was going to get his present.

'Papa,' he said, with a thrilled air of discovery, as if he had only just noticed who he was sitting next to.

'Ha,' father said, ignoring Bedřich. He didn't get his fifty American dollars out, and just sank back into the seat.

'Shitface,' the driver said under his breath.

'I was just curious,' father said.

I couldn't remember the flat. It had been seven years since father had gone away and Bedřich and I had gone to live with our grandmother. Strange people had been living there in the meantime. I hung back when father opened the door and went in.

'Come in,' father said. 'Why are you dawdling?' It was as if he didn't understand what I was afraid of.

We put down our few suitcases in the hallway. I felt we ought to start unpacking and making the place our home. Father walked from room to room, as I followed him.

'Are we going to live here now?' I asked.

'For a while,' he said.

'Is mother?' Bedřich said. Father looked at him as if Bedřich had understood nothing.

It seemed to me as if the flat had been lived in, once, but abandoned so many centuries before that there was no possibility of deciphering the inhabitants' strange lives from the strange detritus of their existence. I did not know if the existences I milked from the air were ours, my brother's, my father's, my mother's and mine; I do not know who had lived there since we had left it.

'What are you looking like that for?' father said. 'Can you cook?'

'Can I cook?' I said. I had never cooked in my life. 'I can have a go.'

'It doesn't matter,' he said. 'We won't be staying that long here.'

Father did not work, and if he went out, he left after I had gone to school and grandmother had arrived to take Bedřich away for the day; he came back before we did, I suppose. There were no presents, and after a few days, Bedřich had taken father into his confused and disappointed world without comment. Father had no idea of housekeeping, and when food came, it came in large amounts, arriving without warning and in crates. If he had a friend who was selling oddly coloured American drinks in boxes of forty-eight, or strange tinned beans, then that would be what we would have. Sometimes he would come home with an unplucked enormous chicken someone had offered him – I remember the panic of trying to handle the floppy beast, father's unstoppable jocosity at its sudden existence on the kitchen table. Once – I shrink from the thought of it – half a pig. We did well enough out of father's strokes of luck and dealings, but our meals, though festive, were quite unlike normal meals.

My father used to tell us often that things would change. One day they did. He called me into the drawing room and asked me if I liked living with my grandmother. I nodded.

'Did you prefer it to this, though?' he said.

'No,' I said.

'Good girl,' he said. 'But you won't mind living with her again, will you?'

'With Bedřich?' I said.

'God, yes,' father said.

'And you?'

'No,' he said. 'Just you and Bedřich.'

'You're not going –' I said. I stopped out of delicacy.

'No, I'm not going back to America,' he said, grinning to show he knew I knew what he meant. 'No, I'll be in Prague still, we'll see each other every day still.'

'Where are you going to live?' I said.

'There's a thought,' he said. 'I think I'm going to live in the summer house.'

I took a while to think about this.

'Why don't you live here?' I said.

'Because somebody else is going to live here,' he said.

'Who?'

'Americans,' he said.

'Why don't you live with grandmother, like us?' I said. I wanted him to be with us. I wanted him to think I loved him best. I wonder why.

Because we lived in the centre of the city, and because there was no garden or anything near us, we had a garden quite near Prague, an allotment, next to a lot of other allotments. They were like gardens without houses or fences. All the time father had been in prison we had kept it, and my grandmother and I had looked after it. These allotments were difficult to get hold of, and you had to wait for, often, years just to get one. So we didn't want to lose father's just because he was in prison. On each plot there was a green-painted wooden hut, with just one room, where you could sit and look at what you had achieved in the garden.

We had a wooden cool-box in ours, where my grandmother and I would put our lunch when we arrived in the morning to work on the garden, and our lunch would still be fairly cool by lunch-time. I had long ago been allowed to paint the box, in stripes which my grandmother had shown me how to keep even with bits of tape and my tongue hanging out. There was a bed which I would nap on when I was small, in the afternoons, and two wooden chairs, one of which had broken and was never used. There was a strange smell to the whole thing; damp wood which, when I smell it now, brings to mind a thought of sun-shaded green, a chill shivering at the end of summer, my grandmother's face, lit with glee as she, long dead now, holds some fine-rooted vegetable from the earth.

Every gardener, I suppose, had a different word for their green hut. We called ours 'the summer house' because we only used it in the summer. It was this that father was going to go and live in.

'What Americans, though?' I said.

'I don't know which Americans,' my father said. 'But lots of Americans are going to come to Prague, you know. They've got to stay somewhere.'

'Why won't they want to stay in hotels?' I said.

'They won't want to when they see our flat.'

My grandmother was indignant when all this was explained to her; she was still more indignant when father moved us in and left immediately. I asked her to explain the situation to me – for my own amusement, largely.

'He wants to make money. As usual,' she said.

'How?'

'It doesn't cost him anything to live in the summer house,' she said, 'and these rich Americans who want to live in Prague are going to pay him rent for the flat.'

'How much are they going to pay?' I asked.

'I don't want to know,' she said. 'All I know is that it won't find its way to you or me or to your poor brother, God help him. And where is he?'

It seemed quite sensible to me, but grandmother was rendered almost speechless by the thought of all the money he would earn from people who knew no better. Father moved out, and we moved out, but nothing seemed to be going on. He kept coming round for dinner at grandmother's flat and sitting, eating her winter stews in a face-down silence while she berated him about how she would have done it, if she had been stupid enough to embark on the thing in the first place, thank god, she wasn't and never would be. From time to time he lifted his head and looked at her with the mournful hostility of a well-trained hound, waiting for the opportunity for misbehaviour.

'You won't be able to rent it out,' she would say. 'You'll have to redecorate, it's far too shabby for Americans. You've been in America, you know what American standards are like, don't you?'

'Indeed.'

He redecorated.

'It's the wrong time of year, who comes to Prague in August? You might as well move back in, take the children off my hands, though God knows, I love having them, and, God knows, how they get neglected when they have to rely on a man like you to keep the poor mites alive, poor Bedřich, do stop that, Bedřich.'

He wouldn't move back in; we kept on living separately. I think all that time, he only had one person living in the flat. It was a woman he got to know somehow. My grandmother kept up a fiction that she had been someone he had known in America, though I doubt if she had ever been west of Karlovy Vařy. In fact, she was the wife of some associate of his, who had left her husband and thrown herself – 'in every sense', I can hear my grandmother saying, smugly – on my father's mercy. She lived in the flat, arriving with *so* many suitcases, my father announced impressively one night over dinner, for exactly one week. I wasn't allowed to meet her. After a week she went back to her husband, preferring his beatings, I suppose, to whatever favours my father expected from her in return for paying no rent, to whatever appalling dampness in the flat's bedrooms. My father claimed for a while to have made money out of her, until my grandmother's calm questioning over dinner revealed that she had lived there for a week for nothing, and had never expected to pay anything.

He was optimistic, that summer, to the point of pigheadedness. Father spent most of the summer in the summer house in the allotments, waiting for rich Americans to turn up to rent the flat. We only saw him when, nightly, he came round to my grandmother's flat for something to eat. I don't really see that he got anything much to eat in the summer house. There was a table and plates which we'd always kept there, but there was no way of cooking anything; we'd always used the plates to eat our cold pickled stuff, our sliced sausages off. Perhaps he just ate raw things; perhaps he ate in restaurants. But when he came round to grandmother's house, she was always cross, and said that he wasn't fair to her, and she wasn't putting up with it, and he wasn't fair to us, and when we were old enough, or, God help us all, if Bedřich had sense enough, we wouldn't put up with it either. We just watched him eating enough for three until grandmother had to tell us to eat as well.

Bedřich didn't like living with grandmother, and it wasn't within his capacities to grasp who father was. Or perhaps he grasped it; didn't believe it. The strange thing was that before too long his favourite people were the Americans who never turned up. He invented a whole family of Americans who were living in our flat. Did he invent them? Did he see them, in his poor tattered head? I don't know. He spoke of them, living their exciting lives.

Usually after lunch, he would say, 'Let's go and see the Americans.'

I humoured him because, in one sense, I wanted to believe in the Americans, as well.

'Why do you want to see the Americans?'

'I like them.'

'Who do you like the best?' I said. 'Grandmother or father or the Americans?'

'Americans.'

'Or do you like bacon best?' I would say, teasing him.

'No,' he said, seriously. 'Americans.'

Then he'd sniffle, and I'd tell him to stop. There were three of them, a girl and two boys, in Bedřich's ideas. One boy was called Tony, and the girl was called Katarina – which was the name of the woman in the flat, the woman who didn't stay more than a week – and the third one was called Dud.

'Dud?' I said.

'Yes,' Bedřich said. 'He's the nicest.'

I went along with it.

'Let's go and see them then. Tony and Katarina and Dud.'

'No,' Bedřich said.

'Let's go and see father then,' I said.

'No,' said Bedřich.

When we saw father that evening, I told him that we went to see the Americans.

First he said, 'Which Americans?'

Then I explained, and he laughed. Then he asked if I'd learned any English words from talking to them, these Americans.

'*Ten nine eight seven six five four three two one*,' I said.

He laughed. I'd never pleased my father so much. 'It was invented by a Czech, the countdown,' he said. 'Did you know that?'

I shook my head.

'Waiting for blast-off, that's what Czechs do best. And do you know any other English words?'

I said all the English words I could remember, all in a line, and a few that we'd made up, and then he laughed again.

'Good girl,' he said. He looked at me as if he perceived possibilities in me; an impresario auditioning an act. 'I think we'll be moving back into the flat pretty soon, though.'

He was right to perceive possibilities in me; they were not, however, possibilities for his benefit. It was worse than ever, that winter. Even Bedřich had decided that the Americans had gone; the Americans who had never been there to start with. We didn't move back into the flat. Father tried to keep on living in the summer house, since he'd finally let the flat. He didn't manage to find any Americans, though. He let it to a Czech civil servant and his plump, small-mouthed family. They paid hardly any money; after a while they stopped paying any at all.

But in a way it was a matter of pride to my father that

he'd found a tenant for the flat, and I don't think he minded at first, since he could hold up his head and talk to his mother-in-law, rather than sit and be lectured by her. For almost a month he lived in the summer house in the cold, with just an electric fire, running off a car battery, to try and keep it warm. Then one day, two panes of glass shattered in the frost, and even he had to admit defeat. Disconsolately, he finally agreed with my grandmother that living in the summer house was impossible. He tried to evict the civil servant from the flat, but, when that proved impossible, as everyone told him, he moved to my grandmother's flat, where we were all living.

Sometimes, when the snow melts, everything seems to change. But when spring came, that year, nothing was different. We carried on living with my grandmother, and we carried on fighting, and arguing. My father never really got any more polite to my half-wit brother, although I can see it must have been annoying when spring came and Bedřich's cold didn't get any better. Usually it could be relied upon to dry up for a few weeks at least, but that year it just seemed to get worse and worse. At first we – my grandmother and I, who were fond of Bedřich, to a point, who treated him as a nice family joke – we made the same jokes as ever. My father wasn't fond of Bedřich; didn't care for him; didn't join in the jokes. I suppose it was the joking which stopped us from taking him seriously. It was my father, who didn't care for his son, who actually noticed when it was getting towards the end of May, and Bedřich was not just sniffing, but coughing quite heavily, and shivering; more or less constantly.

When Bedřich died, I sat down to write letters. But I didn't have anyone to write to, really. Anyone who would have cared knew. So I found myself writing a long letter to Bedřich's invented Americans, to Tony and Katarina and Dud, those funny healthy people. I had not suspected that Bedřich kept our house, until he died, and the house, unkept, went the ways it could always have gone. I told them all about it, a long letter. I wish I could say it was because Bedřich had asked me to in the hospital. But it wasn't; all I remember of Bedřich in the hospital is his scared face. And now I can't say what he was scared of: a lunch he wouldn't be able to eat, a fierce nurse, or death. I addressed the letter to Tony and Katarina and Dud, America, and I posted it. For a while I even looked at the letters that arrived, in case something somehow came back. But it never did, not even the letter I'd written. So someone must have seen it, and maybe even read it.

As for father, well, when we moved back into the flat, the pair of us, after the civil servant had left of his own free will, he decided that he wouldn't move out again, or rent it to foreigners ever again. He started buying odd crates of food just like he had before, and making his money in ways no one really wanted to understand. And he still does. That was in the late nineteen eighties, or perhaps early nineteen nineties. We live close to each other now. I love my father, but I don't see much of him any more.

A GEOGRAPHER

BRUNO WAS A nice boy of thirty-seven. He had kept his looks, and his size in trousers. He had learnt English to a certain firm expertise, of which he was proud. He had lost his hair, which he considered unimportant. He had gained a moustache, about which sometimes he thought one thing, and sometimes another. These were the different opinions he held about the principal changes in his state since the time when he was young.

For five years he had lived in a flat in Golders Green on his own, and worked for five days a week in the London office of a large Italian bank. His mother still lived in Mantua, and was fond of her respectable unmarried banker son as of her respectable dead banker husband. Bruno sent her one thousand pounds every month, of which he knew she saved one half, and did not mind, and every day, in the early evening, he telephoned her.

He had decorated his flat in a style which was briefly fashionable, and which he considered looked attractive in photographs. His cupboards were of polished steel, and his bookshelves were of polished steel. His lights were spotlights from a stage, and his curtains were not curtains, but metal blinds, and black. His occasional visitors found it impressive, but not comfortable. He smiled if they expressed this view, since he knew with perfect security that not comfort, but ease, was his aim. He knew this. After five years of living in the flat he owned, he only sometimes thought he had allowed himself, five years before, to be persuaded of the merits of this style by people he would never meet. He only sometimes wondered if he altogether cared for it, and very occasionally he knew he did not. Bruno was fondest of his stiff-jointed dog, from whom he had only once been separated, when he had first come to England and the dog had stayed in grim institutional quarantine, with only occasional visits. In black moments he wondered if he could bring himself to buy another dog when Pippo died.

Once a week, generally on Friday nights, Bruno allowed himself to put on a black leather jacket and go to Hampstead Heath. There he permitted strangers to perform sexual acts upon him, and, more rarely, he performed sexual acts upon them. His looks, enhanced by his small, distinguished blond moustache, seemed to make him a good deal in demand among the other men who frequented Hampstead Heath on Friday night. He spent most of his time during these encounters calculating the quickest way to escape from the police or from hooligans seeking victims to injure. He knew that men were sometimes arrested, or assaulted by other men.

These occurrences he knew about by repute, but nothing remotely dangerous had ever happened to him, nor did it ever. He did not calculate risk; he merely saw that it was real. Because of this, he did not seem entirely at ease to his temporary sexual partners, nor was he. He was on the heath for pleasure, and not for ease. They occasionally told him, his temporary sexual partners, that he should relax, or asked him to remove more of his clothing than he judged wise. Bruno smiled, and did not act as they suggested.

Bruno did not feel guilty or worried about his participation in open-air orgies each Friday; nor, if a colleague or acquaintance asked him to dinner on Friday night, did he feel he would prefer to be on the heath. It was something he often and regularly did, but it could not be considered a habit. It gave him pleasure of simple and several kinds; he enjoyed the lack of emotional complication in the sexual gratification, but also the beauty of the heath and, occasionally, an encounter which would begin wordlessly and would develop into an intimate, romantic conversation between strangers, looking at London.

When Bruno came back to his flat, his dog Pippo did not seem to look at him in a reproaching, but in a fond way. Bruno rarely thought what was the case, that he had never slept with a man. Nor, if this thought had come to him, would he have thought anything of it.

One Sunday morning, towards the end of May, Bruno was emptying the pockets of a pair of trousers in preparation for sending them to the laundry, when he found a note, in a handwriting not his own. The note said Simon, and a telephone number. It was an odd scrap of paper, and next to his name, the boy who had written it had, out of habit, written a cross to signify a kiss. He put it on one side while he unravelled his shirts and pulled out his socks from their pulled-off balls and did not think about it.

In itself this was not unusual, this note. From time to time boys on Hampstead Heath with whom he had engaged in conversation pressed their telephone numbers on him. He always accepted their telephone numbers, and out of civility gave them a false telephone number, as he had already given them a false name, in return. Once a man at a colleague's dinner party had suggested, when the colleague and his wife were out of the room, that they exchange telephone numbers. Bruno had done so, as if it were a normal thing to do. To Bruno's relief the man had never telephoned him. Perhaps the man, he thought later, had noticed his nervousness. He had been relieved, not because he had not found the man attractive, but because he had.

What was unusual this time – what caused a tiny rippling eruption in his thoughts, like a bubble bursting through viscid black water – was that he had no memory of this card, or of a boy named Simon, or the note being given to him.

Bruno went to work the next day. His desk was as tidy as his flat, because he never left work hanging over from day to day. He arrived at eight thirty, and worked until his lunch-time sandwich which he ate, reading a newspaper, in a bar near his office. He returned and worked until he had finished what he had to do. His secretary went at five, and he left at half past six. All the time he generated work for those around him and beneath him, and he did not think about what he was doing. Once, after lunch, he took out the piece of paper from his pocket and began to dial the telephone number. He stopped one digit from the end, and replaced the receiver. He worked hard; he knew people who worked harder.

The next day he did call the number. It was not easy for him to see why he should. If it was a man from the heath, there were certainly other men who would be prepared to have sex with him on the heath. The fact that he had no recollection of the man suggested that the man was not worth recalling. He had almost decided definitely not to call the number when he found that he was pressing the digits of the telephone number in sequence.

'Are you a friend of his?' the voice at the end of the telephone said, bluntly.

'Yes,' Bruno said. He was not easily daunted on the telephone.

'He's in hospital.'

'Oh, I'm sorry.

'Nothing serious. He's had a bit of a bashing. I'm sure he'd welcome a visit, though. He isn't getting many visitors. His mother's going to come in a day or two, but he's a bit low, to tell you the truth. What did you say your name was?'

'Bruno,' Bruno said.

He permitted the man to tell him the name of the hospital and the ward number where Simon, whose name he knew from a note from a pocket, was recovering, and even asked the man to slow his speech, as if he were writing the information down. He felt a twinge of pity at the idea of the boy with so few friends, lying in hospital waiting for a man neither he nor his flatmate knew. When he put the telephone down, he held the information in his head for a moment, and then, surprising himself, he did write it down.

The man against the white sheets was bruised around his mouth and chin. On his forehead was a large flushed patch, like the ambivalent cursing kiss of a giantess in a fairy tale. It was impossible for Bruno to say if he recognised the man or not. His face was considerably damaged and misshapen. The man looked up. Only in his eyes was there an unbruised softness. Simon – if it was Simon – did not recognise Bruno, since he lowered his head and went on reading his book. When Bruno drew up the chair, he laid the book down on the bed, face down, and looked up with a sigh.

'I'm not religious,' Simon said flatly.

'Nor am I,' Bruno said, surprised.

'You're wasting your time.'

'What do you mean?'

Simon sighed heavily.

'I mean, I don't believe in God, and I'm not likely to, and I don't care how long it takes you to get round to it, I'm not going to listen. So you might as well go away now and talk to someone who doesn't mind it.'

'But I came to see you,' Bruno said. He didn't know what else to say, and it now struck him that he was in an embarrassing situation. 'I found your name in my pocket. I thought you must have put it there.'

Simon looked at him properly. He reached towards the small cupboard to his side, and took a grape from a plundered bunch. He sucked the grape, spat out the pips on the floor.

'I don't care,' he said, referring to the grape pips. 'I'm that sort of person. I thought you were a vicar or something. We get that a lot here. There was a rabbi yesterday, and he went away when I said I wasn't Jewish, but you can't say anything to the vicars to make them go away. Some of them wear their clothes, but most of them dress like you, in a suit and that.'

'How long have you been here?' Bruno said.

'Since Saturday,' Simon said, apparently surprised. He seemed to think Bruno must have known that he was in hospital. 'I'm glad you came, though. No one else has come. They all say they hate hospitals. I remember you now. Your moustache I remember. What did you say your name was?'

'Bruno,' he said.

'Bruno,' Simon said. 'My mum's coming to see me, tomorrow.'

'I'm glad,' Bruno said. 'I came because your flatmate said I should.'

'He's not my flatmate,' Simon said. 'I haven't got a flatmate, actually. I used to, but he went. He was going to be here for a week, the boy you spoke to, but that was two weeks ago and he's still here. He says he's going to go, but I don't think he will.'

'Do you want him to go?'

'Yes,' Simon said. 'Well, maybe. He's being quite useful, sorting things out, and that. You know why I thought you were a vicar? I've just realised, it's because you didn't come with anything.'

'What should I have come with?'

'Well, nothing, really. What I mean is, when people come and visit you in hospital, they usually bring something for you. Like a bunch of grapes or something. Or a magazine. That's what I'd really like. There's a trolley here that sells magazines and newspapers, but by the time it gets up here there's only *Titbits* left. It's only vicars that turn up in a suit and not bringing you anything. And you, which is nice.' He grinned, suddenly, inconsequentially. They looked at each other for a long pleasant time.

'Would you like me to bring you something?' Bruno said.

'Well, only if you were going to come back anyway. The thing is, my mum was going to come tomorrow, but now she isn't coming until Friday. It would be nice if you could fetch me a magazine to read.'

'What do you like to read?'

'*Vogue*,' Simon said, surprised, as if there were only one magazine to read. 'I don't know how long I'm going to be here, or I'd ask you to bring a book. They think when they did me over, they fractured my skull, what they call a hairline fracture, and they're just keeping me to see if I die or anything.'

'They think you might die?'

'No, of course they don't,' Simon said. 'They just think they'd better keep me here. It's really boring, though. It's nice of you to come. What did you say your name was?'

'Bruno,' Bruno said.

'Oh yes.'

Bruno looked at the bruised boy in bed, and suddenly he felt a wave of sex come over him. He liked the boy's wearing a white hospital gown, against which his flesh was furred and dark, when the men in the white beds around him wore pyjamas which they owned. He liked even that he did not understand what had happened to the boy, since he did not know what the boy meant when he said *they did me over*, and he did not understand what his flatmate had meant by *a bit of a bashing*, and shy, did not feel he could ask for an explanation. The boy looked back with his special gaze, tender.

'Can I have your phone number?' he said.

'Yes,' Bruno said, and took a piece of paper. On it he

wrote his name, and he wrote his telephone number. It occurred to him to lie, and he did not.

'In case I think of anything else you could bring,' Simon said. 'Come back tomorrow.'

'With *Vogue*.'

When Bruno smiled it was as if he could see himself smiling with all the charm and pleasure he had never been able to see in himself in photographs. He went directly home on the underground. He got on the first train he saw, without noting its direction. He sat and looked at the progress of black thick wires in tunnels as the trains progressed, and at the embarkations and departures of the people. His mind was blank, or it was not blank at all, and he noted the pleasure he felt, with pleasure. It was only after some time which he could not account for that he saw the station the train was drawing into. He had to get off the train and reverse his direction, to take it again.

When he reached his home it was too late to telephone his mother in Mantua, and rebellious, he did not. He invariably telephoned her at half past seven. She never complained if he did not, but he always regretted it subsequently. He knew this; still he did not telephone. Instead he sat with his stiff dog on his lap and played foolish good games with Pippo, and, when Pippo felt like it, he put a lead around his neck, and together they went for an eager tottering walk. How good Pippo was and how easy.

'Hello,' Bruno said, on the telephone.

'This is Mauro,' the voice said.

Bruno knew no one called Mauro in Mantua who would announce themselves in English, and he waited for confirmation from the voice.

'I spoke to you the other day,' Mauro went on.

'Oh yes,' Bruno said. It still meant nothing.

'I'm Simon's flatmate.'

Bruno recognised the voice, although Simon had said he had no flatmate. 'How did you know my telephone number?'

'Simon gave it to me. He just wanted to know if you were going to see him tomorrow.'

'Don't telephone me at home, please,' Bruno said. 'I don't know you.'

'Are you Italian?' Mauro said. 'Sei italiano?'

'Don't telephone me, please,' Bruno said, and put the telephone down. Terror came upon him. The pleasure he had felt was quite gone.

The next day, he did not go to work. It was unusual for Bruno, although not for the other people whom he worked with. He called his secretary and told her he was unwell. She seemed to accept his word, and asked him if there was anything she should do or any appointments she should cancel. He told her that she should examine his appointments diary, and that if she wished to reach him, she should leave a message on his answering machine, which, since he was in bed recuperating, he would not answer.

Only afterwards did it occur to him that he had not told his secretary what was wrong with him. Nor had she asked. He did not go to bed, but he switched on his telephone answering machine and went out. When he came back, he dialled Simon's telephone number, firmly. But the pip of a ring made him put the telephone receiver down and he did not know if Mauro was there to be spoken to. The day for him was blank and after it he had betrayed both his mother and his firm.

The next morning he did go to work. There was a pile of mail on his desk. While he prepared to deal with it, he sent his secretary out to buy a copy of *Vogue*. He telephoned his bank and checked the balance in his current account. Having done this, he requested them to transfer two thousand pounds to his mother's bank account in Italy. He knew she preferred money to presents; he felt that about himself too, that he had no interest in a present which he might not need or want. Money was better.

'Lovely,' Simon said when Bruno gave him the copy of the magazine. 'It takes me all day to read *Vogue*, sometimes.'

'All day,' Bruno said. 'I read it this morning. It only took twenty minutes.'

'I don't think you can have been concentrating,' Simon said. 'It's easy to read things quickly if you don't really look at them. Anyway, I bet you had other things to do. In your office, I bet.'

'How do you know I work in an office?'

'Your suit, it just screams office. I used to have to wear a suit, but that was in a shop, and it wasn't a proper suit. I never thought you would wear a suit when I met you.'

Bruno felt a violent blush like a slap, unfelt. It was the word *met* that did it. Simon looked at him in a way which is always described as innocent, and is knowing.

'You don't remember me, do you?' he said finally.

'No, I don't,' Bruno said. 'It was very dark, of course.'

'I remember you. Your moustache, mainly. Of course, I've got a bit of a beard now.'

'Don't they let you shave, here?'

'They do, but it's nice not shaving, sometimes. Of course, it's not much of a beard, but I thought I'd let it go for a while, just to shock my mum, when she comes. She's always saying something like this is going to happen to me, and she'll be pleased to be proved right now. Maybe she won't recognise me either, with the beard, or think I've turned into a real man or something. You know. What does your mum think of your moustache?'

'What happened to you?' Bruno said, finally.

'They did me over,' he said. 'They beat me up. They kicked my head in. They hurt me.'

'They hurt you,' Bruno said.

'It doesn't matter,' he said.

'What's your name?' Bruno said. 'Your real name.'

'Simon,' Simon said. 'It always was.'

They were there and stayed there for a while.

'Come and lie down,' Simon said. 'In your suit.'

The ward was full of people. It was full of white, and the boy was asking him to lie on his bed with him. Bruno stayed in his chair and smiled, and he knew before he blushed that it was the smile he brought out and let stay on his face when people said things to him that he did not understand. But, drained of embarrassment, Simon did not mind.

'Who is Mauro?' Bruno said.

'My flatmate. You spoke to him, then.'

'He spoke to me. I didn't know how he knew my telephone number. He just phoned me up.'

'He wants to come and stay with you.'

'He wants to come and stay with me?'

Bruno looked at Simon, but he seemed to be quite serious.

'You see, my mum's coming to stay. She was coming to stay the day before yesterday, but now she's coming tomorrow. He can't stay if she's coming, of course.'

'I've never met him,' Bruno said.

'You'd like him,' Simon said. 'He just needs to get out of my flat and he's nowhere to stay. He doesn't know anyone in London. It wouldn't be for long.'

'I've never met him,' Bruno said. 'I've only met you twice.'

'Three times,' Simon said. 'Here's my telephone number. It would be ever so nice of you if you did.'

He produced a card with his telephone number and his name written on it. This time there was no kiss after his name. Bruno realised he must have had it prepared, as he had prepared the conversation.

'You've given it to me already,' he said, handing it back. 'I don't need it.'

When he got home, he had decided to telephone his uncomplaining mother. He knew she worried sometimes, and knew that, if he did not telephone her, she would not presume to telephone him. He wondered sometimes what fits of sulk and pique she diagnosed in him, and did not speak about; he thought about the reasons she would have for seeing a mood in him not to telephone.

It was his habit not to dial the number of his mother, but simply to press the last number recall button. It was rarely necessary to do otherwise. He did it without thinking, and without thinking he heard the English dialling tone. Only when the ring stopped and he heard, not his mother, but Simon's recorded voice, did he realise that the last number he had dialled had not been his mother.

'Hi there,' Simon's voice said. 'This is Brett. I can't get to the phone right now. I'm at the gym, pumping up my body just for you. So if you wait till the tone, and leave your number, I'll get back to you, and we'll plan some fun, okay?'

There was a short silence, and then an electronic noise. Bruno said nothing; he put the telephone down.

In the fridge there was some meat and some mushrooms. With some onions and a bottle of red wine and a little fennel, Bruno cooked himself dinner, a heavy dark stew. This was something he sometimes did; tonight he did it because it gave him a chance, which he felt he needed, to telephone his mother and ask her how a beef stew could best be cooked. She gave him the information he asked for and then, fond, they had a conversation in which nothing was said and nothing was left out. She did not reprimand him for not having telephoned, and in the end, he apologised, and she admitted she had been a little worried. He did not tell her about the money he had sent her; he looked forward to her surprise and her unelicited thanks, which for him were, he thought, enough.

When the stew was ready, he realised he had cooked far too much; enough for two really. He wondered, while he ate, whether it could be recooked and eaten the day afterwards. Then it occurred to him to give the rest to Pippo, who was, elderly, nuzzling his ankle as if he could not quite identify what the thing he could smell and wanted to eat was. He put some out on Pippo's dish which, since he was a puppy, he had always eaten from, and by the time he had finished, it was cold enough to be given to the dog. He set it down in front of Pippo, who truffled around it for a while, and then hobbled away. Bruno wondered what was wrong with it; he wondered whether Pippo disliked the fennel, or the red wine, and, speaking in dog-Italian, as to his dog he always did, he asked what was wrong. The dog looked, but did not answer.

He left it, and the next morning, when he got up, the meat had been eaten and the plate licked quite clean.

Bruno went to the hospital, for the last time.

'What do you do?' Bruno said.

Simon seemed to be determined not to blush and not to display embarrassment from the directness of his gaze.

'I'm an escort,' he said. 'A masseur. I once took a course.' Then he saw that Bruno's way of looking didn't register understanding, and, his eyes not dropping, he didn't say what he meant.

'I didn't have to do it,' he said. 'I enjoy it. I wanted to go to university. I liked geography, I wanted to do that. I like what I do now. I won't do it much longer. It's a bit dangerous.'

'Is Mauro a masseur as well?'

'Sort of. He's stupid about it. He gets people off the street, and afterwards they won't pay him. They're trouble, sometimes. That's what happened to me. I tried to get involved and he hit me with a chair. Not Mauro. The man off the street. It wasn't Mauro's fault, not really, except for being stupid. I'm cross about the chair. That's why I'm here.'

Simon reached for the bowl where the grapes had been, but it was empty.

'I should have brought you some fruit,' Bruno said.

'Anyway he's gone now,' Simon said. 'This came this morning.'

He handed over a postcard. In capitals it said Simon baby Don't worry about your mother because I'm going Don't worry you won't have to see me again See you again one day I don't know where I'm going I'm sorry about what happened Get well Mauro. Kiss my fat speedy ass honey remember!!!!

On the side of the postcard where there was the space for an address, it said only Simon, and the number of the ward where he lay.

'He just handed it in at the desk,' Simon said. 'Downstairs. Half the fucking staff read it before it got to me. They gave it to some old cunt called Simon halfway down the ward. I suppose he couldn't remember what my surname was, the stupid cow.'

'I've got to go,' Bruno said. 'I'm sorry. I hope you get better soon. I can't come back again, I'm afraid.'

'I knew you were going to say that. Every time you meet someone you like and it doesn't work,' Simon said, 'it seems like your last chance. Your last chance for a nice house and someone who loves you. But it's not like that really, there are always other chances.'

Bruno looked at him. He couldn't think of anything to say. He did not know if Simon was talking about him, or if he was talking about Mauro, and he could not ask.

'There are plenty more fish in the sea,' Simon said, and giggled. 'The thing is, Mauro needn't have gone after all. My mother's not going to come. She never was going to come, I suppose. I thought she was, but you can't trust anyone to do what they say they're going to. So he could have stayed in the flat till I came out of hospital. Still, I can't pretend I'm not glad in a way to see the back of that one. Never visited me.'

He stopped, inconsequentially.

'Do you know how to get in touch with him?' Bruno said, finally.

'I don't,' Simon said. 'I can't think where he could have gone. He can't afford a hotel or a flat or probably even a room. He can't afford to go back to Italy even if his family would have him. I don't care, though. He'll turn up again like a rotten apple. I'm sorry he phoned you up that time.'

'That's all right.'

'You might as well go now.'

Bruno got up, but instead of going, he sat on the white sheets of the hospital bed and put his arms round Simon. Then, as Simon had once asked him to, he lay on the bed, pulling Simon down with him into an embrace, his face into the small haired hollow at the back of the neck. He was glad, in a way, to see the back of this one.

They stayed like that for a moment which went on, before it was time for Bruno to get up and go. He felt Simon, in his stiffness, not especially willing to continue with the embrace, but, as in other circumstances, and other rooms, he was paid to tolerate the embraces of others, he put up with it. Nor did Bruno especially want to continue with it, and he did not quite know why, in this white ward with strangers walking by him and observing the two men in an embrace, he did so.

Like a bullet his knowledge that Simon would get better, and his love would find other chances, was in him, lodged; and it was in goodbye that he craned around the face, so strange at this angle, and his furred mouth found the professionally fond corner of a smile, and kissed its partial and plural goodbyes to a man, and to more than that, to a chance. He had never known Simon, never known his life or the rooms he lived in, and it was to something in himself that Bruno was kissing goodbye. And, before he said goodbye, slower than the break of slow thunder after bright distant lightning came the thought, like no words, of hands moving over flesh in order to know it; like the hands and minds of geographers swarming over the maps and lands of remote and unvisitable continents. They were going to live; forever; severally.

QUIET ENJOYMENT

I HANDLE MY own business. There is not much to handle. My father was a man who didn't get out much, whose whole life was bent on preserving what he could from the daily influx and outward spewing of money; who saved. At the end of his seventy-three years there was a sum both good and pathetic: good for a man who started from nothing, as he was fond of saying, pathetic in the eyes of the world, most of whom could not live their lives on such a sum. It was two hundred and thirty-four thousand, one hundred and sixty-two pounds, on which I now live. He was, in the opinion of many of those people who knew him, who were not many, a classic miser; his words for himself were, by contrast, frugal, sensible, modest.

Besides this sum of money, which provides me with an income which it is my entire occupation to juggle, he left me a flat, in which I still live. It was a flat which, when he was alive, I did not know existed; it is a comfortable flat in a respectable block with a porter. I have discovered, since his death, that he bought it for cash in the last years of the war, when property cost nothing, due to a daily fear of the silent rockets from overhead. In the remaining years of his life, he rented it to increasingly profligate tenants, or so I suppose; I know nothing of such tenants, only of the sums of money they paid to squat on his floors, and the last of whom – a woman of terrible shrillness and horribly dyed Jewish red hair – it was my unlovely task to evict from what, I imagine, she considered her home.

My mother died only five years before my father. But she was a woman worn down by the troubles, as she saw them, of her life, and she made only a dim impression of complaining and round-shouldered exhaustion on those people she met. Myself, her son, included.

I do not work, since the money I inherited from my frugal father was enough to keep me from it. I never expected to work, since no such expectation was transmitted to me, and I was, in fact, slightly surprised when the sale of my father's house and the savings he had accumulated from a lifetime of refusing my mother money for Jif amounted to no more than this. It keeps me going; it allows the weekly journey to the supermarket to restock the freezer and the fortnightly visit to a favourite cinema to see a film, but no more.

The flat I live in is in a part of London which few people have heard of. London is punctuated with the stations of the underground train system like a face with freckles. However, between the familiar names of the underground stations, there are parts which seem, to many, like unreal places. No train stops at Hoxton, in Hornsey, Honor Oak Park or Roxeth. And yet people live in these places, and, despite the lack of a train station, think of themselves as inhabitants of a real place. It is in such a part of London that my flat is, and I welcome the lack of interest from the outside world.

The block in which I live in is, in general, exceedingly solidly built, but there is one wall which, for a reason I have never fully understood, transmits noise from the neighbouring flat. This neighbouring flat is not lived in by the people who own it, but by a succession of respectable and well-vetted tenants. Approximately six months ago, the daughter of the owner of the flat moved into it. I stopped in the hallway and exchanged a comment or two as she came up the stairs, labouring under the weight of a potted plant. It was then that I learnt that she was a lawyer, and was about to begin work for a well-known firm of solicitors in the City.

I had no reason to suppose that she was other than a perfectly nice girl, and I smiled at her when I met her.

For a week or two – for ten days, to be precise – she lived alone in the flat. Her life, I gathered, was simple; she rose around seven-thirty, showered and left the flat between eight-ten and eight-fifteen. This allowed her enough time to reach the office in the City by a quarter to nine. From this, although I know little of the practices of working life except what I read in books, I understood that she was either exceptionally diligent in her working life, or exceptionally keen to make a good impression by arriving early at the office. In these ten days, she mostly arrived home at seven o'clock, and twice came back at approximately eleven-thirty. I would not like to convey the impression that I was observing her. It was difficult not to be aware of her movements.

Ten days after she moved in, I met two boys on the stairs of the flat struggling with boxes. I spoke to them, and learnt that they were friends of the girl, and that they, too, were moving into the flat. A week after that, a third boy began to be seen coming in and out of the flat next door with sufficient frequency to suggest to me that he was also living there, although I had not seen him moving in. I knew that the flat had only three bedrooms. I speculated with a certain idle interest about the sleeping arrangements.

The trouble began soon after that. One Saturday night, I was woken up by a noise repetitive and irritating as a washing machine. It came from next door. I went to the first of my spare bedrooms, to which belongs the wall which adjoins that flat, and discovered that the noise was not that of a washing machine, but of repetitive and irritating music. It was two o'clock in the morning. I shut the door of the spare bedroom, and of my bedroom, but I did not succeed in going back to sleep.

The next morning, on my way out to buy the *Sunday Times,* the newspaper I have always preferred, I met another of my neighbours. I asked her if she had suffered from the noise the previous night, but she said she had not. I realised immediately that this was due to the fact that it was only my wall which both adjoined the flat next to mine and transmitted sound; this surmise was confirmed when I spoke both to the people who lived directly above, and to those who lived below the flat, and learnt that it had only been I who had heard the noise.

I waited until I heard the four young people go out, and I pushed a note, which I had written earlier, through their letterbox. It was very civil, and simply said that they must be unaware that the walls in this block were comparatively thin, and that noise was easily transmitted. I was therefore sure that they would not wish to play their music after ten thirty at night. I did not sign the note, naturally.

Such a note should have had the desired effect, but I

was mistaken. On the Tuesday night following the initial Saturday, I was again woken by music. This time, it was played with a renewed force; there was no possibility of sleeping through this. It was, again, two o'clock in the morning. I thought of what action I could take. There was none. I would not expose myself to danger by asking the inhabitants of the flat to turn the music down; they were clearly indifferent to the opinions of their neighbours, and might even turn violent if roused. I sat in my kitchen and waited for it to end; I sat, trembling with rage and fear until half past four in the morning, when the music was finally turned off.

I was certain that this late playing music would, at least, mean that they would all oversleep and be late for their jobs. In this, however, I was mistaken. The noise of the shower, the noise of breakfast being prepared began, as usual, at seven thirty. I could hear, through the wall, the sound of their voices. They seemed to be laughing, to be discussing the events of the night before. I could not hear the words, but I was sure that this was the case. At eight thirty, one by one, they began to go out. I was exhausted, but did not go to bed in the day.

Since then, my life has been turned upside down. The music begins, in general, at eleven thirty, and continues until three or four in the morning. I am prevented from sleep, and sit in my kitchen waiting for silence. Other people might be able to sleep during the day, I cannot, and even when I try, I lie and contemplate my misery, the assaults made nightly on me. I cannot imagine their lives: I do not need to leave the flat, and am not permitted to sleep; they do need to leave the flat, and do not seem to want to sleep. There is something serious about the regularity of their violence against me. It is as if their whole existence is planned around their nightly four hours of murdering music; it is as if they only live next door in order to persecute me, as if they only go to work in order to torment me with waiting for their return.

It was six weeks into this miserable existence that I began to give way to thoughts of violence. In my weekly trips to the supermarket, I started to find instruments of terrible revenge in the trolley: huge knives, inflammable liquids, hosepipes. My thoughts began to turn endlessly to the acts I might carry out, and bring an end to my suffering. Fire and destruction occupied my waking and my insomniac hours; I grew to fear the turn of my own mind, even while I was indulging it.

They were, I am sure, perfectly aware of what I must have been thinking. Once, before I understood fully the sort of people I was dealing with, I telephoned the owner of the flat, the father of the girl, to inform him of the problem. I reminded him that the legal position was that I was entitled to the quiet enjoyment of my property. This is a legal phrase which I discovered by study. He told me bluntly that I was mistaken, that they all had jobs and were decent young people, and did not stay up listening to music until the small hours. I invited him to come and listen, but he grew abusive. They must have found the information that I was attempting to speak to the landlord the best confirmation of the success of their campaign.

I met them, sometimes, in the corridor, or on the stairs. They smiled at me with their fresh faces, disguising their amusement with what anyone who knew nothing of the situation would have taken for the pleasant greetings of neighbours. I looked back levelly; I controlled my face into a mask, not acknowledging them, not, I hope, giving way to the fear I felt, nor the detestation and violence. I passed on, going back to my flat as they went on to their jobs, letting them continue on to the street, and when I was out of earshot, beginning to discuss the success of their tactics.

I see them now from my window. I see the four of them passing on to the street, often laughing, often seeming to have an ordinary conversation, on their way to their respective places of work. I watch them, with my head full of the idea of petrol and inflammation, of the construction of elaborate traps which will fall on them and injure, of the possible mutilation of flesh. I set none of it down; I merely contemplate it in my head, sometimes weeping a little at what I have come to, at the quiet enjoyment of the acts of violence. I think about these acts which I have not carried out, and the consequences of calm and quiet which would follow them; I watch the four small figures, five floors below my window, as they take their identical black bags, and leave the block of flats in the nameless city, as they move forward briskly into the city, there to prosecute their schemes, as, for one more day before things will be changed, they begin to work against me.

THE NAME ON THE DOOR

HILARY WAS WATCHING the television in his office. It was an American show. A woman with a microphone was asking a woman in an armchair about the esteem she held for her own person. It was shortly after five o'clock on a Tuesday afternoon in December in London.

'What are you like,' Angus said, coming through the door with a file under his arm.

'I don't know,' Hilary said. 'What am I like.'

'I said it was a mistake to install televisions in the offices,' Angus said. 'It would just encourage idleness among the workforce.'

'Am I the workforce?'

'You are. Do you think Ricki Lake is fatter than Oprah Winfrey?'

'Is Oprah still on?'

'On five.'

Angus picked up the remote from Hilary's in-tray, and thumbed a button. 'I don't know,' he said. 'What do you think?'

'Back to Ricki.'

Angus went back. The woman in the armchair had started to weep and the audience were applauding her.

'I don't know,' Angus said. 'I think Ricki may be fatter. But Oprah may weigh more.'

'Do you think so,' Hilary said. 'Did you have something for me?'

'No,' Angus said. 'I just wanted to see if you were busy. How much do you think she weighs?'

'Oprah?'

'Is that the negress?'

'The *negress*?'

'The person of restricted gender of African-American origin. I reckon three bushels or a fifth of a shiny red London omnibus. Are you busy?'

'Not very.'

'So I see. Are we busy?'

'I expect not.'

'Do you want something to do?'

'Not very much.'

'Oh good,' Angus said. 'I don't mind if you don't do anything. It just worries me when people start fidgeting and making me feel that I ought to be finding something for them to do.'

'No,' Hilary said. 'I can find things to do.'

'Oh, good,' Angus said again. 'How is your girlfriend, how is she? Cathy. Cathy?'

'Fine,' Hilary said, stoutly. That was all there was to say, and he looked at Angus with the rolled manila file, stiff as a club, in his hand.

Angus leaned against the bookshelf and looked back at Hilary. He seemed disinclined to go. There was no reason for him to have a file in his hand; he could only be taking it from his office to Hilary's, or from Hilary's back to his own office, since only three people worked behind the frosted glass door lettered with the firm's carefully non-committal title, and the secretary was off with the flu, or with toothache, or down the headhunter's, or skiving.

'How is the house?' Hilary said.

'Oh god,' Angus said. 'Don't let's talk about it. Do you know, I see more of those fucking builders than I do of, than I do of my *mother*. Well, my mother lives in Cornwall in a padded cell and she's a fucking nightmare so of course I do. But you see what I mean. Those builders, four months now, and every day a new problem, like the house hasn't got any foundations apparently and it's built on a gigantic sponge or something so the next strong wind it's just going to fall over. I mean you never hear of houses falling over just like that but I suppose they do from time to time. And if one did it would be this one. You know, it's eight months since I bought it and every single week it's worth less than the week before and pretty soon it's going to be a pile of rubble in Notting Hill and – how much do you get for a second-hand brick, probably about eight pee – worth about eighty-five quid. Let's not talk about it. Are you busy?'

'No, of course not,' Hilary said. 'What do you want me to do?'

'Nothing,' Angus said. 'I was going to suggest closing down for the day and having a quick drink.'

'Well, a quick one,' Hilary said.

It was his third week in the office; his third job since leaving university six years before. The first had been in an office with a view of a car park (those Ford Sierras, stationary chariots, aubergine portents of the unarguably miserable life) which had lasted a year and a half. He had had to leave when his desultory affair with fat Frank, the operator of the photocopier, became generally known; it hadn't produced any bullying or hostility, which he was prepared for, and which he and fat Frank, in his fond daydreams, would face down, heroes against the straight world. In the end, it was just the misty affection which every single secretary in the place had started to direct in his approximate direction. Cold with embarrassment, he came to the conclusion that, for the sake of fat Frank he might be prepared to confront homophobia, but never a cosy, inquisitive and universal sympathy. He changed jobs.

The second job was for twice as much money in the City, was a good position, twelve hours a day, six days a week, officially five, forty-six weeks a year, and he walked away from it for no reason that he could really see; just an overheard conversation. Nothing appalling, nothing, in the end, remarkable, but just a bad day; a situation which he had rescued, but might very well not have been able to rescue. And abruptly, he saw himself not as Hilary, but as an employee of the firm. He was not employed because he was liked, not chosen and included as people chose and included their friends. Rather, in this place, what value he had came from what he did; he was kept on when he produced what he was to produce; dismissed when he failed in his task, valued for what he had not done. And once he saw this, he wondered he had not realised something so obvious before, and immediately knew he had to go.

This was his third week working for Angus, the third

Tuesday afternoon. The job was 10K a year more than the job in the City. Bonuses, too, and they looked promising. But the job was like nothing he'd ever done before. There was just Angus – and Caroline, who'd been there no time either, just since September. He hadn't had his first pay cheque yet. Angus had seemed like a bullshit artist the first time he'd seen him; these days, Hilary had to remind himself that it had been one of the things which had impressed him about his employer, and not a threat to his own future.

'Let's go,' Angus said. 'Is she still here?'

'No,' Hilary said. 'She said she had to go.'

'Yes,' Angus said. 'She had to go. I've just got to make a phone call.'

He got out a mobile phone.

'Use mine,' Hilary said, gesturing at the telephone on his empty desk.

'No,' Angus said. 'This is better.'

'The office phone is cheaper,' Hilary said.

'This is better,' Angus said. 'I pay for it anyway. I mean, mine's the name on the door.'

He dialled. On the television, the programme had changed; Australians were attempting to act in beige rooms. Hilary thought what he had often thought, that if you had never been to Australia, you would conclude from such programmes that the human race was beautiful and fine until the age of twenty-five, and then was comic. He was twenty-eight, solitary, shy; he wondered how the makers of the consolatory afternoon programmes would find a means of representing him.

'Oh, hello,' Angus said on the telephone. 'It's Mr Red here. Yes, hello, how are you. Yes, very nice, thank you.

No, I wondered if you had any candidates there for me to interview. No? Yes, I know it's Tuesday. No, that's quite all right. Yes, I will. Yes, I'll call back later. Thursday? Yes, that's all right. Yes – yes – sorry to wake you – yes – goodbye –'

He hung up.

'Let's go,' he said. 'Shit shit shit shit shit. Right. Where shall we go. Soho. Let's go to Soho. Wait here. I'll be back in a minute.'

'Fine,' Hilary said. 'Yes, that's fine.' It was Tuesday; it was in the wrong direction; but it was the third week of a new job; he agreed.

'I'll be back in a minute,' Angus said again.

'No problem,' Hilary said.

'Hilary,' Angus said, when they were in a taxi and heading over the river towards Soho. 'Hilary. I always thought Hilary was a girl's name.'

'It is,' Hilary said. 'And a boy's. People often say that to me, that it's a girl's name. And write to me as Dear Madam.'

'Do you have another name? A middle name?'

'I do,' Hilary said. 'Yes, I do. It's George.'

'George?'

'Yes,' Hilary said, not knowing how to deny it. 'Do you have a middle name?'

'Yes,' Angus said. 'You could use that. You could call yourself George.'

It had never occurred to Hilary. 'I suppose so,' he said. 'It's my father's name, though. My name.'

'It's your father's name?'

'Yes.'

'What do you mean?'

'Well, Hilary is his name, too, so,' Hilary said, 'it might be a bit awkward if I changed mine. I mean I wouldn't want to say to you I'm changing my name from Angus because I don't like the name.'

'But Angus is a nice name.'

'Yes,' Hilary said. 'Yes, it is.' The traffic was thickening. He leaned forward to speak to the driver. 'I'm sure this will be fine.'

'No, no, no,' Angus said, rapping on the window. 'No, no, keep on going. Just aim for Cambridge Circus.'

The driver made a tiny shrug; the mirror was angled away from Hilary and he could not see his expression.

'The odd thing is,' Hilary said, 'that it's a connection between me and my father. I mean I don't necessarily want to change it just because it's a bit embarrassing.'

'Sorry?' Angus said.

'My name,' Hilary said.

'Oh right,' Angus said. 'I didn't know what you were talking about there for a minute. I can't believe that bastard.'

'What bastard?'

'That bastard,' Angus said. 'The bastard I was just calling just now. I mean, the amount of business I put his way, and he gives me grief because it's Tuesday and he's asleep.'

'Where is he?' Hilary said.

'Clapham, I think,' Angus said. 'I mean, really. You just don't get the service these days.'

'Who is he?' Hilary said. 'Are you interviewing somebody for a job?'

'Interviewing somebody?' Angus said. 'Sorry?'

'I thought you said on the phone – sorry, I was listening when you were talking – I thought you said –'

'Oh God, yes, yes,' Angus said. 'No, no, no. God, Hilary, you are so fantastic, I couldn't make you up. Where have you been all my life. No, I was talking to my *boy*.'

Hilary nodded; the thing he had quickly understood about Angus was that he liked to shock, and he liked people who showed no evidence of shock. Hilary had suspected no *boy*; no friend, no lover, no wife had come into Angus's conversation, and Hilary, having no *boy* to offer back, had kept his own privacy private, had offered a lie in its place. Have you got anyone for me to interview, Angus had said; that was exactly what he had said. Hilary had heard him.

'I've got another number,' Angus said eventually. 'Christ, the traffic. Shall we get out here? Where shall we go?'

'This is fine,' Hilary said. 'We can walk from here, can't we?'

'I suppose so,' Angus said. 'Do you know, there's something so strange about London. How long have you been here? I came here in, God I don't know, ten years ago, something like that. And when you first come here, when I first came here anyway, I got to know it from the tube map and I carried a map, an *A to Z* –' but he said *I to Zee*, cockney to California in three syllables, and as he made his baffling funny joke and pulled his funny face, he looked out of the window and not at Hilary's possible response – 'and went everywhere by tube. I mean if I had to go from Leicester Square to Charing Cross Road I'd get a tube and change twice or whatever rather than do what everyone does and get a taxi.'

'Or walk,' Hilary said.

'Or walk,' Angus said. 'I suppose. Do you still have an

A to Z. I used to have one everywhere I went, in my pocket. I just had no idea. It was so embarrassing. Once I took a client out for lunch. And he looked at his watch and said I've got to meet somebody in Rupert Street in ten minutes and I don't know how to get there. So I said, no problem, and got my bag out and my *A to Z* and was looking in the index. And then he said, as if I hadn't said or done anything, But I suppose the driver will know. And he'd had his driver idling outside all the time. God I was so green then.'

'Did you keep the client?'

'Of course,' Angus said. 'Yes, of course. They like to feel superior. I still don't recommend it, though. Let's stop here. Hi. Hi. Here is fine.'

They got out. Angus paid and took the receipt. It was almost raining. Three men were standing fanning their tickets outside the theatre, and muttering their constant mantra, tickets, tickets, tickets for tonight. Around them the theatre-goers – regular theatre-goers, going to the theatre once a year, a week or two before Christmas – coagulated, paused, moved inwards.

'So horny,' Angus said. 'Horny horny horny. Where shall we go?'

'Where do you think?'

'Golly,' Angus said. 'I don't know. A bar? A club? I love that song so much. Don't you think it's perfectly amazing that in the whole history of the world nobody has written a song until six months ago that just goes So horny, horny horny horny. The profundity of it, really. I mean, it's just what all music is about, someone saying that they're really horny. So where shall we go. God, so fucking crowded with all the office parties, I suppose. Where do you go in Soho?'

Hilary thought. He went to Soho, of course he did. He went home, and took off his suit, one of four, and his respectable tie and the dark blue shirt, and put on a different set of clothes. Not his work clothes; not his student clothes, baggy and easy and nothing special. But clothes for bars. He put on a special set of clothes. They were nothing remarkable; other men put on leather or even rubber, to announce some recondite sexual practice, grotesque and warty fauna calling across the urban swamp in the dim hope of some dim likeness. Hilary aimed for the resemblance of niceness, and, in his chinos and blue button-down shirts and fresh aspect, he probably achieved it. It was not his fault if niceness was not a quality, these days, that many people responded to. And still he went to Soho, like the rest of his kind.

'Do you know the Yard?' he said in the end.

'The Yard,' Angus said. 'No, I don't know it. Take me there. I just want to make another call. I can't believe that bastard. I'm going to try somebody else.'

Angus got out his mobile telephone and, this time, his diary. He turned the pages, and, squinting, dialled a number. He stood outside the theatre on Cambridge Circus, and tapped his feet. Hilary turned away, and looked away down the street, not quite wanting to listen to his boss's telephone call, not quite knowing how to occupy himself while he waited.

'Oh, hello,' Angus said. 'Hello. I'm a friend of Mr Red. Yes, he said you might be able to help me with something. Yes, I have a little problem. I need to have a little meeting. I don't know if you can help me with that? Yes, with Charles. Is he? Is he away? Oh, I'm so sorry. Yes, I know, it's Tuesday. Oh, yes, I quite understand. Yes, not at all. Thank you, thank you. Yes, I'd love to do business with you, yes, of course. Thursday? Not at all.'

'Mr Red?' Hilary said.

'Fuck,' Angus said. 'God, this is such a fucking disaster. Where are we going? Oh, yes, the Garden or something.'

'The Yard,' Hilary said.

'Let's go where we're going,' Angus said. 'Let's go and let's go now. Because I need to go now. I need to go. You know,' he stopped, there in the street, and he looked at Hilary. 'I am so pleased that you and I are going out for a drink like this, and having a chance to have a proper conversation about things. This is really a very very good thing.'

Hilary said nothing. The thought he had been repressing surfaced, that Angus was taking him out to tell him benignly that it wasn't working out and he had found someone better for the job. He swallowed hard, rolled back his shoulders, and kept up with Angus's pace.

Cathy was the business. Yes she was. She had dark hair and skin like soft caramel and eyes of a heavy blue. And her eyelids rolled down slowly when she looked at you and rolled up slowly and she held you in the frank erotica of her gaze. And her figure was tight and her legs were long and her waist was tiny and she had two hands and two feet and five fingers or toes on each. Yes she did.

Hilary could keep this up all day. His powers of description were amazing – at least they amazed him. He sat back and listened to himself telling Angus about his girlfriend, what she had said only the night before about what Angus had said to Hilary and what she had been wearing and what she did for a living, and thought, well, that's really not too bad, that's really quite impressive, I'm quite impressed by myself. And it must have been pretty good, because Angus honestly didn't seem that interested. He didn't seem that bothered by descriptions of Cathy. Normally, perhaps, Hilary would have been a bit worried by this; worried by the idea that he hadn't managed to convey, through the boy-band descriptions and the pub anecdotes, that his girlfriend was in some way extraordinary. But he was, in the event, quite relieved. It meant that Angus hadn't seen the most extraordinary thing about Hilary's girlfriend Cathy. The fact that she didn't exist.

Hilary didn't know about women. He didn't even know any, much, apart from his secretary and his mum and the girls who looked at him mostly and wanted to be his friend until a straight man came along for them. And he certainly didn't know about them. Did people know this? Did they know that he didn't know? He wondered. Maybe they did. Sometimes, they certainly did. Seven years before, a friend had asked him to come to his digs to meet a girl from another hall of residence. He couldn't understand it. Hilary, you're all right, nothing wrong with you, and you've had no luck with girls since you packed in your girlfriend from home two weeks into your second term at university. I wish we'd had a chance to meet her but these things, I know they don't always work out. So Hilary went to have dinner with the boy and his girlfriend and the girl from another hall of residence and a couple from the boy's girlfriend's laboratory.

The varieties of conversational experience among the young. *I got so drunk last night. Do you remember that programme on the television when we were eight or something. I feel like shit after staying up all night to finish that essay and it was terrible and he didn't even notice.* And then another one beginning *When I was younger.* And it was *When I was younger these are the strange things I believed about my own body and about sex.* A favourite one, and one everyone can play in a different way. *I thought my bottom was an enormous slit eight inches long which opened up like a big smile every time I had a poo. I was worried I wouldn't be able to stop myself peeing when I came. I didn't think men had pubic hair.*

And then, halfway through the dinner and the usual run of conversation students have, a girl said the strangest thing about a thing she had believed, when young, about her own body. She didn't think, she said, that she had a vagina. Was it the girl who had been supplied for Hilary? There was an amazed turning of heads; this was a new one. She said it again.

'I really didn't. I thought I didn't have a vagina.'

And Hilary without thinking said, 'But how can you have thought that. I mean what did you think you had been peeing through all these years.'

Another amazed turning of heads, in the other direction, and everyone thought about what Hilary had said, and the girl said, 'But Hilary. Girls don't urinate through their vaginas.'

And they all looked at him and they all knew it and he didn't know it.

Well, he did now. But he had absolutely no idea what else he didn't know about girls. What did they look like? When they took their clothes off? Did they look like the pictures in art galleries? Was that a good enough guide?

Well, no, since he couldn't remember ever having seen a single painting which distinguished the vagina from whatever they pissed through. Not that he would have looked. So, talking to Angus about Cathy, he thought of her black hair and her heavy blue eyes and stuck firmly to things she had said to him, which he had heard other men say their girlfriends had said to them. Knowing all the time that as far as he knew, women nowadays might have a second mouth below their bottom rib. He just wouldn't know about it. Because no one would have told him.

Angus was a strange one. He was not exactly a friend of a friend. More of a contact of a contact. He was starting something up; something in your line, Hilary, because you don't want to be stuck here down this load of crap artists in the City for years, waiting for buggins' turn, waiting for dead men's shoes, waiting for the sack and out on the street when they remember how long you've been in the same office. No, he certainly didn't. So he said he might be interested in a job on the wrong side of the river and the far side of Tower Bridge. And the phone rang.

It was a bad morning; he might not have said yes otherwise. He had been in since seven, knowing pretty well what was going to happen that morning, and since nine he had been watching the piles of figures on the computer screen unravel like knitting; cave away inwards like sand in an hourglass; and he stabbed at the keyboard, helplessly, selling too late, buying too early. From time to time the others came over and stood and looked at him. They might have been awed, but they made a good effort and laughed at his great solitary disaster, making a show of coping as he tucked his telephone between his cheek and his left shoulder, his head lolling sideways like that of a man half decapitated. From time to time between bursts of the telephone he rolled his eyes and sang out his groan, and the small crowd by his desk gave a little cheer, and went off to their own small disasters, their own stored-up triumphs, and loving the thought that *it*, whatever *it* was, was happening to some other poor sap this morning.

It was not a good time for Angus to get through to Hilary on the telephone. He had asked, immediately, if it were a good time, and Hilary had asked who it was and no it was not a good time in the same breath. Angus had said with a mournful expression of regret in the voice, that it was, sadly – and you felt it was sad, you felt this man meant what he said, whatever he said, whatever he meant – a very good time for him, that he could be of help to Hilary, and his telephone number, when convenient, was as follows. Hilary wrote it down, and prepared to say thank you when he realised the man had, with perfect civility, already hung up.

The day, oddly, started to improve from then on. The loss at the end of the day was containable, and when Hilary detached the telephone from its position between his left ear and left shoulder, and put it down, and swung his head round with a practised glorious stretch, it was with a sense of luxury that he picked up the telephone and slowly dialled the number and put the receiver back into its now agonising position; its position in his altered anatomy, altered by work.

Angus was a strange one. The office he had then – the one Hilary went to at eight on a Friday evening – was virtually in the West End. The building it was in was on a road leading to a bridge, as if for a quick getaway, and not planned for any particular purpose, but simply for rent to any temporary and growing business. It was already dark; the evenings had closed in. The entrance hall was plush and quiet; the doorman, in a uniform which might have served for anything and probably had, looked up the neutral name of Angus's business on a clipboard before directing Hilary to the fifth floor. The Edwardian grandiose ambitions, the imperial style of the quiet pre-weekend building diminished at the lifts, and had disappeared entirely by the fifth floor, cream-painted and silently lit. Was the success of the firms occupying these offices evident from the parsimonious upkeep of the common parts, the lush display of the main foyer? Acutely aware only of the tread of his feet, he could not follow the thought through.

There were too many doors; too many firms; too much ambition in this corridor. The names by the doors were unfamiliar, and pointedly unhelpful. GBCB. Facilitation National Continental World Wide. Holmes Wright Carter. Micky Spelicky. Each on the same, uniform plate, each announcing and saying nothing, and by each a door so thick that it could not be seen whether anyone was inside, or whether the building was as deserted as its corridors. It was a jolt when he recognised a name. It was the half-relief and alarm of glimpsing a familiar face in a crowded shop, and taking a moment to know that it is only yourself, seen in an unnoticed mirror. He thought it was familiar, and then remembered it was the name of Angus's firm, Angus who he had come to see.

Afterwards, he did not quite know why he had accepted Angus's job. If his initial unexplained trepidation had quickly vanished, it was replaced by a firmer sense that this was quite a risk. Angus had started it up only a few months before. Other people – the rich – handed over their money to Angus, and he played with it; he made money for them, out of their money, and he made money for himself, out of their money. And soon he would be making money for himself out of his own money and Hilary would be making money for himself out of his own money, and then, and then, after all that, they would retire to some hot silent beach by a hot silent sea, and never have to think for themselves ever again. The speed of growth of his business explained why he was in such a place, having been obliged to find an office, any office, to move to for two months while finding something more permanently acceptable. Speed of growth meant nothing, of course, if you were starting from zero, and, though Angus's client base was narrow, he had some surprisingly big players. Personal attention, that was the thing, and from spring to autumn it had got too much for Angus. He needed someone to spread the load and widen the base. Someone hungry for the kill, keen as mustard, who lives for the client and wants to stitch up the boss.

Hilary sat and looked at this man, in the anonymous temporary office, his eager thin face bright in the room against the unobjectionable and unremarkable furnishings of commerce. He was bony and angular in his suit, his joints and his movements made big by the thin length of his bones, his limbs; he shot his cuffs constantly, as if to place emphasis on his words, *growth, load, mustard*, and as he twitched his arms forward like a practising mantis, the weight of his silver watch jangled like a woman's bracelet against his vein-defined wrist. He wore a double-breasted suit, in a Prince of Wales check. It was a suit not right for the year, a suit, surely, for some Andy-in-accounts, but as Hilary sat and watched Angus talk, it was as if desirability had settled over this Prince of Wales carapace, not condemning its wearer, but rather confirming the certain truth that if Angus wore such a suit, it was surely the right suit to wear; a suit independent of fashion, or appallingly ahead of the game, and he accepted that here was a man beyond the reach of his judgement.

Angus paused, and then excused himself for a moment. Of course, Hilary had heard all this – all this *spiel* before. But he had not always heard it at a point when he had to get out from where he was to where he wanted to be. And now he completely had to get out. He could do the usual rounds, and try and get a job before the word got back that he was looking for out. That would be the right thing to do. He sat and thought of ways to excuse himself. If this had made him think that it was time to get out then it would have served a purpose.

The man came back, and as he came in, suddenly he was not an interviewer, producing the usual line, but overwhelmingly a man, a mere name, defined by the unarguable front of that suit. And, as if to acknowledge his chameleon shift, he began on a different tack. It was fun, here. The money was good and the work wasn't too hard. No getting in before nine, no hanging about after five. He wanted to keep the clients few but loaded. He wanted to take someone on because it was all getting a bit much for one; more money than Angus needed, more hours than Angus could really be doing with. So there you go. How about you, Hilary – Hilary? Married? Kids? A girlfriend, really? Cathy? Nice. You want a drink? A quick one, and Angus could tell Hilary all about the office they'd be moving into the week after next, Angus and Caroline and Hilary if he wanted the job, because the job was his, if he wanted it. Angus excused himself for a second, and Hilary thought that he might as well accept the job, because now he had lied to Angus, and, when you lie to someone, when you say you have a black-haired girlfriend called Cathy when in reality you have slept with nobody since a boy called fat Frank, years ago, who worked a photocopying machine in your office, you establish a relationship with them, you know, so sad, that they trust you.

'What day is it?' Angus said, when he had come back from the loo. They were in the Yard.

'What day is it?' Hilary said. 'It's Tuesday, isn't it?'

'Yes,' Angus said. 'Yes, it's Tuesday. Of course it is. Quiet sort of day.'

Hilary nodded. Tuesday was usually quiet, but not in December; the bar was pretty full with the backs of men, the backs of their cropped heads. Suited, or in the rainbowed slick of a bomber jacket, they concentrated, silently, on each other, waiting to make their move.

'I don't know this bar,' Angus said in the end. 'Gay bar, is it.' And another facetious noise, *guy bar* –

'Yes,' Hilary said. 'I suppose it is. It's better in the summer. I like it. It has a good atmosphere. Nobody bothers you.'

'You don't get hassled,' Angus said. His hand was wandering over his chest, feeling for something within his jacket, the telephone or the wallet.

'No,' Hilary said. 'No, it's all right. It's a myth that you're not safe in these places. It's a good place to come.

They only bother each other, and you get a nice quiet drink.'

'Is that right,' Angus said. 'I've never been here before. Do you not want to go somewhere you might score. Isn't that the point.'

'No,' Hilary said, thinking of his imagined Cathy. 'It doesn't bother me.' He was looking at a dark boy across the bar; twenty-five, maybe. His hair, cactus-stiff and black as oil, his hooded brow, the fact of his shameful and perfect proportionate brevity, standing no more than five feet four, filled Hilary's mind with the certainty that he had had no choice in this matter, that he had been given the obligation to like the short, the dark, the silent, the – yes, that must be it, this waiting Brazilian – as surely as he had been given the obligation to go after men, and the certainty that he would be refused in return. 'We can go somewhere else, if you're uncomfortable.'

'It doesn't bother me,' Angus said. 'I can look out for myself. Hilary Hilary Hilary. You know something. Hilary is usually a girl's name.'

'It is usually,' Hilary said. 'But it can be a boy's name as well. Do you want another drink?'

'No,' Angus said. 'I'm fine. What day is it?'

'Tuesday,' Hilary said.

'Do you ever think,' Angus said. 'That somewhere in the world, all the Tuesdays are piled up together. I mean, that somewhere, time doesn't happen in a sequence. That somewhere all those fucking Tuesdays are in one place. We used to have chemistry on a Tuesday at school and I hated it and ever since then everything fucking awful has happened to me on a Tuesday, every week, without fail. And all those fucking Christmases, all together. And all those fucking ten to fours. Don't you just hate it when you look at the clock and it's ten to four. I always think that ten to fours have so much more in common with every other ten to four that's ever happened than with the moment that happens five minutes later. And Christmas Day is much more like every other Christmas Day than the day before or the day after or anything like that. Do you see what I mean. Do you see. God, I hate time. I hate the passing of time. I really hate it.'

'I see what you mean,'

'I'm going to make another call,' Angus said in the end. He got out his mobile telephone again, and, thinking expansively, dialled. He held it to his ear, and waited; took it away and looked, quizzically, at the visual display. He switched it off. 'Can you get a signal in here, do you know?'

'I don't know,' Hilary said. 'I don't have a telephone. A mobile.'

'Oh, right,' Angus said. 'I'm not getting anything at all. Do you want another drink?'

'Sure,' Hilary said. 'Yes, sure. If you're having one.'

'Oh, I'm having one,' Angus said. He went to the bar; Hilary watched the way he acknowledged, neither by gaze nor avoidance, the possibility of the attractiveness of the men he walked between. There was a perfect neutrality, he saw that, in the way Angus walked; a freedom from the possibilities of attraction or repulsiveness, an inoculation which made the glances of the bar slide over him and the barman serve him with a prompt lack of anything approaching care or neglect. And it was as if he were watching himself; that, despite every difference between himself and Angus, the lack of interest of the bar was confirmation that he was not a sexual being, that the most he could hope for was kindly neglect. He looked down, and saw that, at some point, someone had splashed his shoes with beer, without noticing. He looked at his shoes, as if, though they were merely worn brown brogues, spreading fatly at the joint of the toes, they held some moral lesson for him. It had been eleven months since he had had sex with another human being, and he felt that, if now, another human being took his hand, the long unaccustomed touch of flesh would strike like electricity, loosed, and make him jump backwards, and away.

'I'm sorry,' Angus said, coming back. Hilary looked up. He had almost forgotten that he was here with anyone, so firmly was the association between this place and solitude in his habits. He smiled, and Angus said it again. 'I'm sorry. I mean, for saying don't you want to go somewhere you can score. I forgot.'

'That's all right,' Hilary said.

'No, I'm sorry,' Angus said. 'I forgot you had a girlfriend. Cathy.'

'Yes,' Hilary said. 'Yes, Cathy.'

'Right,' Angus said. He handed Hilary another drink, and they stood there for a moment. 'I don't have a girlfriend,' he said. 'Or anyone. I used to. I just got bored. Better on my own really. Do you know what I mean?'

'Yes,' Hilary said.

'No, of course you don't,' Angus said. 'No, you've decided you're better off with someone. Well, good luck to you. What do you think?'

What did he think.

'Are you looking to be with someone,' Hilary said. 'I mean.'

Angus shifted from foot to foot. 'Naaaaah,' he said.

'With who. You mean with Caroline or someone. Would you? I wouldn't.'

'Not anyone in particular,' Hilary said. 'I'm sorry. I didn't mean to –'

'Naaaaaah,' Angus said again, and Hilary heard with alarm how his voice was sliding, how the daytime telephone clipped civility was setting out into the surprising sounds, the uncharted vowels of fashionable cockney, as if Angus was trying out a tentative and alarming manner on someone who didn't especially matter. 'Naa, mate. Not Caroline. Not fuck some old slapper like that. No way. I'm all right as I am, just me and the cat and me old muvver in a padded cell in Cornwall. That'll do me.'

'Have you got a cat?' Hilary said.

'No,' Angus said, and quite abruptly, he was back to his normal rational voice. 'No, no cat. But I'll tell you something for nothing. I do have an old mother in a padded cell in Cornwall.' He rolled his eyes, as if he had just told Hilary a joke, as if he had just produced a quick punchline from a complex and perilous anecdote.

'Yes?' Hilary said.

'You've got a girlfriend,' Angus said. 'Haven't you. You know something, Hilary. I haven't. I haven't had a girlfriend for years. Not that it matters. It doesn't matter. I'm fine as I am. If I want a girl, I can go and get one, no trouble. I just don't want the bother. What day is it?'

'Tuesday,' Hilary said.

'I know that,' Angus said. 'I meant, what fucking date is it. It's not long till Christmas, is it? What. Two weeks. Yeah, can't wait. Yeah, that'll be great, calling somebody who doesn't want to see you ever again four days before Christmas in the hope that he's going to stop you being on your own for three whole days without a fucking word from anyone except your fucking dealer, just you and a turkey for one and a fucking great pile of cocaine and you can't really be that bothered with the turkey when it comes down to it. Are you listening to me? Are you? Are you?'

'You know,' Hilary said, and then he stopped, hardly knowing what he wanted to say. The man looked at him – his boss – Angus – the stranger – and seemed to be waiting for what he had to say. 'Look,' Hilary said finally. 'Look, I think you can use your phone in here. That man's talking. You must just have been standing in the wrong place.'

Angus turned his head. 'I'll try again,' he muttered, almost ashamed. He got out his telephone, and his diary, and dialled one more time. 'I think it's working. Oh, hello,' Angus said. 'Hello, oh, hello. No, no, you don't know me. You don't know me. I wondered. Well, I wondered. I wondered if you could help me. I got your name from my friend. No. Hello. This is Mr Red. I wondered if you could help me out. With some stuff. I wondered if you could help me to meet a friend of yours. Yes, a friend of yours. Yes, Mr Snow. Yes. Mr Charlie Snow. Yes. Mr MacCocaine. Yes. I wonder if you could bring round Mr Cocaine with his, with a pile of his friends, with three grams of his friends. Mr Cocaine. Do you know what I mean. Yes. Yes, now. Yes. Now. Yes. How much. Yes. Now. Please. Yes. Now. Let me tell you where to come. No. Don't go. Please. Let me tell you. I'll I'll I'll let me.'

Hilary was standing there, and looking at him; and the stranger behind Angus was silent, and the stranger with that stranger, and everyone in a little circle, every solitary man, waiting to meet another solitary man, was standing there, listening, and one or two were starting, even, to laugh, as Angus, at eight o'clock, only, on a Tuesday evening, a couple of weeks before Christmas, closed his eyes and clipped his mobile phone together, in one, and prepared himself. Angus stood, his eyes closed, as if a terrible tragedy had befallen him, and Hilary, waiting for Angus, was seized with the awful consciousness that here was someone worse off than him, about whose fate he could not care, for whom he could not act. He wished – what did he wish – he wished, not for the earth to open up underneath him, but rather for the sky to empty and clear, and his embarrassed roll of the head took in the sky, so clear, so distant, so silent above this evening noise.

'You know,' Hilary said, and then stopped, seeing that Angus wasn't listening. After all, there were ways of talking to strangers, as there were ways of talking to friends, and lovers and family. Ways of talking to the world. And the words *you know* could properly be used to any of them. And yet, looking at this man, this stranger, this employer, this man with his name on the door, Hilary was silenced with the sense of inappropriateness of what he was about to say, whatever it had been. Anything would have been wrong; any comment, just as the interaction between the two of them was too fantastic for any room to contain, any bar, any office. *You know*, he had said, but what Angus might or might not know was too extraordinary to guess at, and, being alone with him was like the sudden understanding of the limits of communication, the limits of epistemology. A blank patience had settled over the man, and Hilary, for a moment, in this London bar, before Christmas, abandoned whatever he had been about to say, and drew a general lesson; the weird certainty that whoever he had known in his life, in the end, at some point, had looked at him with the same blank patience, and waited for him to communicate. He had lied to this man, his boss, about the existence of a girlfriend; he felt, just now, as if he had always lied about everything, lied to his family about who he was, to everyone he knew about what he felt, to everyone he ever met about what he had been, and what he might become, and, as strangers turned and looked at the pair of them, he had very little idea how this state of affairs might ever come to an end.

It was only a moment, and he walked away, hiding what he felt must be in his face, and stood, for a moment, by the door of the bar. And looking back at him was a couple, outside, an unwieldy and unfamiliar sight, a pair of musicians. Each carried an instrument, and each, underneath a beige macintosh, wore a festive set of tails; they looked like party-goers, just before Christmas, before you saw the boxed instruments they carried, with which they made a living. They looked undecided, but cheerful, as they stood at the door to the bar, looking at Hilary with the other denizens, as if he, too, were only an example, a specimen. They stood for a minute, like visitors from another, a normal world, and then exchanged glances; made a silent agreement, turned and went away down the street, dismissing Hilary and his world swiftly, without cruelty, and with justice.

'That's that then,' Angus said, briskly; he unclipped the mobile, clipped it shut again, and put it in his pocket. 'That's that then.'

'Is there a problem?' Hilary said. He was still looking

down the street after the two musicians; he had almost forgotten that he had come to this bar with anyone at all.

'Yes,' Angus said. 'Yes, there's a problem. Do you know about my problem? Do you want to hear about my problem? Let me tell you.'

'You don't have to,' Hilary said.

'No,' Angus said. 'But I will. Let me tell you something. Let me. Don't get to be like this. Do you know what I mean. Don't let your life depend on anything like this. It's no good. It's really no good. Phoning up and asking people you don't know to be good to you.'

'Yes,' Hilary was saying, and he could feel that his eyes would not rest on Angus's face, that they were, in embarrassment or fear or some external imposed truth, swarming away from the sharp-boned face to the men around him, listening to this strange Tuesday crisis, which to them, the strangers, was only interesting, and, for the moment, Hilary could not see why it was any more than interesting to him, this confirmation that it made no difference whether he lied about his girlfriend or told the truth, that whatever he said was of no interest to this man who employed him. It was as if he were standing, not by a man, but by a name, an unreadable and mistakable pseudonym on a plate in a corridor he was always to walk down, knowing nothing from what he read, and the more he read, the more people spoke to him, the less, in the end, he felt he would know or understand or feel. What about me, he felt like saying. What about me.

'Yes,' Angus echoed. 'Yes, listen to me. You know what it is. I used to be a kind of fun guy to be around. You know that? Do you believe that? I used to be. I used to hang out with people and have friends and everything like everyone else. I did. And people used to phone me up and say Hey Angus, come out and have some fun with us, because whenever people wanted to have a party, to party, to have fun, they thought and the first person they came up with was me, because I was the party. So I knew like a hundred people who liked to go out maybe once every three weeks, and every night I went out, and every night I partied with a different lot of people. And it was cool because every time I went out it was different, even though every time I went out it was the same. But you know something. It doesn't last. Because either you give up on it or it gives up on you. Yes it does. It gives up on you. All that partying just gives up on you. And one night you get home and you look at the phone and it's just not blinking. And you think it's not working, that you forgot to put the answerphone on. But you pick it up and it's working. And nobody's rung you, and you do what you can't remember last doing, spending a night at home because you've had no offers. And the next night it's okay, because somebody rings you up. But a week or two later, there's another night, another empty night, and no reason. And then a bit sooner, another one, and another one. And you might start to think, well, I can have a good time on my own. So you have a good time on your own. Because after a while on your own is the only fucking place you can have any kind of time. Because nobody calls and nobody comes. Only people like you who get paid to stick around. Only fucking spongers like you.'

He had seemed to be talking to Hilary, but from the way he now moved his head and shifted his wild wild eyes, it was clear that he had had no idea until now who, exactly, he had been talking to. Hilary looked at him. He thought only one thing. So I'm not going to be sacked. It shocked him, his own thought.

'Sorry,' Angus said.

'That's okay,' Hilary said, and, shrugging, bent to pick up his briefcase. There was no point in staying.

'Hilary,' Angus said. 'Please, Hilary.'

But as he said it, he seemed to understand, Angus, that there was nothing in what he said, and it was almost with a look of patience that he stood there and watched Hilary go. Hilary could feel Angus watching him, watching the new boy, and as Hilary walked off into the street, feeling himself dissolving among the mass, it was almost a cocaine frenzy of his own which dissolved with his departure. The streets were new as he walked down them, solitary, and it was with an unfamiliar sadness at the departure of another that he went, and, saying to himself in a regular way, it doesn't matter, it doesn't matter, he could feel the ripples of Angus's doubt mounting within himself; a doubt linked to the consideration he had for himself and for Angus, a sense that it was better not to be alone. That, even at Christmas, it could be better not to be alone. And then he started to have the faintest pinprick of the wicked, the certain awful conviction that he had had this thought before; that he had heard this certain truth stated once before. One day, he, too, would reach for the telephone; it would be there for him, as it was always there for Angus, and just as he would find he could open it up, half-hearing the voices which would treat him with contempt, he knew he would be able to deal with the wave-like blow that there, somewhere, at the other end of the telephone, was a man who would be prepared to talk to him, who would be prepared to listen, to sell him what he needed, and he went into his evening with the solid truth that he had, without meaning to, made a decision about his future, that his future, for the first time, would turn and accept him.

A CHARTIST

THERE WAS NO one upstairs at all. I went up three times in an hour, in case they had all knocked off for a tea break, which seemed unlikely, but there were just a lot of men with their shirts off wandering up and down. It was three in the morning in a club in Brixton.

You felt the lack of the dealers. The club was full of men dancing in a rather hopeful sort of way, bopping in a sixth form manner rather than the usual, hips-out strut, there were occasional little pockets, islands of men who had obviously planned ahead and brought their own gear, men flailing and grinning, their jaws working. They seemed odd among the cheerily unsorted crowd.

The third time I went up there I bumped into Sean.

'What's up?' I said.

'Nothing,' he said. 'What are you after?'

'Some gear,' I said. 'There's nothing going on.'

'No,' he said. 'I was talking to the barman. He said they've been raided and they all got carried off by half eleven. No chance. Who are you with?'

'Some people I was at dinner with,' I said. 'They sent

me up here to get them enough E for five.'

'No chance.'

Sean was a friend of mine. I'd known him on and off for a year, I'd never been to his house and he'd never been to mine. I saw him in the same two places: in clubs, and at the first nights in galleries. Once or twice I'd been out for a drink with him. He'd never be much more than a half-friend I sometimes had a drink with. He was quite a glamorous artist – the sort people talk about, though not the sort people buy, since his works were too absurd to even contemplate setting up. One man in North London *had* set one up, had bought a room-sized piece for a sum of money which, Sean said, had kept him going for a year and a half. There had been a gratifying stream of press coverage – some of which I'd written – and afterwards a complete lack of any further commissions. Though a fair amount of interest from which anything might come, and a little bit of fame.

The joke of Sean was that I always pretended to be passionately obsessed with him. Friends of mine always referred to him as 'your lover' since he was very good-looking and I liked him. 'Saw your lover the other day.' It wasn't true – I wasn't obsessed with him, though he was a nice man and at his best with his shirt off. He was famous for being monogamous, or almost so; though, as someone once remarked to me, sometimes it was hard to believe when you saw him in a club at five in the morning. I knew what I thought, and didn't say anything to anyone about it.

'Where's Joe?' I said. Joe was his partner.

'No idea,' he said. 'Haven't seen him for a week.'

'Is he away?' I said. I shouted a bit over the noise and

the thump as the first swathe of the number dissolved into accelerating beats, before the dance music cut back in.

'No,' he said. 'I don't think so. He moved out.'

'He moved out?'

'Yeah,' he said. 'It's a bummer.'

'Come on,' I said. 'Let's go and talk about it.'

The club has a room slightly insulated from the dancing floor, so that the music comes out as a dull thud rather than the speakered shout that makes your ribs thud. People go there, it is said, to chill out; I never heard anyone use the expression, except in the same ironic way that they might say, 'Had some well dodgy gear Sat'day'. So Sean and I went into this room without a proper name. There were three bespectacled drag queens practising their low-level bitchery in a corner; one man who had overdone it was lying on his back on the floor, quite ignored, quite unaware that he had lost a shoe.

'I don't know what happened,' he said. 'It was my fault.'

'I'm sure it wasn't,' I said. 'Come on, tell me.'

We'd never slept with anyone else, Sean said. You know he was the first man I ever slept with. And he was late coming to terms with it, and he'd only ever had one other man before he met me, in York. Joe was a really shy man. He didn't look it; he was. He liked going to clubs, and to bars, but he would do anything to get out of going to a party. He hated going to dinner parties, he hated giving dinner parties. When he changed his job, he lost a lot of sleep just thinking about how he was going to get on with the people he was going to work with.

It was mad. He wasn't the most confident person in the world. No one would have thought he was. But he was easy to like. It was the combination of a man who went out all the time and one who was self-deprecating, shy, easily embarrassed by small difficulties. No one found him intimidating, or hard, or anything; everyone saw the little problems he had, and didn't talk about. People liked him.

The thing was, what people didn't see, was that he'd turned his shyness into a kind of virtue. He didn't see any reason to try and get rid of it, though he'd rather not have been shy. He just thought that was the way things were and there was no altering any of it. That was really where the monogamy thing came into it. We'd decided that we weren't going to sleep with anyone else, we weren't going to pick up a boy at a club and say to each other, well, see you tomorrow. There's nothing wrong with that, I don't think. It used to be the way things were.

But he wasn't doing it because he thought it was a good idea. We decided that we wouldn't sleep with anyone else because he didn't believe he could pick someone else up. It was all because he wasn't confident enough. Of course he could have done. People used to come on to him here, when he was dancing, or whatever. Whenever I went off somewhere, when I came back there was always some really gorgeous boy grinding his arse against Joe's crotch, and him with this apologetic look on his face, as if he couldn't help it.

You'd think that would have persuaded someone that they could score as easily as anything. But it didn't. When I said this to Joe – I only ever said it to cheer him up, to make him think that he wasn't as hopeless as he thought he was, I never said it to persuade him to go ahead and sleep around – he'd only ever say, 'Oh, the thing about this place is people are always playing weird games with each other. It doesn't mean anything.' He seemed to believe it. He really seemed to think that if he'd said to one of these boys who was coming on to him like that, 'All right then, come home with me,' they'd have laughed at him for taking it seriously.

And it was the same everywhere. Once there was this guy who was coming on to him to this unbelievable extent at some dinner party – not just flirting, but, by the end of the evening, asking him for his phone number, and not believing him when he said, 'I don't think that would be a good idea.' When we got home, he said to me, 'Oh, he was just saying that,' as if the man wasn't serious. I really had to persuade him that it was a bit more than that. Crazy. That was where the monogamy came from, not from wanting only me, or thinking not having every man on a dance floor wasn't, in itself, a good idea. What really scared him was this idea that if we started saying, like everyone else, 'Oh, well, we can have it off with some Spaniard now and again without worrying about whether it's going to mess up our relationship,' then we'd set off and I'd score and he wouldn't be able to.

The weird thing was that I didn't particularly want to tap off with anyone else. I was just mad about Joe. I know it sounds completely unbelievable, but still after seven years, he'd take his shirt off and I'd be struck with lust. I just wanted to fuck him the whole time. Even when he was being a complete pain in the arse, I still wanted to fuck him. I fancied other people, of course I did, but I never wanted to get off with them particularly. And I never thought of myself as being particularly faithful. It was like monogamy had been forced on us by something outside, something outside our control. For him it was just the fear that there was no one else for him; for me it was this lust I couldn't control, just for him. We'd both rather have been without it. But there was nothing we could change, and it looked like such a good idea from outside, we never really talked about it, we never really complained about it. Maybe there was nothing to complain about. Probably there wasn't. You never know what holds people together, what that glue is.

About a year ago, I met this man. He was all right. He wasn't mad, or anything. I saw him around and we always talked. He was funny, and everything; a nice man. It wasn't that I ever missed him if he wasn't at a party, or down here, but when I saw him, I thought, oh, right, he's here, good, I'll talk to him in a bit. Joe met him and he thought about the same of him that I did, nice man, nice-looking, let's have him round to dinner some time. And that was it. Of course, we never did have him round to dinner, just carried on bumping into him. You think the same thing about probably twenty people at any time in your life; you think, oh, must get him round, but there's no particular reason to.

Last November I was down here and bumped into him – I remember when it was, it was when there was that big storm. I'd been here since midnight, and when I came out at six, I'd no idea anything had happened. There were all these trees just lying all over the place, and I remember coming out and just looking. There was a car outside with its windscreen shattered – a roof tile had just gone straight through it. I'd met this man that night. It stuck in my mind.

'Do you mind if I talk to you?' a boy said to Sean and me. He had just come up.

'We're just talking to each other,' Sean said.

'Oh, I'm just looking for someone to share a cab to Trade,' the boy said. 'Are you going there?'

'I don't think so,' I said. The boy was too skinny to be nice to.

'Only I've just come up for the night,' he said. 'I've never been here before. I was looking to see if I could get any E but there doesn't seem to be any about.'

'No,' I said. 'No one takes drugs here.'

'Get away,' he said. 'I know better than that.'

'Well, I've no idea where to get any,' Sean said. Then he leaned forward and put his face right against the boy's. 'I'll tell you a secret. We're not clubbers. We're not queers, either. We're plainclothes policemen, and we're looking for poofs who take drugs.'

'Get away,' the boy said. He turned from us and went out of the room, looking for someone to share his taxi with. Sean rolled his eyes, and went on with what he was saying.

He was someone I sort of knew, this man I met. I used to meet him most weeks down here. Anyway, we danced a bit together, then I said, I'm knackered, come and have a sit down. We were both off our faces, and you know how everyone seems then. So we were sitting here – Joe was away, I think – anyway, he certainly wasn't there. And I don't know why, but this man started telling me about what seemed like his main hobby.

'I like to know who's had who,' he said. I didn't know what he meant. 'I like to know who's slept with who.' I didn't understand why anyone would want to know something like that. Well, I could, I suppose. It's quite interesting when you hear that two people you know have just started sleeping together, or when you hear that two people you know used to sleep together ten years ago and now just bump into each other at parties and are just friendly with each other. So I can see that's quite interesting. But this man had taken it a stage further than that. He'd actually drawn up a chart of who'd slept with who.

'Why are you telling me all this?' I said.

'Wait,' Sean said. 'There's more.'

He didn't have the chart with him, Sean went on, but he drew a little example of what it looked like, and explained how you got on to the chart. A name would be connected to another name by a line, which would lead on to someone else. The aim was to establish how many fucks you were from anyone else, anyone you hadn't actually fucked or would want to. He was quite proud of the fact that he was only three fucks away from Leonard Bernstein in one direction, and seven from Prince Charles in another.

Then he explained how you got on to the chart. He had a word for people who had got on to the chart. He called them chartists. It was a joke – at least he thought it was funny. I did, too. I'm talking as though I despised it from the start, but I definitely didn't. I thought it was a funny thing to do. I thought it sounded as if it was full of these kind of scandalous glamorous people. I sort of wanted to be one.

I didn't stand a chance, though. You didn't get on it by fucking just one person. You had to be connected to two people. And I'd only ever fucked Joe in my life, so that was that. And he wouldn't get on the chart because he'd only ever fucked me and this man in York. So I laughed and said I'd like to see the chart some time and forgot about it.

About a week later I was in Soho and saw this man in a bar. I went up and said hi again to him. Like you do.

And there was something the next day, something or other I thought he'd be going to. I asked him if he was going, and he said yes, and let's have a beer afterwards. And then I said, hey, bring your chart along, I'd like to see it. He looked at me in this weird way. 'I didn't know I'd told you,' he said. 'Well, you did,' I said. 'Last week. I remember even if you don't.' He came along the next night and afterwards we went out for a beer. I didn't think he'd have brought it, but he had.

I don't know really why I was interested. Most of the people I'd never heard of, apart from a few people we both knew, and a few people everyone's heard of, like Cary Grant or whoever. It was like this huge piece of paper – I remember being in the Café Pelican and everybody obviously thinking we were completely off our heads with this piece of paper twice the size of the tablecloth, and laughing like hyenas. We'd been laughing about who'd fucked who for about half an hour when I noticed this name. 'Who's that?' I said. 'Oh, it's just some bloke in York this friend of mine fucked and then told some friend of his who went up and fucked him too. It was about a year ago. He's quite a useful link.' 'I'll say,' I said. The thing was, this bloke in York was Joe's ex-boyfriend.

It wasn't much of a coincidence, and it didn't mean anything. But anyway, I said Joe had gone out with this man, and things started getting interesting. 'We could get Joe on to it,' he said. 'If he's fucked him and you. But you're not on it.' 'No,' I said. 'I've never slept with anyone else.' 'You're joking,' he said. I wasn't. 'Is that true?' he said. 'I thought that was just your line. You've never had anyone else?' 'No,' I said. 'Not that I wouldn't mind.'

Till I said that I didn't know I thought it. It really

annoyed me, in a way, that I couldn't be on the chart because I'd never slept with anyone. It doesn't sound now like much of a reason to shag someone else, because you want your name on a piece of paper. Maybe I always wanted that, to have my name on a piece of paper, to get noticed. To be history. Now I am history. That's funny. It isn't much of a reason. But you only need one.

'Just never had the opportunity?' he said. 'No,' I said.

That was the opportunity. The opportunity I needed to fuck up my life for good, get rid of someone I loved and who loved me for no reason at all. Well, you know the rest, or you can guess it. I went back with the man and fucked him. No, I didn't even go back with the man; I never went to his place, and he never came to mine. We fucked in the alley behind a bar in Covent Garden. You know the one. Yes, you do.

Two days later, this packet came through the post. I opened it. It was a new chart, it was exactly the same as the old one, except now it had two new names on it, a new series of lines, drawing connexions.

I opened the chart at breakfast. Joe wanted to see it.

He moved out about a fortnight later.

Sean stopped talking. He closed his eyes. The room seemed terribly small; the music thudding too close to me. I didn't know what to say.

'Why have you told me this?' I said.

'Because you didn't know it,' he said.

'Yes I did,' I said. It was almost true. 'I knew that I'd told you about the chart, and I remember having it off with you. It was only three months ago.'

'You didn't know what happened.'

I didn't know what to say. I could hardly bear to listen

to him telling me a story about myself, I could hardly bear to listen to my own actions, and their consequences.

'I'm sorry,' I said. It was just a joke, the chart; it was an idle amusement, and it had never occurred to me that having a name on it, that having recorded someone's bland liaison could in any way affect anyone else's life. For a bizarre moment, I stopped thinking about Sean, and Joe. I wondered about the other two hundred names on the chart, the two hundred chartists. I wondered what had happened in their lives because of what I had written on a piece of paper, and I wondered what that piece of paper had caused. 'I'd never have done it,' I said.

'You didn't do it,' he said. 'It was me really.'

'What's the time?' I said.

'Four,' he said. 'It's going on late tonight.'

I took his hand in mine.

'I can't do anything to make it up,' I said. Perhaps I was sincere. 'I would do anything to change things for you, but I can't.'

'No,' he said. 'The thing is, that this was always planted in things from the beginning. The way me and Joe would end was there from the start, because he wanted faithfulness for the wrong reasons, and I wanted faithfulness for the wrong reasons, I suppose. Maybe not.'

'I think fancying someone is a good reason for faithfulness,' I said. 'It's the only one – it's the only free one.'

'I'm thinking about going,' he said. 'Have you got money for a cab?'

I got out my wallet. I looked in it for twenty quid among the usual detritus of receipts and bills and notes of phone numbers. In there, among all this, was a little snap-fastened plastic sachet. I fished it out.

'Look,' I said. 'I'd forgotten about it.'

'What is it?'

There were two pills in the sachet. I had bought them last week; I hadn't got round to taking them. I had forgotten about them. They might be the only two pills left in the club; in the world. They would do for me; one now, one in two hours' time. They would.

'Do you want one?'

'Go on then.'

So things were different. I took him in my arms. We danced till dawn. All that.

ELEKTRA

THERE IS AN oddly festive atmosphere between the eight of them; unaccountable, since the room – a disused office – has the brown-edged light which windowless rooms always have. It seems grubby to Anna, though it is, in fact, perfectly clean. The three men, two of whom have not spoken and will not speak, are similarly dressed, each in a dark grey suit, with a white shirt and dark tie. Care, on the other hand, has been taken to make the clothes of the five women not just similar, but identical. This in itself is not unusual; the five women are police officers, and used to wearing uniforms. But these clothes are not their uniforms. They consist of an ugly blue dress and a knitted cardigan. Anna feels she must look conspicuously unaccustomed to these uncomfortable clothes. She looks at the others. They do not; she probably does not. The clothes have successfully turned them all into high-security prisoners.

In any case the real high-security prisoner – somewhere in the building, behind probably no more than half a dozen locked doors – has had only a week to get used to the uniform.

The man in charge of the operation looks again at his watch. He is, like them, either nervous or excited. It is not clear what could go wrong, but things have gone wrong before, and must not again. The telephone rings and he picks it up. He does not speak. The voice at the end can be heard to say a few things. The man says 'Yes', and puts the telephone down.

'The witness is in place,' he says. 'It is fully understood what is to be done by the participants.'

Having no leader, the women say nothing. Anna tries to look alert, keen, capable. Until she joined the police force, and for almost a year afterwards, she was an enthusiastic amateur actress; she enjoyed the evenings with the group, pretending with her lines to have relations with people she did not know, entering into the imagined life of someone who probably never existed and making them real. She liked, in between rehearsals and during them, to sit around with the other amateur actors, and pretend for a while to be a real bohemian, to complain about trivial things, about the play and the director, and be late for things. She never thought she would act professionally, although years ago at school, people had sometimes said perhaps she should. She had never wanted to. She had always wanted to be a police officer. And now, she thinks irrelevantly, she can be an actress too, just for the afternoon.

The man in charge doesn't seem to take their silence as meaning that they understand and remember what they have been told. He lives, in fact, in an apartment block next to the one Anna now lives in. In the months she has lived there, in a quiet part of Zweibrücken, she sees him getting into his car, at much the same time as her, a minimum of three times a week. He does not acknowledge her, although he knows who she is, and speaks to her when they are in the station together. Anna has mentioned it to her husband, Peter; he was interested mainly in who the man was that she was talking about. She described him, as if he were a suspect – muddy blond hair, average height, inclining to plumpness – until Peter said, teasingly, 'No distinguishing features' and they forgot about it.

In any case he is going to explain once more what their task is this morning.

'Instructions from the top are that the prisoner has repeatedly attempted to refuse to take part in an identity parade,' he starts. 'Refusal has not been granted. The prisoner will be placed second in the parade. Each of you will go in separately. The conduct of the prisoner will be observed carefully by each of you. Each of you will go in three times in the same sequence.'

He pauses, and looks at one of the other two men. Anna is obscurely irritated by him saying 'refusal has not been granted'. She cannot think of the right or sensible way to say what the man means.

'It is understood that the prisoner will attempt to protest in the course of the identity parade. Legal advice has been received that protestation may be taken by the witness as identifying the prisoner over and above the witness's memory of the prisoner's appearance. It is therefore necessary that protest be anticipated and enacted by the participating lady officers.'

'Is it known,' Anna says, irritated by almost everything this man says, 'what form the protest is likely to take?'

The man looks from side to side. Each of the other men moves his head almost imperceptibly.

'Not in precise detail,' he says. 'It is presumed that physical resistance will take place. It may also be that the prisoner will attempt verbally to identify herself in an attempt to invalidate the identification procedure.'

'In which case –'

'In which case it will be necessary for the participating lady officers likewise to identify themselves.'

'To identify ourselves?' says one of the other women, obviously not understanding. 'As police officers?'

'Naturally not,' he goes on. 'As Ulrike Meinhof.'

The prisoner is already in the large cell which serves as anteroom to the identification room when the five women enter. Ulrike Meinhof looks very unlike her photograph in the newspapers. There, she looked defiant, healthy, well-cared for, even – Anna thinks with a tinge of amusement – even rich. In the flesh, she is pale, her skin sallow, with a rash or with spots, perhaps from a poor diet. Or from lack of exercise, and, Anna thinks, she's not likely to get much of that for a few years. Her hair is dry and unkempt like a dog's. She is surprisingly thin. She, too, is wearing the ugly blue dress and knitted cardigan. She looks up as they come in, perhaps in surprise at seeing people dressed identically to her. Of course, she has seen no other prisoners since her arrest. She quickly looks down again.

Also in the cell are six women prison officers. Two of them are holding Ulrike Meinhof tightly, although there is little imaginable way that she could escape. Still, things have gone wrong in the past, and things could go wrong again. It is not known how, precisely. It is merely known that it is possible.

The cell, though large, is now almost uncomfortably crowded. One of the warders looks at the five pretend prisoners, then at Ulrike Meinhof.

'Her hair,' she says. It is true. Ulrike Meinhof's hair has not been brushed for many days, and is in a mess. The five other participants, however, have neatly cared-for hair. She stands out. 'We need a hairbrush for her.'

'I refuse,' Ulrike Meinhof says.

'We need a hairbrush,' the warder says. Another warder goes out.

'I refuse to permit my hair to be touched,' Ulrike Meinhof says. 'The forcible brushing of my hair constitutes assault. Specific regulation must be made to allow such an act of abuse.'

'I thought you didn't recognise regulations,' the warder says as the other returns with a hairbrush.

'You live by your own rules,' Ulrike Meinhof says. 'It's all shit.'

'Language, madam,' the warder says ironically, as she starts to brush the hair. 'Hold her head.' Her hair is obviously knotted and unkempt; the hairbrush sticks at once. She pulls a little, and then, so as not to hurt more than necessary, she lays the flat of her hand against the root and tugs. She need not have troubled; as soon as she took the hairbrush, Ulrike Meinhof started to scream. An oddly feminine, panicky scream, high-pitched and, in the bare cell, deafening. It must be painful, to have your hair brushed like that, Anna thinks, but the screaming has nothing to do with pain, continues after the brush is taken out. She remembers her mother in their small flat, how she liked to brush her daughter's hair; the quiet pain she endured as she pulled on the scalp, the exquisite feeling of drained cleanliness, of new blood in the head when it was finished.

The warder takes two or three minutes over it, though the noise is unpleasant. She puts the brush down, and abruptly Ulrike Meinhof stops screaming. She looks up, balefully.

'My lawyer should be here,' she says finally.

'Your lawyer is in the identification hall,' the warder says. 'We are ready now.'

Anna has been married for only a few months now. She and her husband both work hard. They want to get on. Often, they do not see each other for long in the week; when one is awake, the other is asleep. They sometimes eat together; they speak every day on the telephone, speaking ordinarily about ordinary things. Sometimes, holding the telephone receiver in the police station, Anna feels a wave of love and smiling tenderness come over her so strongly that she has to close her eyes, so that Peter, who cannot see her, will not hear a change in her voice. Sometimes he wants to go on talking to her, when there is nothing to say, and she is reassured that it is not only her who feels this about him, but he who, looking at her, is submerged by her love for him, as she is in his love for her.

Only at the weekends do they have time together; they like to visit the public parks and semi-urban castles where they walked before they were married. They do not find a routine in their trips, but each time a new pleasure, an old pleasure revitalised. Their weekly trips to the same six or seven places are like the pleasure she takes in his body; it is utterly familiar, and yet she looks at the hair on his body and realises she could never know every single hair on it, never count them, never exhaust what there is to know about his flesh, the dark smiling eyes in his dear round face, his love for her.

Their routine Sunday morning is to sit over breakfast,

a meal which never seems to stop, just to pause for half an hour before he gets up and makes more to eat, pours more juice or slices some more cheese or ham. He likes to sit in his dressing gown; she likes to dress. Mostly he gives way, and puts on some clothes, though she would never ask him to; sometimes he rebels, grinning at her without justifying himself, without comment on his unshaven face and well-worn, too-small green dressing gown. That is nice too. They read the papers to each other. He is interested in what she is doing today; they have read a great deal about Ulrike Meinhof and her killings, her planted bombs and her aims to overthrow society with her associates. It seems quite strange, quite distant, but frightening in an immediate way, like a remote thunderstorm, approaching at an incalculable speed, unstoppably. It is something they read a lot about, and talk a lot about. They do not quite understand it.

'It says that a man arrived at the flat of Joachim B., a teacher in Wuppertal,' Peter reads, 'and asked him if he would be prepared to shelter "comrades in the struggle" for a time.'

'Was he a friend of the teacher, the man who turned up?'

'No,' Peter says. 'It says he did not recognise him.'

'What did the Joachim say?' Anna says.

'He said he would,' Peter goes on. 'But then he talked to his wife, and she thought there was something strange about the request.'

'Well, there was,' Anna says. 'If a complete stranger arrives and rings our doorbell, and asks if some more complete strangers could come and stay with us for some time, well, what would you say?'

'Or even not complete strangers,' Peter says, because the

week before, his brother had asked if he could come and stay, and, with no reason at all, Peter had said that it wasn't convenient.

Anna smiles; they, too are conspirators. 'What happened?'

'His wife told the police, without the teacher knowing, and they turned up and lay in wait for the Baader–Meinhof people. But they never came. And the teacher is in prison under suspicion of knowing more than he says. You wouldn't do that, would you?'

'Tell the police?'

'You are the police.'

'Read me my horoscope.'

There are six of them now, identical, waiting to be ushered into the room. In the hall is a witness who saw a woman in Hamburg who might have been Ulrike Meinhof. They have not been told whether this witness is crucial or trivial in the case. The identification will proceed, anyway. Ulrike Meinhof is second in the line. The door is opened.

The first policewoman to go in resists her guards, trying to pull away from them and moaning slightly. Anna observes her; she is very unconvincing. Ulrike Meinhof follows, and she is also unconvincing; she has been standing sullenly, silently in the wings, as it were, and as soon as they start to lead her forward, she begins to struggle and to shout, as if enacting a part.

'I am the Meinhof,' she shouts. 'I am the Meinhof. *Das soll eine Gegenüberstellung sein?* Is this supposed to be an identification? I am the Meinhof!'

She attempts to turn her face away from the witnesses, while shouting her name. She is struggling, although why is not clear. She cannot escape. She turns her head, pulling at the guards who are making an ungainly progress across the room, like a three-legged race. As she does, she looks up, away from the witness, and for a tenth of a second her gaze sweeps over Anna, standing next in line in the wings; and for a tenth of a second, Anna seems to see all the things the Meinhof has seen, all the suffering and cruelty and violence she has seen in society, all the suffering and cruelty and violence she put into society, and what, for a tenth of a second, she sees in the eyes of the terrorist; the terror of an animal in a cage who does not understand its captors, thinks that their restraining is cruelty, the restrictions it finds are deliberate torture. They stumble on, awkwardly, the group; she twists so much that one of the officers almost falls to the ground, bringing the others with her.

Anna is next. She starts shouting 'No,' before the Meinhof is out of the hall. She invents a line; 'I am the Meinhof' is too banal, and has been used before. 'Don't you see,' she shouts as she goes into the hall, struggling convincingly, 'Don't you see it's me you're supposed to look at? It's me, you swine!'

On the whole she is quite pleased with herself. The other three do not do so well, not trusting themselves to shout convincingly; they merely struggle and turn their heads.

On the second time round, they all seem to relax a little. Anna recognises the ease which settles over actors after the interval. They all start shouting this time; Ulrike Meinhof tries to make what is perhaps a joke, shouting '*Und hier ist nochmals die Meinhof*, here comes the Meinhof again.' They let themselves be dragged across, they refuse to walk and are carried. The Meinhof's antics seem quite moderate, compared to theirs. Anna, who this time is first, tries 'It's all a sham. It's me, it's me.' And then a line comes to her, like a prompter whispering through the din and struggling.

She shouts, 'Can't you see, it's all a performance?' She tries to hit one of her guards; she notes the surprise and flash of fear on the guard's face. She will remember the sign that she has been real to him.

Afterwards, Ulrike Meinhof is taken off to the cells, and they go back to the office of the man in charge. He has a bottle of schnapps, and they have an unexpected but necessary drink. They do not, quite, toast each other. He does not congratulate them; they were, after all, doing their duty. But, before doing anything else, he sits down and fills out a form quickly, while they stand with their glasses, and speaks as he writes, as if dictating to himself.

'In the opinion of the undersigned,' he says, breathing heavily as he writes, 'it was impossible that the witnesses and the officers in the hall deduce from the behaviour of the women paraded the identity of the prisoner.'

They all understood that this is his way of saying that they did well. He offers them more schnapps.

'Do you have a hobby?' he says to the nearest of the policewomen.

'I like playing tennis,' she says. 'At the weekend.'

'Ah, tennis,' he says. 'A funny thing, tennis. I've never tried to play tennis, not for years. I've always been convinced that I'd be no good at it if I tried. I don't know why. I just think that. I don't think I'd be very good at tennis, maybe it's something to do with the temperament.'

They do not quite know what to say.

'I like to collect things,' he says. 'I have five collections of different small things. Well, I say they're small, but together, they take up a lot of room in my flat. I don't know why I started, really, but they just grew and grew, and now, I find a lot of relaxation in it. It's relaxing, really, going round, finding an example you haven't got, something you'd never seen before. One day, I suppose, one of my collections is going to be complete, and then, I don't know what I'll do. My wife often says that. She says, You, if you ever finish with your collecting. I don't know what you'll do with yourself.'

Anna is thinking about Ulrike Meinhof. She knows what she did; she read it in the newspapers, every day, every week, something else. Something every day, something every day, and, quite abruptly, like a light being switched on, she knows why. It is because she is unhappy. It is because she wants things to come to an end, not start again, that she is killing everyone, that she wants to kill all men, every father she can find, starting with her own. And when all the fathers are gone, that will be nice, she thinks; she will sit down on a rock and look around at the nothing that is left and plan a society which is no longer there to be planned. But there is no end to the fathers, just fathers begetting fathers, and there is nothing but an end to the Meinhof; an end which anyone, once they began, in a cold hall behind the locked doors of a police station, to act out her life, could see, just as the Meinhof, struggling, identifying herself to stop herself being identified, can see her own end, and struggles against it.

Peter is already asleep when she gets home. He works at odd times, starting at six in the morning. He is usually in bed by nine o'clock. Anna stands at the bedroom door, looking at his dear face in the half-light from the hall, beyond happiness, beyond worry or fear, in sleep. The novel he is reading and likes to read in bed has slipped from his hand and lies abandoned on the bedspread; he will roll on to it and wake up. She leaves the light on in the hall – she likes to sleep with a little light filtering through – and quickly undresses. She puts the book on the bedside chair, and gets into bed with her husband. She moves against him; he does not move or resist. She eases herself back against his body. On his side, his knee bent, it is as if he is waiting for her, for her to fit herself into his body. Right now, though she does not know it, she is pregnant. Their lives are new, and they will always be like that, for decades to come, for generations. They have been married for four months; they have now owned a single item of their furniture for longer than that. They barely have to trust each other. Their hands touch. One sleeps. The other, for a few more moments, before joining her husband, is still awake. *For her brother*, she thinks, with amusement she cannot, for the moment, quite explain; *for the sake of imaginary brothers*. Her eyes are shut.

FORBIDDEN ÉTUDES

I MUST HAVE seen her children before I took any notice of her. They were conspicuous, those two boys, and might even have been notorious in the neighbourhood. At least eight years apart in age, they seemed to have no friends, and were always idling up and down the road in the other's joyless company. Nor did they resemble each other in the slightest, and you had to know they were brothers. The elder had a certain furtive obesity, a plank of greasy blond hair falling over his face like the unlovely New Romantics of my own adolescence; the younger was more rancid, twitchingly mobile in his emaciated and blood-drained features. Jason, the elder, you felt, longed only for a locked bedroom and limitless supplies of pornography and crisps; the younger, fancifully named Claude, his peak of ambition might have been the largest possible animal he could safely torture to death. I noticed them, but I doubt I would have connected them with a slight nervous woman who I could only have glimpsed in the newsagent's or in the garden of a house fifty yards beneath the indisputable tide-mark of respectability which so marked the road my parents lived in.

Hepatitis had come at an inconvenient time for me. I'd always more or less accepted that the career I had chosen, of concert pianist, would mean years of fruitless struggle and then failure, disappointment, the garret and an embittered old age. But it hadn't happened quite like that. I hadn't even finished the year at the music college before a concert agent heard me play and signed me up. It all seemed to be going a bit too fast. He produced a date at a hall – not a quiet one in the suburbs, but a big hall, a famous one. And it was soon. We put together a programme, and I bought a proper set of tails, and got used to the way the other kids looked at me. It was wondering, and not particularly envious. And then I got sick.

It was really bad luck. I still didn't know how I got it – it might have been a terrible holiday in Spain, or a girl called Janice who seemed nice but who, in the end, turned out to have given me a false telephone number. Anyway, it doesn't really matter. There was no question of doing the recital. I was weak and yellow, papery and hideous. 'Go home,' my agent said. 'Go to your mum's. Get well. Everything can be put off till you're better.' I kind of knew he was just getting rid of me, that he was glad to have been given an excuse. But I didn't have an alternative. I went back to my parents' to get over it.

My parents had a piano, of course they did. It was the same one I'd practised my scales on when I was a boy, a nice 1920s domestic grand from a Leipzig firm called Zimmermann. The touch had gone and the keys were yellow as my eyes, but I wasn't home to practise. I was home to lie on the sofa and watch daytime TV and get better. All the same, if you carry out the same activity for six hours a day for ten years, every single day, and then suddenly stop, it gives you a pretty bad itch. I'd be sitting with my mother, working on one of the recuperative ten-thousand-piece jigsaws she'd got, and suddenly she'd say, 'You're trilling.' And I'd look down and there, on the table top, my fourth and fifth fingers were executing a perfect left-hand trill in triplets, as recommended by Brahms, and I wasn't even thinking about it.

One day, a piano tuner came. My parents said nothing about it. I suppose they must have asked him to. He spent a couple of hours going up the keyboard, followed by five minutes of extravagant arpeggios, and one of the easy Chopin waltzes, the one in C sharp minor, to impress the idiots in the kitchen. Me, sitting idiotically in the kitchen, I didn't say anything, though it had been a waltz I'd been playing since I was nine years old.

So a day or two later I left the jigsaws, and went into the dining room, where the piano was. If you play an instrument – if it makes up your life – it isn't a metaphor, and won't become one. It is just what it is. So I won't say that it seemed to grin at me sardonically, with its gaping top, its crocodile-yellow grin. But a couple of weeks out of the presence of the beast is enough to make you realise how big it is; and, since I was alone in the house, I stood at the door in my dressing gown, and looked at it for five minutes. And then I went over, and sat down, and played, very slowly, just to myself, some Schumann. It was just what came into my head. It was the slowest of the variations he wrote and then removed from the Symphonic Études. The most beautiful of all the forbidden études, so difficult, so beautiful. No one knows why he took the best five variations out, but I sometimes thought I knew; they are too beautiful to listen to, they are only to be played.

And I played the most private of them, to myself, in the empty house, and thought, here is Schumann, and here am I, unaudienced, and here are the forbidden études.

After that I played quite often, though never really practising. It was a few days before I realised I had an audience. The window of the dining room, at the front of the house, was behind your back as you sat at the piano, and you were not disturbed by the sight of people walking up the road. I played all the old favourites, since I could only play what I had in my head and the music I had left at my parents'. I played the first of the Liszt *Années de Pèlerinage*, the Swiss book, and the *Appassionata* and the *Pathétique* and the *Adieux*; I played preludes and fugues by Shostakovich and Bach; I started on the Ravel *Miroirs*, which called my mother into the room, concerned I might be overdoing it; and each day I finished with that beautiful showstopper, the Chopin *Berceuse*, which begins so sweetly, and works up to such an exquisite muted firework display, doing your passage work in thirds no end of good. The only thing I did not play were those forbidden études of Schumann. I didn't want to. They were never out of my head, and my mother had to go on with the thousand-piece jigsaw – a view of Milan cathedral, as I remember – on her own.

I had just finished the *Berceuse*, and got up, not tired but replete. I turned round. The two boys were there, on the street, gawping, one big, one small. I scowled at them, but it seemed to have no effect, and, unembarrassed, they just stayed there. They were young and idiotic; I stood there too, and stared out of the window at them. After all, this was my family's house, and it shouldn't be stared into by the neighbourhood oiks. But they wouldn't go, and after a minute I couldn't stand it any longer, and left the room. They might have been there, unobserved, for hours.

A few days later I was in the post office. 'You look a bit better,' my mother had said. 'Would you like a little walk? Ten first-class stamps.' I'd hit a bad day and a gleeful crowd of pensioners were mobbing the desk for their weekly forty quid, or whatever.

'Oh dear,' the woman behind me in the queue remarked. I vaguely nodded. 'Terrible, isn't it.'

'Yes,' I said. 'Yes, terrible.'

'Hello,' she said. 'I know you. At least I know your parents. I'm Sylvie.'

'Hello, Sylvie,' I said. I was tired; it took me at least a minute to remember to tell her my name in return.

'You play the piano, don't you,' she said. She was a small woman, dark and frail, perhaps younger than she appeared; her general nervousness, her frayed overcoat, two years overdue for replacement, may have aged her. She took one little bony hand in another, left in right, right in left, incessantly, and I thought of the American proverb, one hand washes the other, thinking that this woman would never be done with the patient washing. 'I heard you do. I know you're good. My children, my boys, they said you're good enough – well, I won't say what they said, it would embarrass you.'

'Thank you,' I said.

'I was musical,' she said. 'Once. I mean I still am a bit. I used to play the cello. I don't get much time now, with the boys and everything –'

'You ought to keep it up,' I said, conventionally.

'Do you think so?' she said, and now her hands stopped folding each other over and over, and she looked up at me, her eyes shining. 'Do you really think so?'

'Of course,' I said.

'But I have no reason to,' she went on. 'You know – I hate to ask – please just say no if you don't want to – but I would love it so much if someone like you would just strum through some music with me.'

'With pleasure,' I said. It didn't seem a lot to offer, just there, in the post office.

'I used to be good,' she said. 'I have Grade 8.'

'I'd love to,' I said, since Grade 8, to me, meant an exam for children, one I now could barely remember. 'Come round any time. I'd love to. I really would.'

'My goodness,' she said; and her gratitude, so real, so overwhelming, as if she had lost some long-preserved virginity, made you wonder about the rest of her life. 'I can hardly wait.'

My mother wasn't exactly discouraging, but it would be hard to say that she greeted the news that I had made friends with Sylvie, who lived thirty houses down the road in some nebulously different social class, with any enthusiasm. She knew quite well who she was. 'There's a husband,' she said. 'Hangs his jacket on the hook in the back of his car. And two boys. Never seem to go to school.' I shrugged; it wasn't my business.

I saw the boys the next day, though, as I was sitting in the front garden to take advantage of some sunshine, early in the year. They were mooching up the road, zigzagging from one side of the pavement to the other like stage drunks. The elder saw me first, and straightened up, and they began to walk, head down, as if expecting some punishment.

'Hello,' I said confidently as they came up. 'I think I know your mum.'

'Our mum,' the elder said, and then was overcome by

a fit of giggles, in which the younger less quiveringly joined him. 'Our mum – knows you.'

'Yes,' I said. 'Yes, we met in the post office.'

'He's called Claude,' the fat boy said, pointing at his brother.

'I see,' I said.

'But he's – he's – he's –' the younger one began, unable to get it out.

'What's your name?' I asked the fat boy.

'I'm called Jason,' he said.

'I see,' I said.

'Nothing wrong with that,' he said.

'No, indeed,' I said, and after a moment in which we all stared at each other with massive and inexplicable hostility, they continued up the road. I sat down again.

Sylvie came round the next day. My mother stayed firmly in the drawing room, and let me answer the door and take her into the dining room. She probably wanted to make a point, but you could see it was lost on Sylvie; though she started babbling, almost before she was in, about how lovely the house was, her single-mindedness was almost appalling. I recognised it; the way she checked herself, almost forced herself to accept a glass of water to keep up the fiction that this was some kind of social encounter, corresponded to something in me, the part of me that wanted only to be alone with music.

She was a musician, you could see that. And she was a musician despite being no good at all.

The cello was a horrible beast, an orange job made, at a guess, in Bulgaria, and behind it she had an anthology of the horrible epics of the cello's repertory. 'You must know this,' she kept saying, 'but tell me if you don't.' But

I knew them all; the Brahms E minor and the Elgar concerto and the Debussy and the Beethoven A major. I'd played them all before with a succession of no-hopers, and relaxed into them without really thinking. She could play, she said, the easier movements, and we gave up at the first sight of a fugue. To be honest I found it best to concentrate on what I was doing. She was terribly bad; out of tune, uncertain of anything higher than the G above middle C, with an ugly, breathy, stubby sort of tone. But she was loving it, you could see that; and though a blind man would not have thought much of her abilities, a deaf one might have loved it. Her platform manner, polished in how much solitude, in how many desperately snatched hours in quiet upper rooms, was awesome, and she gestured over the tangerine instrument until you felt like throwing a tarpaulin over her. As we went from Elgar to Brahms to Haydn, I went in my head from embarrassment to silent amusement to something like pity. We said little between each piece; I just looked at her flush, and wondered at what my mother would be overhearing.

The beautiful but rather demanding coda of the Shostakovich sonata came to an end, and I looked at her, wonderingly.

'That was so good,' she said. 'You really are –'

'Yes, wasn't it,' I said.

'Did you ever play –' she said, leaning forward, her eyes shining, both hands around the neck of her cello. 'Have you ever played – the sonata – the sonata I always call – you'll think me silly – the sonata of sonatas? Did you ever play that? The Chopin cello sonata? I never have. Only on my own. Do you like Chopin? Do you?'

'Of course,' I said. 'Yes, I do. I love Chopin. I knew

there was a cello sonata, but I've never played it. I don't think I've ever heard it even. It's a late piece, isn't it?'

'Oh yes,' she said. 'Oh yes. It's very late. So beautiful. I don't know – I don't know how to ask –'

'Ask away,' I said. I was getting annoyed with these mock-withdrawals, this absurd and unnecessary shyness; if she wanted something, she should just ask for it. 'I'll only say no. I mean, I can only say no.'

'I'm sorry,' she said, 'but it's my dream, really, to play the Chopin sonata with someone, someone like you who can play so beautifully. I never thought it would happen. I mean, I have the music here. Do you think – if I left the music with you. I don't want to impose, I really don't, but if you could spare the time to look at it, and perhaps in a week we could –'

She stopped, and closed her eyes. There was something behind her, you could see that; something invisible, blocking her mouth. All she had wanted to ask, it seemed, was if I would play a piece of music with her, but it seemed to me then, as I looked at this stranger, that I had given her more than I knew, that a couple of hours with me and with music was something she would carry on thinking about for years; and I thought this with a tang of shame, that it had meant so little to me, that I had given her as little as I could and would have given her less. I wondered what had silenced her: husband; children; a life she had not chosen. The strings of a cello are taut, and respond quickly to the movements of its player. She held her instrument firmly, taking a deep breath, and the strings blurred, silently, into vagueness with the perfect vibrato of her trembling.

'We could have a go now,' I said reasonably. 'It might

not be very good. But I can sight read pretty well. I'd like that, to be honest. I really would.'

Sylvie, looking down, handed over the music. I opened it up and looked at it for a moment. I didn't know this piece; there is more Chopin than you know, and this had somehow escaped me. Late Chopin, rich Chopin, Chopin writing for himself, and I took a big breath and started. Someone had tried to play this piece with Sylvie before, and over the copy was written a web of increasingly desperate numbers, fingering, exclamation marks, spurious simplifications and omissions of the demanding inner parts, and, every ten bars, symbolic spectacles to remind a hopeless pianist to watch the hopeless soloist. I hadn't gone far before I realised that, with this one, I was being stretched.

We got through the big first paragraph, and I slowed a little at the tiny *piano* interlude. I could vaguely see the thing getting pretty black later on. She didn't come in at her cue, and I paused, looking at her, doodling a little on the chord; she looked at me, her eyes shining.

'I'm sorry,' she said. 'It's just – it's just so beautiful – and, you know – playing this, with you, playing this, so well, I feel as if – well, I'm not very good, I'm really not a very good cellist, don't try and persuade me anything other, but playing with someone so wonderful, I just feel so privileged, so lucky, that I know I'm playing better than for years. And that bit, just those eight bars, you know. Could we just – I know we should press on, but if we could play them just once more – it would mean –'

'No problem,' I said. 'What is it? Seven after B?'

'Exactly,' she said. 'You see, you see. You know.'

I wasn't sure that I did; it was just a big tune in A flat. But we played it – I tried not to look at her, she was flinging herself around the dining room to such a degree – and she stopped again at exactly the same point.

'You know,' she said, a bit breathlessly, 'I'm not sure that was quite right. Could we –'

'Of course,' I said, and we started again from the same point. It meant nothing to me, just a small problem in fingering, and I was almost angry that, selfishly, for some reason I knew nothing about, she wanted to play the same few notes over and over again. 'Let's go on,' I called as, at the same point, she half-faltered, but continued. I was concentrating, and only really marking her beats, but it can't have been more than a dozen or so bars later – a minute in real time, in the sort of time which exists outside music – when I looked up at a clatter on the wooden floor, and saw that she had dropped her bow, that, stricken, she was looking at me, that big in her was some great solitary confession which already frightened me; and frightened me because in a second I could see that it had nothing to do with Chopin, or music, or, to be honest, with me.

The door opened.

'Am I interrupting?' my mother said, coming in firmly. 'I just wondered if you were near a break.'

'A break,' I said, thankfully.

'I hate to say it,' my mother went on remorselessly, 'but we mustn't let our wunderkind exhaust himself. I'm here to make sure he recovers.'

'Oh no,' Sylvie said. 'Oh, I'm ever so sorry,' and her accent, grating against my mother's like lemon on glass, made me despise, momentarily, my family. 'It's been such a treat, I've been too demanding. Let's call it a day, shall we? You've been ever so kind, more than kind, really –'

'I think that would be best, to be honest,' I said, and it

was as if I had slapped her face. 'We can do it again some time.'

She flushed, more insulted than I had meant. I sat at the piano and watched her loosen her bow, put her music, her instrument, the rosin, the bow into their appointed places.

'Would you like a cup of tea?' I said eventually.

'No,' she said. 'No, thank you, that is kind, but I must be home for the boys. This has been such a treat for me. It really has. Really wonderful. I hope I haven't tired you out –'

'Not at all,' I said, and then she went.

And that was it. We didn't play again; I saw her a couple of times by chance, and we were perfectly friendly, for five minutes or so. And about a month or two later, when I was feeling much stronger, almost myself again, I was down at the park for a walk by myself. I was miles away, and didn't notice the boys until they were right on top of me. One of them was fat and blond and fifteen; the other may have been seven. They blocked my path moronically, and stared. I smiled.

'Our mum –' the younger one said, eventually.

'You –' the elder one said, with no seeming intent to insult, but, apparently, just trying to attract my attention. Yes, I thought, going on, walking around the unattractive brace, that's about it; you –, yes, you –

The odd thing is, I've played the Chopin cello sonata quite a lot since, and come to like it. It's a strange sort of piece. There's a peculiarity about it. It's much easier for the soloist than for the accompanist. The cellist has an easy time of it. She just comes along and does what she has to do, plays a simple sort of part. For her, there's nothing surprising, nothing awkward, just the same sort of thing she plays every single day of her professional life. Every single day of her life. Believe me, it's the pianist, the one in the supposedly secondary role, who has the hard job, really, in the end; he is given one problem after another, and has to unlock all the difficulties, has to make what he can of it, and all the time, something he has never seen before, something he can hardly begin to know how to get round, to come out of with credit.

Sometimes you play it, and almost start to think that your fingers are going to be bent into a completely different shape by the end of it, by the sorts of demands it makes, demands you never expected. But you look down, and there, at the end of your black sleeves and white cuffs, there are your hands, and they are the same hands they ever were. Of course they are.

Well, I got better, after a bit, and got my strength back. Luckily, the hall had a slot they hadn't filled, eight months after the original date, and I made my début, a bit later than planned, but with pretty well the same programme. I remember my tails feeling loose with all the weight I'd lost, that night, but it went well, and it's gone on going well since. You've probably heard of me, if you take an interest in these things. I'm twenty-six. I don't know if I mentioned that. But I am. I'm twenty-six. I've got years ahead of me.

WORK

I WAS AVOIDING Quentin.

I could see him approaching across the crowded course at Heathrow. An unmistakable figure, tall and loping, he moved between the late holiday-makers and the unserious flocks of unicoloured stewardesses, like the only man in the terminus with somewhere to go, and something to do on this October Sunday evening. He hadn't seen me yet; it was important that he should not see me just yet.

'There's Quentin,' Richard said.

'I know,' I said from behind my newspaper. 'Don't let him see you.'

'Why not?' Richard said. 'Shouldn't you be telling them all where to go?'

'Yes,' I said. 'Quentin's going to have to get himself through security. I can't speak to him until then.'

Richard – whose first select committee trip this was, who, there to explain any technical points about financial policy and the European Union, could not be reasonably expected to take an interest in the finer points of select committee protocol – gave me an old-fashioned look. I didn't care. It was me who had to get half a dozen Members of Parliament halfway across Europe and back without losing any.

'And, if it can be helped,' I said, 'it would be better if you didn't, either.'

'Too late,' he said. 'He's spotted us. Here he comes.'

I liked Quentin, I liked his humourless intelligence, so redundant and so excessive in a Member of Parliament. His braininess, his interest in aspects of economic policy – which nobody else would pay attention to – was, twice weekly, on display in Committee Room 6 of the House of Commons. The rest of the committee had, long before, decided that Quentin was one of the better jokes which had been afforded them by the chance delivery of elected Members. It was common for Quentin to inflict his ruthless line of questioning about methods of measuring inflation, or whatever, on some hapless and clueless witness while the rest of the committee flung themselves around in abandoned merriment.

I liked him; I thought his forensic manner and periodic intense social charm went together in an unexpected, pleasing way. But, I suppose, it could be understood why such an intelligent man had never quite made it to being a minister. He reminded you somewhat of the comment made in Burton's diary on the famously dull seventeenth-century Member, Serjeant Wylde, that 'in the time of the Long Parliament, he was always left speaking, and members went to dinner, and found him speaking when they came in again'. His suspect origins as a Foreign Office official, and his failure to understand that people in error do not, always, need to have their errors explained to them would have seen to any ambitions for office. And, right now, unknown to him, he was being a complete pain in the arse.

About a week before the Treasury Committee left on

its visit to Prague and Rome I had a useful but irritating phone call from a contact in the House of Commons travel office. She confirmed all the flight details; I sat, ticking things off on the latest agenda for the visit.

'And Mr Davies is coming back from Rome two days early,' she finished.

'Not as far as I know,' I said.

'Hold on,' she said. 'Yes, that's quite right. We had a request to change his ticket, bring it forward by thirty-six hours.'

'Not from this office,' I said. 'Are you sure?'

'Yes,' she said. 'I've issued the ticket. Haven't you had it?'

'No,' I said. 'Did you issue it to us?'

'Oh, now I remember,' she said. 'He came in himself last week and asked us to change it and send it directly to him, so we did.'

'Well,' I said, 'you should have checked with us first. That's quite infuriating.'

'I can't very well refuse a Member,' she said.

'Well, you should have let us know,' I said.

'I'm letting you know,' she said. 'I'm letting you know now.'

The problem was that it just couldn't be done. The rule was absolutely inflexible, I knew it perfectly well, but I looked it up anyway in the Red Book, the little manual of guidance for Clerks of select committees. I knew the rule because I'd helped to write the Red Book a year or two before. I wished now I'd had the sense to cross out the sentence, but there it was. *Members must take part in the whole of a select committee visit.* No skiving off early; no late arrivals; no bunking off to visit mistresses in Trastevere (a possibility greatly enhanced when another rule, *Members' wives may not take part in a select committee visit*, had been introduced in the late nineteen-eighties). So Quentin's unilateral decision to come home two days early presented a problem.

'Oh, I don't know,' my boss said, panicking in her turquoise suit. 'What do you think we should do?'

'Tell him he can't do it,' I said.

'I suppose so. But we don't know about it.'

'Yes we do,' I said. 'The travel office told us.'

'But he hasn't told us.'

'Does that make a difference?'

My boss looked at me, helplessly. It could not be suggested that, in possession of this information, we should tell Quentin he couldn't go, or couldn't come home early. On the other hand, we could always forget anyone had told us anything. Which, in the House of Commons, was always a useful standby.

'The problem will be,' my boss went on, 'if he tells you that he's going to come home early before you set off. Then we couldn't really say that we didn't know. But if he doesn't tell you until you're on the plane, let's say, then it would really be too late to do anything about it, if anyone asks about it later.'

'So we cover our backs by pretending not to know anything about it until we've set off,' I said. 'Just one thing. At what point could the trip be reasonably said to have started? How early?'

'Well, when the plane's taken off?'

'Check-in?'

'Security check?'

'Done,' I said, the haggling between propriety and face-saving complete.

Unfortunately, all that, which seemed to solve the problem, would be quite technical if Quentin managed to ruin the whole plot by telling me he was coming home early before he had even checked in. Then, I couldn't see how I could avoid telling him that he couldn't go, and therefore precipitating a huge row. If, having been told this, however, I didn't tell him in return that he couldn't go, there would be a huge row when we got back to England, from the big boys in the department. Neither seemed very appealing prospects. I had decided, then, to avoid Quentin altogether until he had passed through the airport security, and then to acquiesce in the bad news, knowing that I could do nothing about it. It was this perfect scenario that was in danger of being wrecked by the fast-approaching figure coming through the check-in queues towards us.

'Just going off for a second,' I said to Richard, getting up and walking briskly in the direction of the Sock Shop.

As I stood among the racks of undesirable hosiery, I could see Quentin talking to Richard. He looked round and seemed to glimpse me. I smartly turned, leaving the Sock Shop and ducking into the next franchise, which happened to be a chemist; in case this was not enough, I walked to the back of the shop, left by a side entrance and went into the public lavatories.

Five minutes later, I emerged cautiously. There was no sign of Quentin; Richard was still there.

'Where's he gone?' I said.

'I told him you'd gone to change some money upstairs,' Richard said. 'What's all this about?'

'Nothing,' I said. 'Just can't quite face talking to Quentin right now. Let's go through.'

He looked at me sceptically. 'He said he's leaving early. I said he ought to mention it to you.'

'You didn't tell me that,' I said. 'Let's go through.'

'They haven't all arrived,' Richard said.

'They're all grown-up,' I said. 'They've been to an airport before. Let's go.'

Standing in the queue for the X-ray machine, I made myself only dimly aware of Quentin, ten paces behind, gesturing in my direction; it wasn't until we were on the other side of the barrier, standing by the duty-free and the luxury goods emporium that he caught up, or was allowed to catch up.

'Hello there,' he said. 'I don't know whether Richard said anything, but I'm going to have to leave early.'

'How early?' I asked, as if it made any difference.

'A day and a half,' he said.

'Well, it isn't really permitted,' I said. 'But I can't see what I can do to stop you. Of course, I can't re-arrange your ticket, much as I would like to be helfpul.'

Quentin beamed, it occurred to me that in his youth in the Foreign Office, he, too, must have put himself in the position of wilful ignorance, of not making the formal gesture of being informed of what he already knew to be the case. Now, we had completed the contract, and I wondered whether he, in fact, understood the contractual agreement quite as well as I did; that he would tell me when I could no longer prevent a breach of the rules; that I would allow myself to be told when the information was no longer of any direct consequence.

To sceptical strangers, it was not always easy to justify my job or the purpose of the committee I worked for. I'd done the job for about five years by this time. The House of Commons has never been much good at looking at the detail of government; and in particular it's always been hopeless at looking at how the Government spends its money. In 1979, in the first flush of excitement at being new in government, the Conservatives set up a system of committees, one to each government department, of Members of Parliament. The idea was that each committee would look at its department's spending, administration and so on in detail and at length; it would act as a collection of well-informed Members, ferreting out and disseminating vital information to the press and public and to the House at large.

That was the idea, and had it worked efficiently, the Government might have had cause to regret it about once a week ever since. Of course, though, it didn't work. My purpose was general bag-carrier; I thought up questions which they might like to ask, I sucked up the expertise of people who, unlike me, knew something about the subject, and, in the end, I wrote reports which sank like stones. As far as I could see the whole thing was driven by personal obsessions, a strong desire to get into the headlines and the desire to irritate or mollify the whips, according to taste. It was a moderately entertaining job, and I had been far less jaded during my first months in it. My partner was pleased I'd got a job at all. But the idea of what a select committee might achieve baffled him.

'The thing I don't really understand is, what do select committees do, exactly?' He looked genuinely puzzled. But they didn't have select committees where he came from, and, though I'd only been working for one for a month, I would do my best to justify it.

'They scrutinise things.'

'What things?'

'Government spending, government administration, that sort of thing.'

'What do they do when they've scrutinised it?'

'Issue a report saying what the Government ought to do.'

'And then the Government has to do it?'

'No, but it probably would carry out the recommendations if that was what it was going to do anyway.'

'Can the committee insist that anything be done?'

'No.'

'Can it tell the Government to pass laws?'

'No.'

'So it just tells the Government to do things, and if the Government was going to do them anyway, then it does, and if it wasn't, then it doesn't.'

'That's about it.'

'So what's the point?'

'Well, it represents informed opinion in the House of Commons.'

'Meaning?'

'Gives people a chance to talk indefinitely about a pet obsession or two.'

'I see.'

I hadn't quite managed to put the point across, I felt, but he now seemed to have grasped what the committee did to his own satisfaction, if not mine.

In black moments, I thought that the real reason select committees were so popular was that they could say anything they liked in the sure knowledge that anything too mad would not be followed by any consequences, since the Government would simply ignore it. Fantasy Government, I sometimes thought, watching a lot of unpromotable people saying, 'If I ruled the world, if I ruled the world', over and over again. Sugaring this futile situation were a number of small treats. Select committees could talk to anyone they wanted, and some committees behaved like small boys, summoning all the glamorous and famous criminals and celebrities they'd always wanted to meet and chat with. They could guarantee a certain minimum audience for their opinions, and, if the opinions were really ridiculous, or strongly opposed to the opinions of the Government, quite a big audience. Among the journalists who had to cover the work of Parliament, at least.

Not the smallest of the treats afforded committees by the Government was the ability to travel abroad. If they could justify a trip, a committee could go wherever it liked. The carnival air which always surrounded a visit produced its own recklessness, and frequently a series of fairly predictable disasters and embarrassments. Select committee trips abroad, and, in fact, any kind of trip abroad, gave rise to a double record, in the minds of the parliamentary officials, the Clerks of the House of Commons, of which I was one. In the first place, there was the series of official records of what was done; where was visited; which eminences were seen; what expenditure was incurred. From the initial proposal, set down in two or three lines in the minutes of proceedings of the select committee – *That the Committee do visit Martinique in February* – to the ambitious agenda, drawn up, fought over in committee – 'I think we ought to have lunch with the Governor of the Bundesbank' – and finally reduced to more modest ambitions, sketchy notes made in overheated or overcooled rooms, over lunch, over dinner, over, sometimes, even breakfast, and finally to the polished and absurd summary of what the committee discovered on its jaunt to be printed in some unreadable report, the committee presented the acceptable face of its travels, in writing, to the outside world.

But, apart from the written record, the Clerks preserved, like a small tribe, an oral tradition of catastrophic or spectacular happenings when a select committee travelled abroad, or when they, free for a week of their hopeless charges, travelled to Strasbourg to work, for vast and tax-free sums of money, for the Council of Europe. This wasn't supposed to happen; part of the ethos of the Clerks' department is that, however badly members of the department behave when overseas, something informally referred to as 'Strasbourg rules' meant that it wouldn't be chattered about when back in Westminster, and, however fascinating the story of some Member or Clerk insulting a distinguished foreigner, getting drunk or arrested might be, it was not quite the thing to discuss it.

Like all such rules, it never worked, as I discovered when, on a trip to Paris, I picked up a boy in a bar in front of ten quite distinguished colleagues. Somehow, though such disgraceful behaviour shouldn't be gossiped about back home, each individual story was just too good not to retell in some form, and, like most of my more drunken colleagues, I found the narrative – in my case, how I ended up at eight in the morning at Charles de Gaulle airport, without the faintest idea of how to get back to my hotel, back into a pinstriped suit, and back down to the Western European Union to start minuting its proceedings by nine – going effortlessly into the rich oral tradition of anecdotes about Members and Clerks. Any Clerk coming back from abroad would be expected, over the cold meat pie and tinned potato salad in the Tea Room, to produce some spectacularly salacious story about his own, his colleagues', his Members', or the whole committee's misbehaviour. It was part of the genuine, as opposed to the written ethos of the palace; the only unbroken rule was that none of these stories ever be written down.

These stories formed a tapestry of anecdotes, told and retold, looked forward to eagerly. Some Clerks had a repertoire of stories, one had a whole series about his amazing luck with women abroad; a luck which, alas, never seemed to be quite so potent when translated to the Stranger's bar and to a victim of his malodorous charms who was not an exotic foreigner, but some new secretary, uninformed, but quickly wising up to the company she found herself in. Others had a single party piece, brought out on high days and holidays and anticipated, and greatly relished, by an audience who had heard, many times, the epic of the Member who lost his shoes in Paris, or the Member who was robbed by a prostitute in Rio, or the simple, colossal tale of a committee's two-week trip to the Bahamas to look at nothing in particular, at the delicious height of the season.

I'd added in a small way to this tradition before. The committee concerned with energy policy had a slight, ongoing worry that it could only quite rarely justify a trip abroad, and then, only to very unexciting places. The Agriculture Committee could always go to a Caribbean island to watch bananas grow, the Trade and Industry Committee could go, if they had insufficient shame, to Brazil on no better excuse than that they wanted to think about British trade with Brazil. But, whatever the Energy

Committee decided they wanted to look at, they always seemed to end up going to Düsseldorf to look at some power station, and it was hard to see how it could be managed otherwise.

The trip I went on was a characteristically unexciting one – burning rubbish to generate electricity in Germany, Sweden and Denmark over five days – but was greatly enlivened by a fine source of Tea-Room anecdotes, Geoffrey Dickens. Dickens was a Member much admired by those who didn't know him, who found him an amusing fellow, full of blunt speaking and common sense. Most people who had to work with him thought him a buffoon who never said a sensible thing in his life. Most of those anecdotes came from him directly – I forget the number of times I heard, in the five days, the story of how he came to write 'To my dear horse-face' on a photograph of himself and sent it to a lady admirer. The only intelligent or perceptive thing I ever heard him say was his account of how he canvassed any given old people's homes in the minimum time possible.

'The first old dear who says to me, "I bet you can't guess how old I am," I always say, "You must be at least a hundred and fifty, you old witch." The thing is, any old lady who says that to a visitor, she's always going to be the one they all hate. So you lose one vote but you gain twenty-five. Saves a lot of time.'

Dickens was regarded, in the House and by the Clerks, with opinions ranging from amused tolerance to unamused contempt. How he ended up on a committee passing judgement on energy policy was a matter of some mystery.

His most impressive moment came in Germany. There is a certain sort of Englishman to whom Germany is not the country of Goethe, Beethoven and Caspar David Friedrich; nor indeed, a country which perpetrated and was torn apart by a series of terrible historical tragedies, the Kaiser Friedrich, the Great War, the Holocaust and Partition; but to whom it means only a joke about goose-stepping, don't-mention-the-war and a nation whose defining characteristic is their lack of a sense of humour. Dickens was very strongly one of these people; it had been apparent, even from his conversation on the aeroplane, that he would need to be watched quite carefully and, if necessary, apologised for.

A day or so passed without incident. On the second day, the committee visited a major power plant where some innovation or other was being put into effect. It had been impressed on us by the embassy that the man who we were to meet was exceptionally distinguished, of almost inconceivable importance and greatness; that we had been very lucky to find such a terrific fellow free to talk to us at the very short notice of six weeks. The terrific fellow came in, and smiled benignly while one of his underlings explained, with the help of a yard-high perspex model, the workings of the power plant. By the side of the plant, there had been placed, by the thoughtful model-makers, two human figures in orange plastic, one waving at the other, to show the scale of the thing. The explanation went off without hitch; the committee, after lunch, was rather subdued, and the meeting dissolved into coffee with Dickens looking rather pensive. I felt an unexplained danger signal when I saw him heading straight for the grand panjandrum, and followed in his wake.

'You know what I thought,' I heard him saying, 'when I first saw your model, and those two little chaps. You know, I thought, that one on the left, with his arm raised, I thought, is he supposed to be giving the Hitler salute or something?'

I shut my eyes. The man from the embassy, standing alongside, seemed momentarily beyond speech or, indeed, movement. The big cheese, however, did not seem to be responding at all. What was quite clear was that he didn't think that this comment from this extraordinary figure was intended to be funny; nor did he think it intended to be offensive; he simply failed to classify the comment as any kind of meaningful utterance at all, and continued to talk about new methods, ever more unlikely sources of generating electricity. Dickens, however, was delighted with his own brilliant sally, and three days later, in Denmark, was retelling the story of how he had successfully punctured the pomposity of the German nation with a well-directed shaft of wit to some very bewildered Danish civil servants.

The Treasury Committee, my current posting, were famously argumentative, famously unsparing of the sensitivities of whoever they might meet, but they weren't buffoons on that scale. On one occasion, a few years before, they had unforgivably engaged a tremendously grand ambassador in a row while eating his food, and, still more unforgivably, insulted him by telling him that he was a traitor to his country's, to British interests. The accusation of unpatriotism was bad enough, but might have been worn, if not exactly laughed off, had it not been made in front of a lot of foreigners. The ensuing row was of such proportions – telegrams to London, a formal meeting of the committee at eight in the morning in the chairman's hotel bedroom to discuss the bounders' misbehaviour –

that it was judged wise not to return to the country in question until the ambassador had retired.

That was always a danger. It was still more acute, on this occasion, because the committee was supposed to be inquiring into European monetary union, a subject guaranteed to produce twelve separate opinions among any given eleven Members, and to produce ample opportunities to insult anyone the committee happened to come across. I had decided that none of this was my problem, and that I shouldn't worry about it.

What I further trusted to was the chairman, who I thought a genuinely decent man, and one who could be relied on to have a quiet word if things were getting out of hand. The chairman of the committee, to his face always referred to as Chairman, always behind his back as Tom, was invariably quite excellent at this sort of thing. He had been catapulted into a position of slight prominence by a great deal – a quite unnecessary amount – of horse-trading. Tom, an improbably rakish fellow who wore red socks and tasselled loafers with his sharp suit, said little, intervened only when necessary, and, I sometimes wondered, might very well have regretted letting himself in for two or three meetings a week of desperate dullness. Sparked off by a sudden sense of the absurdity of the whole thing, he was capable of strange spasms of laddishness which ensured fondness in anyone who worked for him; for the rest of the time, he seemed, like Nancy Mitford's Lady Alconleigh, to float in a cloud of boredom, only occasionally to descend with a comment of such sharpness as to make one wonder whether, after all, he wasn't the most attentive of all of them.

'Why are we going to Prague?' he said to me, once we were all ensconced on the plane.

It was difficult to answer. Sitting around a couple of months earlier, the six staff of the committee had been thinking about where the committee might like to go to find out about the prospects for monetary union. Of course, the real answer to the question was that the committee shouldn't go anywhere, they should stay at home and read some of the papers they were sent. But that wouldn't do as a proposal, since that was what they were supposed to do anyway.

The lunch-time proposal we came up with in a spirit of mild hilarity was that the committee should go on a grand tour of Europe, going not only to countries that were in the European Union, but to countries which weren't in the European Union, but perhaps hoped to be, and countries which might one day start to think about it. The lunacy of this idea, which culminated in a proposal for a tour of Europe and beyond – 'Have we thought about Morocco?' someone said, only partly joking – unsurprisingly went down pretty well with the committee, but less well with the authority which granted money to select committees to travel. By the end of the bidding process, we were left with a trip to find out about the prospects for monetary union which would go only to Italy and the Czech Republic.

The ambassador to the Czech republic was civil, driving into Prague, but slightly bemused concerning the motives for a select committee to visit a country where membership of the European Union was an only distant possibility. The Czechs, on the other hand, were all completely delighted to see us.

'You are the functionary,' a man said at the tiny Parliament, a glittery toytown affair of brightly dressed guards and Ruritanian riotousness where we were having lunch with the Czech finance committee.

'I am,' I said.

'I too,' he said. 'Look, your chairman is making a speech.'

'I know,' I said across the table. Lunch was just beginning, and the formal exchange of greetings and thanks just under way. It didn't occur to the Czech Clerk not to talk, nor to most of the Czech Members, and the lunch began in a cheerfully unstructured manner. A beer-drinking hearty joined in.

'I speak little English,' he began. 'Why do we as Czechs wish to join the Union? I do not know.'

It went on, the lunch, moving from clear soup with slightly gritty dumplings, to an elaborate dish of chicken with half a tinned peach on top and a slice of processed cheese. The beer was good, though.

'Czechs are a very proud people,' someone else added. 'No Czech would join the Union to take money out of it. We would only join if we could add to it.'

'Well, why join at all?' I said. 'Why not aim to be a sort of island, making money out of your freedom of action, outside the Union? Do you suppose Brussels would have your best interests at heart?'

'No,' he added. 'There is something true there.'

'No,' someone else said. 'It's not true. Like everyone else, you talk as if we were you. You talk as if we were an island, like you. You must remember: we are not an island. The options which you see for you are not always there for us. You must try and understand, you English, the point of view of the rest of us, the point of view of anyone apart from you.'

I was aware, somehow, that I had said something tactless.

'Why do we want to join, in the end? It is for political reasons, and for reasons of security. We live at the edge of Europe – or, you think we do. And our neighbours have not always been very nice. And we worry about that, and we want to know how we can bind ourselves in.'

'So, politics again,' I said. A kind of weariness came over me. I had a sense that nobody wanted monetary union because it would work; everybody who wanted it, wanted it because they thought it would save them from themselves, from their neighbours, from politics.

'This man,' the Czech Clerk said cheerily, 'he has his own point of view.'

The ambassador had a dinner for us that evening. The Czechs invited were almost entirely people who had lived outside Czechoslovakia for years, in Canada or America, returning when communism fell and Slovakia so conveniently offloaded, to the slight chagrin of quite a lot of Slovakians. I couldn't work out, and couldn't think of a way to ask, whether the guest list was because that was who the important people were, or if they'd been selected because they all spoke good English.

'We privatised everything,' one said. 'We gave it all away. We could have made money, and we didn't. We wanted a real popular capitalism, but we knew no one could afford to buy shares. So we just gave shares away – the same number for everyone – in whatever utility people wanted. And then people were free to sell them, and make a little money immediately, or hang on, or start to deal in them. And people have.'

'But you must have lost a lot of money which you could have made.'

'We did.'

'So why do it? You must be in need of a lot of capital.'

'The great problem for us is that no one has felt that the state has anything to do with them. People here always felt helpless, that the way things were run weren't their business, and they were at the mercy of some distant figure behind a desk.'

It seemed a bit unimaginable to me. Prague was so small that the institutions seemed unthreatening. Government buildings went semi-guarded, and we wandered in and out, bumping by chance, or so it seemed, into unretinued ministers. The informal place could not be imagined as it had been ten years before.

'The important thing was to try and use the sale of the utilities for social reasons. For cohesion. Look at it another way. We lost – or we spent – a lot of money. But if your Government could buy social cohesion, don't you think they would?'

'And it worked?'

'It's working.'

I looked at his bright face, his thrilled excitement at the possibility of success, and I, too, felt excited at the idea of something which, this time, might just not go wrong.

The first morning in Rome went entirely to plan, both the official one and the one I had quietly envisaged, of blunt statement of opposition, or, at worst, a row. The issue at question, for the whole trip, was simply this. The Maastricht Treaty had set up four conditions, to do with the state of each national economy, which had to be met before a currency could be admitted to monetary union. If you applied these four conditions strictly – and the

Treaty seemed to say that they should be applied strictly – then hardly any country now in the European Union would qualify. Britain probably, but it didn't look as if Britain would want to. France maybe (but we wouldn't talk about that). German pretty definitely. But, when it came to the crunch, without anything resembling a partner in monetary union, why on earth would Germany want to abandon the most successful currency in history, and one which was such a focus of national pride that patriotic discontent could easily arise?

Italy, by the rules of the Treaty, didn't seem to stand a chance. Their economy was shot to pieces, the much-vaunted *sorpasso*, or overtaking, of the nineteen-eighties seeming rather a quaint delusion by now. The situation shouldn't really have been complicated by the fact that they all wanted desperately to be in monetary union, almost as a demonstration of national pride; it shouldn't have had anything to do with the fact that almost every Italian one ever meets says, with varying degrees of honesty, that they'd rather be ruled from Brussels than from Rome. And yet it was. Talking to the Treasury, talking to the Bank, the constant sense was 'Brussels can't leave us out.' The committee was growing a little testy.

'What about the conditions in the Treaty?'

'The conditions in the Treaty are flexible.'

'They certainly are not flexible. That's the point of them.'

'We think they may prove to be flexible.'

'How flexible do they have to be?'

The man – tremendously elegant in an English blazer and cream trousers, oddly dressed, to an English eye, for the occupant of such a crucial position – smiled, faintly.

'We think they may be flexible enough. We think that if

matters turn out to be improving, even if they have not reached the limits specified, the Treaty may allow us to join in any case. Imagine it from our point of view. It is an absurd situation; if the criteria are interpreted strictly, we may not join even though we wish to; you may join, but you do not wish to. In these circumstances, the idea of monetary union can only be described as a confrontation between the unwilling and the unable. That is why we think the criteria will, in the end, be interpreted flexibly.'

'But, but, but, but –'

One of the Members was almost purple, flicking through the Treaty in search of the crucial passage. Richard leapt up and showed him the passage. I wrote down *a confrontation between the unwilling and the unable*. A jesuitical debate followed about the meaning of the crucial sentence, to nobody's satisfaction. Smoothly, the Italian moved on to something we were, officially, not interested in; political union. Things quickly degenerated.

'You see, our political institutions are very young. They are not ancient as yours are.'

'How old do political institutions need to be?' someone asked, quite fairly.

'And we need to learn,' he went on, 'from other traditions, intellectually richer institutions.'

This complete balls seemed to stun the committee into silence, or perhaps they simply feared that entering seriously on to this ground would spark a row between them, and lead to nothing. So nobody managed to point out the absurdity of a man with a thousand-year-old name explaining to us why it was necessary that Italian political culture, so immature, should take on the immense historical experience and practice of the European parliaments.

I'd heard all this before, from my partner, an Italian economist. Like most Italians, he was of the view that the Roman political culture was corrupt, and beyond reform; he viewed the prospect of abdicating responsibility for ruling a nation and handing it over to what seemed to me the barely less corrupt and patronage-ruled culture of Brussels and the Commission with less alarm than the prospect of carrying on being ruled as before. Vain to suggest that people have a responsibility for themselves; vain to suggest that the reason given by Italians for giving up power – that it's the least bad option – is not, and never will be, a good enough reason. Perhaps it's all a matter of perspective. From Rome, Brussels looks like a model of good government. From London it looks very much like a place where patronage is institutionalised. It reminded me that in India I had once seen an advert for a television, or perhaps a car, with the slogan 'Greek technology!' It would not work in Britain, but no Indian, looking at it from quite a different angle, could see why it struck an Englishman as being so funny.

Lunch was rather chilly – both metaphorically and literally, since the opening speeches of welcome and the responding speech went on so long that the waiters started openly rolling their eyes in despair at the plates of quite delicious pasta congealing in front of the gentlemen. Even Tom's graceful speech couldn't rescue the occasion, and the committee went off for its afternoon sight-seeing, clutching the favoured gift of Italian institutions, boastful, expensive catalogues of the art collections of the Bank of Italy or whoever, with a vague sense of unfulfilment. I went for a walk with Richard, in the general direction of the Piazza del Popolo.

'What are we doing here?' I said.

'You tell me,' he said. 'Fact-finding mission, I thought.'

He twinkled, slightly.

'Well, quite,' I said. 'I mean, what have we found out this morning?'

'I thought you were taking notes.'

'Yes, and I've got pages and pages about Quentin's opinion and the Italian opinion of Quentin's opinion and some question that the Chairman asked which I hadn't heard before, and about three lines of that cynical twat's views on Europe, which mainly weren't what we're here to find out anyway. And we got a good phrase for the report about the unwilling confronting the unable.'

'Only three more days,' he said. 'Why would anyone build two identical churches next to each other?'

'No idea,' I said. 'One of them's got the most brilliant Caravaggio in it – a sort of dead body right in the bottom third of it, and the rest of the picture's just completely black. Though you can't really see because the lighting's so bad.'

We looked in the church, and then in the other, mirror-image church, and then I remembered that the painting wasn't in either, but in the church, scaffolded up into cubes like an architect's initial sketch, on the other side of the square. And then I remembered that the picture I was thinking of wasn't in Rome at all, but in a grubby little museum in Messina.

The ambassador's house in Rome is a villa of astonishing beauty – it's one of those Roman buildings which have belonged to an almost comic sequence of grand names out of history: Pauline Borghese, Goebbels, that sort of thing.

There aren't many houses in Rome with an aqueduct in the garden. But the paradoxical effect of all this splendour was to egg the committee on to newly impressed heights.

The small talk at table lasted about a minute. With the arrival of the *sformato*, Quentin speaking horribly wonderful Italian, began straight away on the Maastricht criteria, to the slight puzzlement of his neighbour, the wife of a smart industrialist. The harangue continued, and went on; the table fell silent. Finally, as if by some mysterious, bridge-players' telepathy, one of the Italians from the Bank seemed to be elected to respond, and something resembling a conversation began. I concentrated on my food and acknowledged to myself that the dinner was going to follow the usual course of these things: delicious food, slightly too cold; not enough wine; and, worst of all, condemned to silence.

As quickly as I could, I went out to the cloakroom to fetch some fags; a flunky would be out with all this on a silver tray in a moment, but I wanted an excuse not to listen to anyone's opinion for a moment or two. Outside there were some waiters, having a sit down and, like me, a smoke; they made a desultory gesture of standing up and putting their cigarettes out; I made an equally desultory *non si disturbi* gesture in their general direction. There was no one minding the coats, but, as I began to rifle through in search of mine, a boy about my age appeared. It wasn't clear whether he was the coat attendant or a waiter or, indeed, another guest at the fairly enormous dinner.

'There it is,' he said, plucking out my coat. I was impressed.

'How did you know which mine was?' I asked.

'I noticed it when you were getting out of the car. Beautiful coat.'

I was quite delighted with this, getting praise for clothes from an Italian. I'd bought the coat a few weeks before in a fit of extravagance, and it was, it's true, a striking object; furred like a teddy bear, falling in three unpunctuated sheets of cloth plainly to the ground, it was almost the thing I loved best in the world just at that moment, and, though it wasn't really cold enough in Rome in October to justify wearing it, I couldn't imagine leaving it behind.

'Do you like my suit?' I said, daringly, knowing that Italian men talk readily about clothes and mean almost nothing by it. It was a green tweedy suit bought, like most of my suits, in a fit of irony, a sense of how comic the idea was that I might work for the House of Commons, that I might very well be obliged to wear a green tweed suit on Fridays, a charcoal flapping pinstripe the rest of the week, and which, in the end, reached a charred and sorry end when, three months after this conversation, I leaned back on a windowsill at a drunken dinner at Roxy Beaujolais's dining room in Soho and learned, not from the sensation of burning, but from the smell of burning tweed, so like the smell of burning hair and flesh, that what I was leaning back on was a lit candle.

'Very nice,' he said, fingering my lapel, and knowing nothing of any of this. 'You speak Italian well. Unusual for an Englishman.'

'Not well,' I said, truthfully, and observing how strikingly his very blue eyes set off his very black hair. 'I had an Italian lover.'

It was late; my spirits were high. In high spirits, I used a word the Italians would probably not use. In conversation, they said *boy*, or they said *friend*, and they did not fear to be misunderstood. I feared being misunderstood; I feared the slightest possibility that this boy would think I had used an inappropriate word, which meant only that I had a friend who was Italian. So I used a poetic, an over-emphatic word, wanting only to be understood.

He carried on looking at me in an amused way.

'*Anch'io*,' he said. 'Me too.'

'I'm staying in the Belvedere,' I said. 'We are here for three days.'

'*Lo so*,' he said. 'I know.'

And not wanting, especially, to know what he had meant by *anch'io*, not wanting to know what he meant by *lo so*, I turned my back on him and went back into the ambassador's party, quite forgetting my cigarettes.

'So, what have we learned?' Tom said suddenly the day after next, on the plane.

I answered him, somehow, but I didn't know. What did we learn? I think we just went abroad, and told people what our views were, and were not listened to; and then they told us their views, and they were not listened to in return.

'What do *you* think we learned?'

'I think,' Tom said, 'we achieved a frank and informative exchange of views.'

He twinkled, very slightly. The oldest and absurdest of the dreams of the Enlightenment died here, for me; the dream that one could understand the world by seeing it. We had seen the world, or a fragment of it, and we had only seen ourselves in it, only talked about our own views. We were both unwilling and unable; unwilling to listen to other people, unable to do so. But I could not see why we had travelled at all, only to fail to understand strangers;

we could have stayed at home, and failed to understand each other there. I did not understand what made Quentin set his interlocutors right; I did not understand why Richard, or Tom, or the boy in the cloakroom, acted as they did, and I could not imagine ever understanding the motives of such people; of any people.

A few months later I lost my job, for writing indiscreetly about it. It was very sudden, although I had been expecting something rather like it for a while, and I had no chance to say goodbye to the other Clerks, let alone the committee. I'd never quite got round to writing up the trip to Prague and Rome, and the blank notebooks were not so much a reproach to a lack of industry, as an honest account of our inability to understand what people meant when they talked to us.

A friend on the committee gave me a little summary of what happened when the subject of the abrupt loss of a Clerk was discussed in the committee.

'I hope he wasn't dismissed for his sexual proclivities,' Quentin remarked.

'No,' Richard said. 'He was sacked because he was in blatant breach of his contract.'

There was a little muttering. Another Member seemed to rouse himself from a conversation with his neighbour.

'Sorry,' he said. 'What did he look like? Did he have a beard?'

Someone set him right, and the discussion came to an end. Well, what then? What do they do? I suppose they begin to divide up the questions someone else has written for them, and begin to make a few notes about points they would like to make to whoever that day's witness is. I suppose they tease each other, and then ask a member of the committee staff to go out and fetch the witness; I imagine the witness, a grey-faced, bald man, perhaps nodding and smiling at the committee as he sits and begins to sort his papers, hoping that this time it won't be too bad, knowing that it probably will be. I imagine the committee facing the man's bravado, seeing how little it means, I imagine the chairman nodding at the shorthand writers in a sign that they should start, and, as they begin to write, as ever, the committee begins to talk.

TWO CITIES

CAROL ALWAYS LOVED Basil. She loved his narrow shoulders and his thick glasses. She loved his uncombed hair, his air of neglect. She loved the scattering of dandruff on his blue serge shoulders. She loved the way he read, his mouth open, making a faint panting noise. She even loved his giggle, she even loved the way he never looked at her, could never meet her gaze, though it made her wonder how, never having looked at her, he would ever recognise her. And though she did not love him the first time she saw him, and certainly did not love him the last time she saw him, there were plenty of other times. Plenty; well, enough to assure herself that she always loved Basil, and always would.

The last time she saw Basil . . .

Carol had to ring the doorbell twice before the door was opened. The chain rammed, holding the door to an eight-inch gap. Before her was the vertical third of a face. It was Mary, Basil's wife. She looked at Carol, and said nothing.

'Hello, Mary,' Carol said. Mary said nothing. Before the door could be shut against her, she continued smoothly.

'Basil lent me some money. I came to give it back.' She had put on her cleanest and most flowery frock for the occasion, a pair of flat Mary Jane shoes, a headband which might have had GOOD GIRL emblazoned across it. There was nothing in her appearance which Mary could reasonably object to. She wondered what it was. It must have been her.

'We don't need it back,' Mary said quietly, her red-scrubbed hand, its nails unpainted, holding the door tightly.

'Oh Mary,' Carol said, and smiled. 'I didn't mean, Mary, that you needed the money. I only thought you might want it back. I only meant that, Mary. I didn't mean to insult you, Mary, or Basil.'

The hand tightened. Mary made as if to shut the door, her face screwing up with courage and determination. Carol quickly said, 'Anyway, here it is.' She pulled out two fifty pound notes, and, quickly, thrust them through the narrow opening of the door, into Mary's face. Mary leapt back; Carol had almost touched her. But the money was on the floor of the hallway, and Carol turned round and went back up the garden path, thinking luxuriously how hideous the garden was, really. God, she wanted to insult these people. God, she already had.

The two notes were exactly the same notes Basil had given her six months before. She had not used them; they had lain, untouched, on her bedside table. She had had the feeling that if she spent them in an ordinary way, the gift would start to seem like a piece of cheek on his part. As it was, they were only two pieces of paper, which she had looked after for a while.

Carol had promised herself that she would not look round as she walked away from the house. But, as she got to the gate, she found she was too curious. Mary was still there, at the wedged-open door. Upstairs, a curtain shivered as someone moved away from it. Carol walked off down the quiet dusty street.

Carol was the eldest child of six, in a way. Her parents had married when her father was young, and her mother was younger. For five years they had no children. A doctor told them that they would never be able to have children of their own. They believed him, as people often believed doctors twenty years ago. They went to a local authority, and, after having their lives thoroughly gone into, were declared fit and proper people to adopt a child. Carol was blonde and blue-eyed and two months old. Her mother – her real mother – had been little more than a child herself. She would do very well.

For a year she was loved best of all. Carol was not the name her adoptive parents would have chosen, but it was, it seemed, already the child's name, and they loved her best of all. They accepted the name, as they accepted the fact that she was given, and not made; as they would have accepted a harelip or a limp. They were fit and proper people to adopt a child. She was a fit and proper child to be adopted by them. It was only a year, however, before her mother felt less well than usual, and went back to the same doctor who had told her that she could not have her husband's children. After examining her, he looked grave and declared her to be pregnant.

And after that, it was as if Carol were a changeling, swapped in the night for some phantom child they need only have waited for; an invader, bearing no gene, no virtue of her family. She found herself belonging to a family which, unknowingly, had been adopted by some cuckoo-child with ambitions of its own. A boy was born, and, in time, four more boys, and Carol was no longer loved best of all. She knew, in fact, that she was not loved at all. She ended up with five rowdy brothers. Or, rather, step-brothers. They were all like her small, dark, slightly hairy parents. She was big and blonde, and stood out. Children do not usually learn to read the expressions in faces until long after they can read print, having nothing to read but love. From the beginning, she knew how to read her parents' expressions. Her parents said nothing unkind, but she learnt from their anxious gaze what they really thought of her. She said later that she had no place in their affections, but she did; she occupied a small cramped nasty little place between embarrassment and shame.

Her mother told Carol the story of her adoption, years later, out of motives Carol could not quite disentangle. Her tone was reassuring, but the story was a fable of cruelty, unavenged, which might have begun with a horse's head over the western gate of a city and ended with the bound-up stepmother being bundled into a black deep pool. The only thing Carol thought of, when she remembered growing up with these strangers, was her father's characteristic greeting, when he met his changeling daughter. He would mark her approach, in a room of the house, on the stair, in a street of the neighbourhood. 'Good girl,' he would say vaguely. To Carol it always seemed like the reassurance a conspirator takes care to give to his victim-to-be.

She never knew, as it happens, what became of the doctor who ruined all their lives with a stupid mistake. Some adopted children seek out their real parents. Carol had a conventional interest in that reckless girl-mother, but, in search of some kind of explanation for herself, would have done better if she had gone and found the GP. In her mind she could see him, a little man, writing with a silver fountain pen in a sunny panelled room filled with flowers. Still ruining lives with those 6 p.m. diagnoses.

It was clear to Carol, as soon as she realised the helpless limits within which her parents' fondness was contained that, once she was able, she would need to leave home and fend for herself. She worked hard at school, with results that were not extensive. She was not successful, and her teachers took much the same notice of her, she always thought, that her parents did. She left with a small clutch of examination results, and a resolve that she would manage with what she had.

'You can type, I expect,' Basil said.

'Yes,' she said. Instead of amplifying her answer, she slid a certificate across the desk to him. He made a show of looking at it.

'And word processing.'

She told him of the strange names of the various systems she had used, and a couple more she had merely heard of. 'I could easily learn more,' she said. 'I've often been told that I am quick at adapting myself to new tasks.'

'Your strongest virtue is –' Basil said, running a pen down the list of typed questions on the sheet of paper in front of him – 'adaptability. Right. Mm. What would you say are your main faults, if you have any?'

'It's difficult to say,' Carol said, 'because I like to take a positive attitude to everything. But perhaps I am rather too much of a perfectionist.'

She was inexpressibly bored, and the man was, it seemed, only half listening. She hoped it was because he had already decided she would do. She looked at him while he was trying to find the next question on his list. She nearly helped him out – she had been reading them upside down for the last ten minutes. He turned his attention to the one-sheet list of accomplishments and examination results which she had sent with the letter of application. She noticed that his hair had been brushed at the front but not at the back, and had not been washed that morning. A small scattering of scurf was on the shoulders of his slightly shiny suit. A single man, then. She was silent, seeing no reason to say any more. She did not dislike him, she found.

'Yes,' he said. 'Yes.'

She did not reply. This was the third job interview she had been invited to. In the first, she had felt shy and had said almost nothing. In the second she had felt she could talk more fully about herself, and had, until the interviewer, his hand edging nervously from the centre of the desk to the side and back again, called an end to what had become a conversation. This time, she had decided, she would describe her abilities and suggest charm by smiling, and see if that was more successful than the other strategies she had resorted to.

To this end, she had been making the effort to smile all week, as if in charm, to strangers. The smile, on her face, still seemed to her like an ill-fitting and unflattering wig, placed on her head by a malicious stranger. Shop assistants and bus conductors, before, had taken her money without noticing her; now they stopped and looked at her smiling face with suspicion, alarm or simple dislike. The nearest to a successful outcome had occurred that morning, with the nice-looking boy who had been deputed to lead her from the front door of the firm to Basil's office.

'Hi,' she had said. 'I'm Carol. I hope I'll be working here before too long.'

'Simon,' the boy had said, walking a pace or two in front of her, and not turning round. Though she could not say exactly what success her attempted charm had had on him, it had not been directly expressed revulsion, she was fairly sure of that. He was the sort of man, with his height and his dark hair and his confident absurd striding, who she wanted to have success over.

Basil's room was beige; the walls like porridge. The desk was bare, apart from Carol's papers, a craning lamp and a single hardback book. It gave no suggestion of the business the firm pursued. They sat there in silence.

'I like your suit, by the way,' Basil said finally, without looking up. He surprised her; she hadn't thought he would stop the interviewing and just say something to her, as if he had human likings.

'Thank you,' she said.

'Very nice,' he said. 'You live near here?'

'For the moment,' she said. 'That's my parents' house on the CV. I'm looking for somewhere else near to live on my own. It's difficult, though. Things are tight at the moment, and I have resigned myself to staying where I am for another month, against my will. I mean, until I have been working for a month, or thereabouts.'

Was he offering her the job?

'It is difficult. I remember what it was like,' he said. 'My wife and I –'

Not a single man, then.

He paused for a moment, and then, blushing, got out a grubby wallet and said 'I wonder if I can help at all.'

Carol looked at him directly. 'I'm sorry?'

'I wonder if I could lend you some money,' Basil said, putting the wallet down on the desk. 'I mean, I was just about to offer you the job. If it would be helpful I never have any objections to offering help. Or the firm perhaps might be prepared to give you an advance. If you were unhappy about taking a personal loan . . . I'm sorry, I've embarrassed you and said something improper. I only meant well. I'm extremely sorry, you must think me very strange indeed.'

'No,' Carol said. 'No, it was a very kind offer.'

'I don't know what I was thinking of,' Basil said. He brought the few papers on his desk together in a pile, squared them with the palms of his hand. Only the brown wallet disturbed the empty symmetry; his activity made her realise that he had embarrassed himself; that he was taking himself out of an awkward moment. 'But if you would like – if it would help you out – a hundred pounds –'

'I would be very grateful indeed,' Carol said. 'I find that the more one can make simple arrangements in a simple way, the better. A hundred pounds until my first pay cheque would be an enormous help. If you are offering me the job.'

'If,' Basil said. 'I mean, if you would like it, or like to think it over.'

She looked up at the ceiling, as if considering it. She often found herself prey to small fetishes and superstitions of her own devising; she was a counter of stairs, a woman who, at twenty-two, still avoided cracks in the pavement. If the ceiling was as immaculate as the rest of the office, she thought, she would refuse the job. If, like the occupant of the office, it was not immaculate, she decided she would accept it. Basil looked at her as if not quite understanding why she wasn't saying anything. In one corner of the ceiling, she saw, there was a small stain, as if, one particular jocund morning, Basil, had preferred to throw a cup of coffee in the air than drink it.

'I would be very happy to accept,' she said.

Basil reached into his wallet and took out two fifty-pound notes. She took them, feeling that she was doing him a favour by appearing to place herself in her new employer's debt. If you knew that presents were only ever given in the hope of turning the recipient into a debtor, then, at least, you were a step or two ahead of the game. She knew all the dodges. She really did. And she seemed to see herself, sitting in this same room, in a month's time, listening while this man told her that his wife did not understand him; and, six months after that, listening to the same man telling her that his wife had understood everything. But for the moment she smiled, as if in politeness.

Her parents seemed surprised that she was going to leave the house, and had already found a job. She told them in their doggy drawing room, around the edges of which casually acquired piles of old novels had a knack of accumulating. The youngest of her step-brothers, the annoying eight-year-old, kept wandering in and out and bothering them, quite uninterested in her momentous announcement. They didn't oppose her, but then, she hadn't expected them to. The next day she spent a depressing morning in Clapham looking at a succession of flats where she could live on her own. She took the last, which was no more deplorable than the others. It was empty, and had been cleaned, but was not immaculate. Cigarettes had been stubbed out on the cheap carpet by a previous tenant, and across the powder-blue was a scattering of small shiny black circles, like a dropped and valueless fistful of holiday coins. The flat was relatively near where she was to work; it had two rooms, which were enough. She moved in with her things, and told her family where they could reach her.

The first day at the firm, the business was explained to her. The firm placed advertisements in the pages of colour magazines inviting punters – the customary word – to purchase small decorative objects. The small decorative objects were mostly made out of china or glass, in theoretically limited editions. A plate was the first thing she had to deal with, with a highly detailed and realistic picture of an aeroplane on it. Animals, less realistically depicted, formed the bulk of the firm's business; a lifesize kitten with a bashful smile; a small rhinoceros made lovable with a small piece of glass under its left eye to simulate a tear. Kittens do not smile; rhinoceroses do not cry, but Carol did not trouble herself with thoughts like these, any more than she speculated on the lives which would be improved by being ornamented in such a manner. From a warehouse somewhere nearby, large numbers of such objects were despatched. Nobody from the office ever seemed to go to the warehouse, and Carol had never seen the objects themselves.

There were fine matters of judgement involved in the selling of such things, in which matters of judgement Carol was instructed. A man two offices down from her had the job of deciding how much demand there would be for a dying unicorn with a genuine silver horn, or for a golden retriever puppy, a third lifesize, batting a butterfly from its nose. When he had decided this, the appropriate number was ordered from the factory in Mexico which made the objects, and Carol was informed of the number. In the advertisements, this number was described as the size of the limited edition. The same man also had the task of deciding the price to be demanded for each object. This was a mysterious process, and Carol could not see on what basis he settled on any sum whatever for objects so perfectly worthless.

Carol was to work next to Basil's office. His job consisted of negotiating with the magazines which published their advertisements. She was employed to type his letters. It was understood that, as Carol became more experienced in the work of the firm, she would occasionally find herself called upon to write the paragraph in the advertisements which described the object and tempted the *punters*. Basil explained this to her on her first morning, and she had the impression that she would not be asked to do this for some months, if not years. In fact, she discovered, the rest of the firm assumed from the beginning that she would take on the job of writing the advertisements. The secretary of Basil had done it since time immemorial – or at least for the last three years, since no one now working for the firm had been there for longer than that – and, by the middle of her second week, she found herself trying to describe a bun-faced Edwardian infant with a balloon in a paragraph of a hundred and fifty words.

'Having trouble?' Basil said kindly as he came in.

'Just thinking,' Carol said.

'You'll get the hang of it,' Basil said. 'The first one is always difficult, and I'm letting you have plenty of time. There's no need to think about deadlines with this one.'

'That's very thoughtful of you,' Carol said. She had finished the paragraph an hour before. It was only a hundred and fifty words; it had taken her ten minutes. 'Do you mind if I confess something? It's simply that it seems rather an important thing for me to be doing so quickly.'

'It is important,' Basil said, and as she had guessed, he seemed gratified by her helplessness. 'It is important to get the copy right. But you oughtn't to worry, because I'll see it, and the third floor will see it. We'll all stick our oar in, and by the time you see it in the *Sunday Times*, I'm afraid you probably won't recognise what you wrote. Which is not to say that what you come up with won't be good. I'm sure it will be excellent. But we all need to justify our existence by making supposedly helpful changes.'

'I see,' Carol said.

'Don't be downhearted,' Basil said. 'Listen, I'll let you into a tiny secret. I'd never say this to anyone else. But I have a terrible suspicion that people would buy these things whatever we said in the advertisements. I honestly think it would be harder to put people off buying our things than it is to persuade them.'

'I think the copy might take me another two hours,' Carol said. 'I might need to think about it.'

Copy was the word they used for any writing which would in the end be printed. She had quickly learned to say it. After she had written eight or nine advertisements, she started to understand the right way to do it, and, following a formula which she worked out for herself, she began to enjoy doing it. First, she would describe the photograph of the object which was sent to her. In a naïve style, she suggested some kind of simple story, saying that a kitten had temporarily lost its mother, or that a china girl in a china crinoline was preparing for her first ball in the Victorian era. Then she would stress the workmanship, the fine quality of the materials (genuine crystal, genuine porcelain, genuine paint). She would point out that it was the work of an internationally famous designer, or an internationally famous sculptor in porcelain. You were required to state the exact size of the object, and then Carol would make a point of saying that the object might bear no resemblance whatever to the photograph in point of shape, size or appearance. She stressed the very small number of copies in the edition, and outlined various methods of paying a large sum of money for the ornament. Finally, she would indicate that the object should be viewed as an heirloom and would be treasured by future generations. This approved form of words was to overcome a fact which nobody in the firm quite admitted to, which was that upon purchase all these objects would reduce in value to nothing whatsoever. The advertisement was not allowed to mislead by stating that it would increase in value. But you could say *should be viewed as an heirloom* and *will surely be treasured by future generations.* Carol had no trouble with that. She did not believe in the existence of future generations.

What did give her trouble was coming up with the names of the internationally famous designers. It was with some surprise that she learnt that there are no such people, or not really. There is no reason why such people should exist, nor any reason why, if they existed, they should become famous. Instead of troubling, then, to find out the name of the person who had imagined that a unicorn with a silver horn cast in porcelain would be an attractive addition to the home, she used the names of the employees of the firm. Secretaries found themselves being described as famous for their poetic imagination; senior executives were acclaimed across the world for the delicacy and beauty of their creations. If she had imagined, in doing this, that she would become popular, she was mistaken. These people were not flattered, or amused; once their attention was drawn to Carol they looked at her, as people always had, with a mixture of nervousness and fear.

In Carol's head were odder things than the advertisements she wrote. She often wondered what it would be like to go to your first ball in the Victorian era if your dress was not bone and cloth, but if you were entombed in porcelain, untouchable. The image held her; a girl who could not be embraced, who looked out helplessly from what her flesh had been baked into, a white casing, an upright sarcophagus.

The end of her first month came, and her first pay slip. She did not give Basil his two fifty-pound notes, and the nearest he came to asking for them was, every so often, to stand by her desk, and rub his thumb along his lower lip, saying nothing for a minute. And then he would say 'Nothing,' and go back into his office. She continued, serenely; he had hoped to establish power over her with the strange loan; she would embarrass him by making him raise the subject, and making him see that she had no shame.

He did the same thing five times in two weeks, and then stopped. She kept the two fifty-pound notes, and never thought of spending them. She thought often of what Basil had said at the interview. It had been nice of him to comment on her suit. As time passed, she wondered why he did not say something like that again. He was someone who, unlike most people, had surely perceived that her exterior, substantial, half-smiling and firmly impermeable, disguised her vulnerability. She believed that compliments struck her with greater force than most people, since they came her way more rarely, and she believed that she stored them up longer. She could not compliment him back; there was little to compliment him on. Beaky, unkempt and thin, with a suit seemingly made for a larger person, he was not someone very likely to stir her feelings. But she liked him. There was something nice about him.

When he came, as he often did, into the room to talk, she made an effort to ask his advice about some trivial aspect of her life. She liked him in these moods.

'How's the flat coming along, then, Carol,' he would say. He came in as if he could hardly wait to say her name, and she liked the careful way he said it. She smiled.

'It's coming on,' she said. 'I don't know, exactly, what it needs. Perhaps a pet of some kind.'

'Perhaps,' he said. 'Good idea.'

'What do you think,' she said. 'If you had a pet, and you were me, what would you get?'

'If I were you,' he specified. 'It depends I suppose on what you like. Cats are nice, though dogs can be too. If that might be a little demanding, you could think about a fish, though they're not terribly exciting, I mean, something swimming up and down and round and round. If you have to look after something – I mean – if you had to look after something, you might value it more – and then you might like it because it took so much trouble, do you see, and then –'

'By that logic, I ought to get a giraffe,' she said demurely, looking at the absurd photograph of this week's ornament on the desk.

'Yes, quite,' Basil said. 'Yes, that would certainly, that would certainly be very difficult to look after, in

Wandsworth, or wherever.' He kicked the furniture, his bright gaze sweeping the room like a lighthouse in fog.

'Clapham, in fact,' she said. 'Do you have a pet at all?'

'Well, no, but I can't say that I've never been tempted by a dog,' he said.

'A dog,' she said. 'What sort of dog?'

'Nothing very big,' he said. 'I would love a dachshund. They are quite adorable.'

'A dachshund,' Carol said.

'Yes,' Basil said. 'Yes. I always thought so. But apparently they are more trouble than they are worth, someone told me. They have back problems.'

'Well, you would, wouldn't you,' Carol said, going on typing. 'With a back that long.'

'I can almost see it,' Basil said. 'I even thought up a list of names for it. I thought Caspar would be nice, or Pushkin, or –'

'Pushkin,' Carol said. 'Why don't you get one, then?'

Basil got off her desk, briskly. 'I don't really know,' he said, walking away. 'It would be difficult, right now.'

'Difficult?' she said.

'My wife,' he said.

'Your wife?' Carol said. She thought she knew very well what he was going to say. She knew he was about to say that his wife didn't understand him, as men say to their secretaries in comic films. He surprised her, when he spoke.

'My wife has problems,' he said. 'We never had children. It wouldn't be fair on anyone, really.'

'How sad,' Carol said. 'I'm sorry to hear that.'

He looked for a long time at the paper on her desk, then, standing up, he yawned; yawning, his startlingly good teeth were revealed, and the clean thick root of the tongue opening before the faint thunderous scale of vowels, like the ecstatic cries of doves, from his thick red throat, before he seemed to remember his manners and flapped a hand at his open mouth. He looked down, a little abashed.

Carol could understand how she had surprised him. She didn't have problems, and her lack of problems was on her face. She liked her job. She no longer saw her parents. She was happy to live in her small and adequate flat. She liked working with him; she liked that best, best of all.

There was nothing to find out about him. His clothes told their own story, and his appearance the same story. Once, she stayed late in the office after he had gone, and went through his desk. There was nothing there; just boring letters. Only the book on his desk was strange; it was an anthology of poetry, a book of English poetry. It had his name in the front, and nothing else. She let the book fall open, and read it where it fell. It might have been supplying her with a meaning, an explanation. She did not know, and went on reading until it no longer made any sense to her.

On Sundays Carol usually went for a walk. For a few weeks after she had left her parents' house, they had asked her to come back for lunch on a Sunday. She always apologised for having arranged something else. There was no temptation on her part to go; there must have been little on theirs to ask her. She formed her own ritual of the Sunday walk. Not a country walk – not hiking to sit on gates with dry sandwiches, or to brighten up some ugly low-ceilinged pub with electric-orange cagoules. She liked, instead, to walk in the city. She walked the pavements of the quiet Sunday city. What she needed she carried; what she saw interested her; what she did not see she did not think of. Those empty Sunday streets of the city; Carol with her thoughts of Monday.

She knew where Basil lived from the telephone book. It was in the far suburbs, and one Sunday she found herself walking without a plan in that direction. It was long, the walk, crossing twenty named districts of the city, and it took her an entire morning before she reached the street where he lived. It was a quiet street; you might have thought the houses were large, if you had not understood that each one was divided in two, each huddling against its neighbour. The trees which lined the street were young and spindly, and, recently trimmed, looked stumpy, ungainly, wrong. As she walked down the street, she looked into each house and saw that the owners had made a determined effort to paint their most visible room an interesting colour, yet each room remained the same proportions in each house, still confirming only what she knew, that most people are what you would expect. What was she doing here? Perhaps she just wanted to see the street he lived in; perhaps, she thought, she just wanted, out of curiosity, to walk the route he took to the newsagent's, to the tube, to the pub. Out of curiosity; but she was fooling herself, and she knew it. She was well out of curiosity by now, and into something else.

She rang the doorbell. There was a long wait. She could hear something which might have been a movement, or a whispered conversation. Someone began to unbolt the door. There were four bolts to undo; when they had been shot back, and the chain undone, Basil opened the door. He looked so different in his Sunday clothes.

'Carol,' he said, in dull lack of surprise.

'I'm sorry to drop in like this,' Carol said, smiling. 'I was in the area, and I remembered you lived here and I thought, well, nothing ventured nothing gained, and I might as well say hello since I was in the area, as I say –'

'That's all right,' he said. She sensed that she was not completely welcome here. She didn't care. 'Why don't you come in?'

From the way he had half-welcomed her, the house might have been in a mess, but it was not; it was, in fact, almost savagely tidy. There was nothing more than a bare table in the hallway, and, as she followed him into the kitchen, the usual pans and kettles were absent from the bare and scrubbed work surfaces.

'It's very quiet,' she said. 'Are your children out, or something?'

'Actually, we don't have children,' he said, looking out of the window. 'Would you like a cup of coffee? Mary – my wife – she's still upstairs. I think she's cleaning the bathroom.'

He fetched a polished kettle out of a cupboard, filled it with water and plugged it in. With a cloth out of another cupboard, he wiped up a little splash of water made by the tap. He opened another cupboard, and got out two cups, then a third, then instant coffee, artificial dried milk, sugar.

'I'll just call my wife, shall I,' he said. He went out into the hall and made a strange cooing noise. The faint susurration of scrubbing brushes from upstairs stopped. 'How are you getting on with those fairies?'

'Those fairies?' Carol said.

'You know,' Basil said. 'The ones that came in on Friday. I wondered if you'd had any thoughts about what we were going to call them in the adverts.'

'I haven't quite made up my mind,' Carol said. In fact, she hadn't seen the photographs of the ornaments; they must have been in the folder which arrived at half past four.

'No hurry,' Basil said. 'Mary.'

'Hello,' his wife said. She stood in the doorframe like a guest, raw and frightened.

'Hello,' Carol said. She got up and took Mary's hand. Mary didn't respond. Carol ran through her explanation of how she came to be in the area, but the wife said nothing. Carol bent all her practised ineffectual charm on her. She didn't respond, and quickly Carol thought she might as well go now that she had seen the wife, and seen Basil.

'Mary liked you,' Basil said the next day.

'Really?' Carol said, with the appearance of pleasure. 'Well, I liked her too.'

'I'm sorry she's so shy,' he said. 'She liked you, though. She really did.'

'I don't mind shy people,' Carol said. 'I'm shy myself, really.'

He looked at her, as if to ask for elucidation before leaving the room. She lowered her eyes, to demonstrate her shyness.

Simon came in without knocking. The pictures of fairies were all over the desk.

'Horrible, aren't they?' he said cheerfully.

'I like them,' she said.

'You know, Carol,' he said, unabashed, 'in all the time I've been here, I've only ever heard of one person buying any of this rubbish. And he didn't buy it for himself. It was because his girlfriend had left him for some other bloke. Have you heard the story?'

'A million times,' Carol said.

'Stop me if you have, won't you,' he went on. 'Anyway, out of revenge, he took down her credit card details and ordered seventy-five little china people, just like that, that picture there, and glass dogs, the works, stuff you'd never in a million years want in your house, all that rubbish, all on approval. She returned them all, of course, but, you know, every day, there was a new horrible little china person for her to pick up and open. She must have just wanted to throw it at the wall, but she'd have to open it and pack it up carefully and send it back. Imagine, every morning, having to face something like that.' He pointed at a smiling goblin, and shuddered. 'And I've never heard of anyone else ever buying any of this stuff for any other reason at all.'

'But they do,' Carol said. 'Did her new boyfriend leave her in the end?'

'I don't know,' Simon said. 'Why do you ask?'

'Because – perhaps she herself had very bad taste and she would actually have liked all these unexpected gifts. It might have been agreeable to think that one had a secret admirer, willing to pay for these things.'

'At least until the bills started to arrive.'

'Yes, that is true. But by that time, she might have decided that she liked the ornaments so much she would keep them, and pay for them.'

'A hell of a lot of money, though.'

'She might have thought it worth it. Or she might have been rich. Some people are, you know.'

He stared at her. It was as if she had said something very strange, and, sitting with her composed face, she ran what she had said through her head, to make sure it contained no inadvertent obscenity, no breach of the rules. *Or she might have been rich. Some people are, you know.*

'I don't know,' he said after a while. 'I can't imagine. Carol –'

'Yes, Simon,' she said, starting to type again.

'Where do you live?' he said.

'I live on my own,' she said, turning the screen towards him. 'What do you think of this, as a name for this one? The naughty-looking troll on the tree trunk?'

He looked at the screen. There, she had typed, in 32-point capitals, occupying the whole screen, the words THE GREAT FUCKING PONCE.

'It might not do,' he said nervously. 'You –'

'Yes, Simon,' she said, composedly.

'You're too much,' he said, leaving.

She stayed in the office, again, until everyone had gone. She saw Simon go; he walked briskly past her open door. Basil came in with his bag and his coat on.

'How's it going?' he said. 'Nearly there?'

'Nearly there,' she said.

'Don't stay too late,' he said. 'There's a good girl.'

'No fear,' Carol said. 'No, I'm nearly there with this advert. I just want to finish it off.'

'Have you got a name yet? Basil said.

'Almost,' she said. 'To be honest, I was going to wait to see if the rain stopped. I forgot my umbrella this morning.'

'Nice weather for ducks,' Basil said. 'I've got a spare one you could borrow.'

'That's very kind of you,' Carol said. 'But I'd rather not.'

She looked directly at him, and caught his gaze; and suddenly he blushed, remembering, no doubt, the other loan, unrepayed, and hurried away.

She sat and waited until she could hear nothing in the building. Only the corridor was lit; the rooms were dark, apart from hers. *There's a good girl*, she said to herself. She got up, and went into Basil's room. It was as it always was. She sat in his chair and picked up the book of poetry. Again, she let it open where it would, and began to read. She read with all the attention she could spare. She relished the shuttlelike to and fro of the lines, the neatness of the noise. And after a moment, she reached down, and up her skirt, and dragged off her knickers. She dropped them on the floor, and, spreading her legs, pushed her skirt up. The seat of the chair was coarse tweed, and, her legs on either side, she rode it, pressing herself against Basil's chair, and all the time reading Basil's book.

> Then prostrate falls and begs with ardent eyes
> Soon to obtain and long possess the prize
> The pow'rs gave ear and granted half his pray'r
> The rest the wind dispers'd in empty air.

And that was her. Half-prayers in empty air. That was Carol, given up to her wishes. It spoke to her. She was silent.

It seemed to have worked, calling on Basil like that. He asked her if she would like to come to their house for lunch, and properly.

'That was delicious, Mary,' Carol said. 'You're a very good cook.'

Mary blushed and said nothing.

'Oh,' Basil said. 'That's not Mary, I'm afraid. No, neither of us can cook. It's all pre-prepared.'

'Could you cook if you tried?' Carol said to Mary.

There was a long pause. Mary started fiddling nervously with the table cloth.

'I think I might be able to,' she said in the end. 'But ready-prepared is so much easier all round. I really think it's nicer now than it's ever been before.'

Mary smiled, gratefully. It was turning out to be a success. The room the three of them sat in was the dining room. Like all the rooms in the house Carol had seen, it was entirely white. She had seen no pictures in the house, no ornaments, and the nearest thing to colour were the beige carpets, the cream table cloth. Everything here had been chosen so that it could not hide the dirt, so that dirt had no hiding place here. Carol took her glass, smiling back at Mary, and then, quite deliberately, let the wine spill from it on to the cloth. Mary leapt up, and started dabbing at it with her napkin. All the time she was talking. She might have been talking to anyone or anything.

'You mustn't rub, that's the thing, you get it all up if you press and soak, just that, not by rubbing, just rubs it deeper into the cloth, just a dry cloth, just hold it like that, just firm against the stain, it'll be all right . . .'

Carol carried on eating. Basil let Mary talk for a few minutes, frantically pressing against the tablecloth and the table and then, finally, said, 'Let me see.' Mary looked reprimanded, and, with her cloth in her hand, sank back into her chair.

'That's fine,' he said. 'Honestly. No one could ever tell anyone had ever spilt anything on it.'

She shook her head and made as if to press again on the cloth. He made a little gesture and, as if slapped, she shrank back.

'Carol's thought of a good name for those fairies,' Basil said conversationally. 'You remember, Mary? She came up with a very good name. We're going to call them "The Light Militia of the Lower Sky".'

'I don't understand,' Mary said, sitting down again. 'I thought they were just fairies.'

'No,' he said. 'Make an effort please, Mary, please. Carol found this name for the fairies. She found it in a poem. Don't you think it's clever?'

Mary, saying nothing, was obviously unhappy.

'Well,' Basil said. 'I think it's brilliant. I think it's clever of you to have found that. I didn't know you knew about poetry.'

Carol didn't know what to say, but she relished what he said. 'Have you seen Simon recently?' she said in the end.

'No, why?' he said.

'I think he's dyed his hair,' she said.

'But I saw him yesterday –' Basil said. 'Do you know, I thought there was something strange about the way he looked. I couldn't pin it down.'

'That's just men for you,' Carol said. 'You men, you never notice when someone changes their appearance. No, he's put in blond streaks. He looks absolutely terrible.'

'Why's he done it?'

'I think he fancies himself a bit,' Carol said. 'I think he thinks he's a bit of a ladies' man.'

'What, Simon?' Basil said, and he was off laughing. Carol couldn't help joining in. It wasn't that it was obviously ridiculous, Simon being a ladies' man. He was a nice-looking boy; nobody could have blamed him for trying to make the best of himself, even by making the mistake of the blond streaks. It was just Basil's laugh; it was infecting her, and egging her on. Mary didn't laugh, and she wouldn't; she wasn't prepared to laugh at someone she didn't know, someone her husband and her husband's secretary knew and she didn't. Carol looked at her, briefly.

'I like a ladies' man,' she said.

'Simon, a ladies' man,' Basil said, still laughing.

'I like a man who's not going to break in two,' Carol went on. 'I like a nice beefy man, not someone like Simon who's going to be worrying all the time about his hair – are you going to touch it, are you going to spoil it.'

Basil had stopped laughing; he looked over at his silent wife.

'I like a nice big man, a big dark man,' Carol went on. 'They're the best. Sometimes I just feel I need someone who's going to take me and overpower me. That's what I like. I like to be fucked. Do you know what I mean? I want to be hurt, to be taken, to be made to do things I don't want to do. That's what I want. Do you see?'

'Carol,' Basil said.

'It's been so long,' she said. 'I can't remember – and it's never been right, it's never been someone who doesn't say they won't damage me, they always say they'll look after me, and always, they end up hurting me, they say they don't mean to, but they always do. And I always hurt them first, hurt them before they can hurt me, that's the best thing. I just need –'

'Carol, please,' Basil said. There was fear in his face.

'Basil,' she said. 'You know what I think.'

Mary got up and left the room, quite calmly. Carol barely glanced at her. Basil shied away, but did not follow his wife.

'No,' he said. 'No, I don't know.'

'Yes you do,' she said, with scorn. 'You know what I feel for you.'

He looked at her. In his face she saw only desire. She went on, as confidently as someone reading from a script.

'And I know what you feel for me.'

'You mustn't –' he said. Then he moved away from what he might have said. 'You mustn't upset Mary.'

'I never would,' she said immediately.

'You've just made a mistake,' he said. 'That's all. I thought maybe you and Mary could be friends. That's what she needs.'

'No,' Carol said. 'That's not what you thought, not really.'

He looked at her. He might never have seen her before.

'I think you'd better go,' he said. She got up. He did not mean what he said, she knew that.

All the way home, walking the streets, she feared what lay above her, she feared the turning of the angels, the spirits there to guide her, to guard her. She feared the spirits she had named, and had thought, with naming, to control. Their desertion of her, and the transparency of their vengeance, those denizens of air. Those lucid squadrons. How well it came to her.

It was so unfamiliar, that day, that new city, and filled with apparitions and constructions. Nothing she saw was as she had previously seen it. It was as if, in love, she had not observed the world around her, as if things had changed at every point, and she had not seen them. Her new love had hidden the world from her, and this new world was not transformed, but revealed. The city of yesterday and the city of today were two cities; the city where Basil lived, the city where she lived, they too were two cities. And the city of work and the city where she merely sat and brooded, those were two cities as well. There was no limit to the doubling and halving of cities, each twisting away from its shadow, facing, like a great coin, away from what it could never become and could never share. As she walked over the bridge which divided the city where Basil lived from the city in which she had to live, she saw something she had never seen before. It was a huge Ferris wheel. She thought it was being built; broken into segments, the parts of the wheel hung from the central spoke like a dangling Meccano fan. She thought how wonderful it would be, in the days to come, when the wheel was complete, and whole, and spinning, each small car loaded with those in love. It shone.

As Carol opened the door to her flat, the telephone was already ringing.

'It's Simon,' the voice said. She could not understand. She could not think of a Simon, and just carried on listening. He was asking her out for a drink. She refused, saying that she was too busy. It was untrue. She had nothing to do but think about her thoughts, think about Basil. Love is always strange, and it had come strangely for her; come with a passion for a man with glasses, dandruff and no shoulders. He was perfect; how perfect he was; how his perfection exceeded anything his sad wife could perceive. And his patience, which made him keep his feelings from her, and from that sad wife; that confirmed her in her emotion. She had never known love, would not have accepted it if it had been offered. And she would never have chosen to offer it to anyone, fearing acceptance as much as rejection. It had slapped her, and, composed, she had let it topple her, unperceived by anyone around her, had let it overwhelm her quietly. She plotted, alone.

The next day she sat on the upper deck of the bus which took her to work, and remembered to look for the Ferris wheel, to see its progress. She turned in her seat, and looked out for it. But she had been mistaken. It had not been in the process of construction. Between the previous afternoon and that morning, the wheel had been taken away. It had been in the process of being dismantled. She had simply not seen the wheel in the previous weeks, when it was whole and working.

Basil was not at work that day. She had not expected him to be. He had called in and left a message with the switchboard. She realised that this was so he would not have to speak to her. It could not be left like that. In the afternoon, Carol told Simon that she, too, was feeling unwell. She took a bus to Basil's house. She had nowhere else to go.

'No,' he said immediately when he opened the door. 'I'm sorry, but –'

'Please,' she said.

'There's no point,' he said. They stared at each other.

'Basil,' Mary said. She had come up behind him, a pale figure, patient with waiting and love. 'Why don't you ask Carol in?'

'I don't think that would be a very good idea,' he said.

'I think you should,' Mary said finally. 'Since she's come all this way.'

Basil let Carol in, gesturing limply in front of him, and she led the three of them into the kitchen. Carol sat down; Basil and Mary both stood. As if in reflex, Mary moved over to the sink, where the washing-up stood half-finished.

'Are you all right?' Carol said. 'They told me you weren't very well.'

'There's no point to this,' he said.

'I don't know what you mean,' she said.

'You'll just upset yourself,' he said. 'And me. And Mary. I can't have you upsetting Mary.'

'Why don't we ask Mary what she thinks,' Carol said. Mary's back, at the sink, quivered.

'There's no point to any of this,' he said. 'I'm going upstairs. You'd better go.'

He left, almost running from the kitchen. Mary, at the sink, had a knife in her hand. It was clean, and she was washing it slowly, as if in anticipation of its soiling. It was a carving knife. Carol could not imagine, in their diet of ready-prepared, clean and frozen dishes, that it was something which would ever be required. Mary was a figure of pale terror, a figure from which every defence, every confidence had been drained. But Carol saw immediately that Mary was terrified, although it was Mary who was holding the knife, and it ought to have been Carol on whom the terror settled.

'Basil,' Mary said. 'You're very fond of Basil, aren't you.'

Carol shook her head. She was not fond of him; she ached for his weakness. She wanted him, and she wanted him gone, never to have been there.

'He won't stay upstairs for long,' Mary said. 'He'll be down in a minute for you.'

Each word she spoke bore its own emphasis, as if she were reading from the successive entries in a dictionary, and not forming part of a sentence. With a sudden deliberate gesture, she turned and placed the carving knife on the kitchen table, almost in front of Carol. It was unimaginable that she would leave it there rather than put it away with the other knives. But that is what she did. She left it carelessly in front of Carol; left her with a task to carry out, for her own benefit, and for Mary's. With a series of abrupt, unrelated movements, she hurled on her outdoor clothes; actions quite unlike the normal process of dressing. She was at the door in an instant.

'You know,' she said – her eyes shone – 'we never had children.' Carol knew it. And she was alone in the immaculate bare kitchen, waiting for her man to come downstairs, with one shining thing out of place and waiting. Her tool.

'We don't want it back,' Mary said.

It was three weeks later. She made as if to shut the door, so, quickly. Carol said, 'Anyway, here it is.' She pulled out the fifty-pound notes, and stuffed them through the narrow opening. The money was on the floor of the hall, and Carol turned round and went up the garden path.

Of course, Carol kept the job. Basil, some time later, announced to them all that he and his wife were moving away from London. He hoped to make a new start in the North. Nothing unusual; no one worked for long in this place, everyone said. Carol wished him and Mary the best of luck, and signed the card. We'll miss you, she wrote. Good luck and best wishes, she wrote, and passed it on to the next person to sign.

And Simon. Well, she fell for Simon. No; that's not right. For a time, she used to sleep with Simon. No, wrong again. A few times, she fucked him. A word, *fuck*, she would never say, and a word she would never write. And in the end they weren't good enough for each other.

She learnt all about the violence in fondness from Simon. And from herself, when she was with him, but the lessons she learnt went back into the past, taught her lessons about Basil and Mary and Carol. She was better off on her own. Simon, probably, was worse on his own, but that hardly mattered. There are still telephone calls in the night; telephone calls which say nothing, and mean nothing. She is woken by the telephone, and picks it up, and listens to the three seconds of silence, like the silence that comes after weeping. It annoys her, but less than people did. She knows that people call in the night, but knows also that they will never come after her. She knows this because, in the past, they never did, and they never would.

DEAD LANGUAGES

I DID NOT know when I was a boy that most people in the world went away to school. I only knew that no one from my family had ever left the stilted house in the forest river, to travel fifteen miles in two days to arrive, with the mud dry on my bare feet, at the big white school where they laughed at the way my family had always spoken.

They kitted me out with clothes which scratched and made you sweat; clothes which either gripped you like ropes and made you want to pluck and itch, or hung loosely over your hands and feet and got in the way of running. And a pair of brown shoes which, eight months later, my father would take from around my neck, where they had been hanging during the journey back home, and sit with them for an entire week, looking at them and thinking his thoughts no one ever asked about.

The mister of the school was a Christian and had a wife. They lived in the school, in a separate wing, which the boys called the House. It was the way of the school, and the mister, for one of the younger boys, or one of those less accustomed to shoes and stuffed square beds, to be taken into the House to learn its clean domestic ways, the ways of what I learnt to call civilisation. I was the youngest boy, at least at first, and unused to the life of the school, and of schools like it. So, like boys before me, I was taken into the House to work.

When I first went to see the mister to be told of this, I shook in my shoes. I stood at the end of the long dark wood room and waited to be shouted at. But the mister did not shout; he said good morning and, with his way of pausing before speaking, asked me to come closer. He asked about the place I came from, and he asked how old I was, and my family, how was it. And then he stopped asking, and in the room there was silence for so long that I raised my head, and I looked at what he looked like. He was just looking at me, in silence, without talking. And his big black eyes were sad in the way the eyes of animals are sad. Or look sad, when you know that in the fact they are really nothing of the kind.

There were few duties for me, and they did not interfere with what I had to learn. I learnt that I lived on an island, too big to walk around. I learnt not only what I knew, that you could add things and take things away, but that things could be multiplied and, more often, because it was harder, divided. I learnt that there were languages which were dead, and civilisations which were gone, and I chanted the words which humans once spoke freely and in feeling, to say *I love* and *you love*, and I felt nothing except what I happened to be feeling at the time. And I learnt other things, in the mister's House.

Every day, at four, I would walk around the trim square of grass to the House. For two hours, I was supposed to do the housework. At first I dreaded going round there, because the boys of my age told me stories about the mister and the mister's wife. They said they would fight in front of you. They said he would punish you. They said the mister was afraid of his wife, and he took it out on you. I was afraid that these things would come to pass, and then quickly I saw that they would not. It did not occur to me to tell the boys who said these things about my meeting with the mister; it seemed to me then that nothing happened, when he said nothing and gazed at me.

I was intended to dust, to tidy, and to iron clothes; to make certain preparations for food. But in the fact, I did not do these things. After some time, each afternoon, perhaps no more than half an hour, the mister's wife would call to me. 'Come and sit,' she said. And I went and sat, and drank *totosa* with her in the heat of the late afternoon, and we talked. I liked to listen to her.

The mister was immensely tall and his limbs were immensely long. They were insect-like, or lizardy, his limbs, in the way they gave the sense that through sheer length they would easily break, or easily turn themselves backwards. When I think of him, I think first of his loping vaguely across the thin lawn of the school; but then I think of his wife. Because the mister's wife was round and sweet and idle like a sweet yellow bun, and reminded you of the mister because she was so unlike him.

'Come here, Bobo,' she would say. A silly name she had for me. Her voice comes to me, it still comes to me; her husk and hint of a rattle which made your throat ache with the urge to cough, and clear it. And her conversation, the silliness we let ourselves jabber about. She would ask me things which I was certain, once I knew enough, I would be able to answer. 'Why is the sea sometimes blue, and sometimes not at all?' Or she would ask me about my family, and I would tell her about my tiny mother, no taller than I, and my little brothers, and my new sister or brother who now must be born, whom I knew nothing about, and the long stilted house no more than fifteen miles, and no less than half a world away, which my father and his father together built. I did not talk too much about my family; I had a constant fear that one of them might have died, and I would know nothing about it. It would be bad to sit and talk fondly about my father and laugh about what now seemed to me the funny way he had of putting a little yaw in the middle of words. A bad thing, if he was dead and I did not know it.

We talked once about death, the mister's wife and me, and it was like another fancy of hers. 'If there was a day,' she said once, 'when nobody in the world died, nobody anywhere died, who would notice?' I sat and thought about that world without death, for one day; how it would be happy and untouched by suffering, and yet no one would know until long afterwards, when suffering and death and pain had returned. Enchanting, these conversations, and a secret they were, from the mister.

I came to understand that he slept upstairs after he had finished teaching, while his wife talked to me in the dark cool rooms with their resiny smell of teak. The creak and lollop of his coming downstairs was, for me, a sign to rise and be busy with the furniture and a rag; and, for her, a sign to sigh and stretch and smile for her husband.

'Who built the school?' I said once.

'Long long ago,' she said. 'It belongs to me now.'

I digested this.

'It was the mister's,' she said. 'But he thought he would lose it, so he gave it to me.'

'How could he lose it?' I said.

'It could be taken away from him,' she said. 'He was afraid it would be, so he gave it to me.'

I thought about it. It made no sense, to give something away because somebody would otherwise take it from you.

'And now he'd like to be off, to be rid of his old baggage, but he can't,' she said. 'He's stuck with me, and I'm stuck with him, because the school is mine.'

I thought.

'If you gave it back to him,' I began.

'They would take it away from him,' she said.

It made no sense. In the dark corner of the sitting room, I heard the quick creak of the ceiling which meant he was getting up, and I reached for the duster.

The boys in the long room where I slept laughed at me at first, and soon I learnt to speak as they spoke, and to wear my shoes always, and not to scratch myself, under their laughter. And soon I joined in with their fanciful talk about the mister and his wife. The tales of shouting, tales of hurled insults, the names of vegetables and beasts they yelled at each other, the throwing of objects in their epic rows; I listened, and soon I too found I could tell of arguments I had not heard. I joined in when the boys said that they knew of a machine for punishment the mister kept in his upper rooms, and they knew of a boy who, five years before, had died of fright when he had merely seen the terrible machine. I thought that there was probably no such machine, but in my duties I did not go upstairs. I did not know what punishment and secrets and humiliations lay in the bedroom of the mister, and the bedroom of the mister's wife, and I kept quiet.

'Does the mister ever speak to you?' she said to me once, one afternoon, as we sat with our cooling *totosa*.

Her conversation was like that, simple questions you could not understand.

'Yes he does,' I said.

'Does he speak to you when you're on your own?' she said.

'I don't know,' I said, after a while.

'If he asks you to come to the House when I'm not here,' she said.

There seemed to be nothing more. She was looking at something, with sudden fierceness. She was looking at a big fly, making a noise like thick paper tearing at the far wall. I sat and waited for the next thing she would say. But she said nothing more. And in six months, I was no longer the youngest boy when I came back from my six weeks with my family in the quiet stilted house in the mud by the river. Before long, the fat progress of the creamy yellow flesh of the mister's wife through the shady cloisters was as comic to me as to every other boy. For years behind and years to come.

That was the way to talk about her, in a funny story. Because I told the stories to the dormitory, the stories of how she talked to me. But it was no story, and the boys in the long room after dark laughed at me for thinking it was something to be told. And yet it was.

Years passed; they always do. And the time came to go; and I was exactly the same. Except that I knew more, and I talked differently; louder, I suppose. And I knew my father, when I jumped out of the boat back from school, would, as he had every year, seem smaller. I knew his way of talking would have suddenly developed a funny, unexpected yaw I would want to correct. The dead languages we learnt at school, we guessed at their pronunciation, I knew, and guessed wrongly; and I knew that if a speaker of those dead languages was to leap out of a boat and talk to us, his way of saying even *I love* and *you love* would seem strange to us. But it would be a way of speaking we had once known, and had forgotten; a way newly unfamiliar to us, because we have so changed.

The time came to go, and not to return, and I did not know whether I was supposed to go. The mister asked me to go to his room, once more, and I went. He was sitting behind his desk, as he had before. This time I looked at him, but his eyes were dark and sad as they always had been; and we looked at each other.

'Here,' he said eventually to me. 'You've been good. We ought to be proud of you.'

'Thank you, sir,' I said.

'I'd like to give you a leaving present,' he said. 'Something you will always keep.'

'No need, sir,' I said.

'No need to call me sir now,' he said.

'I would like to say goodbye to your wife,' I said after a time.

'My wife is out for the afternoon,' he said. I did not understand the mister and his wife. I did not know what contracts passed between them in the dark. And, in the fact, I still do not. He reached for his wrist, and unhitched his watch. He glanced at it, as if checking it still told him what Now it was, and offered it to me, across the broad expanse of his desk. I shook my hands at him. His smile insisted, and I carried on shaking my hands at him. And I did not know whether my refusals were the sort of polite refusals which always intend to finish in acceptance, or if I did not want the watch. I did not know, and on either side of the desk, I shook my hands at him, and he smiled at me, and proffered.

The mister's tiny wrist-machine was what I once called *tiktik*. Knowing no better. And with every *tik* another second gone, and another moment, and a chance lost, and, perhaps, no new chances to take their place. Once I wanted to learn and learn, until I knew enough. But now I know that I will never know enough; that the exams in that unmastered subject, Enough, have never yet been set; that they have never been passed, and never will be.

IN THE NET

MATTHEW WAS FORTY-SEVEN when his heart, as they say, was broken. His wife died, with no more than the usual inadequate warning, and he decided to go and live as a widower in a Suffolk village.

He could quite imagine it, a widower in a Suffolk village, living behind a kempt front garden, a regimented frontage. For the first time, he would occupy a position in society. A Suffolk widower; it was a position secure, and as little needing explanation to the world as a vicar, an MFH, a prostitute. He made his decisions; to go and live in Suffolk, and to live and announce himself as a widower. And he made them, understanding that, from now on, this was how his life was going to be. Things had turned out oddly for him, all in all, turning him into a widower, killing his wife off like that. It was not the first time he had declared himself a widower. A more pensive man might have wondered whether this was the role the world had decided upon for him; decided upon it before his wife had been killed, before he married her, decided upon it long before he had even declared himself bereaved of the wife who, as yet, did not exist.

Matthew had not married Catherine until he was almost forty-five. He was an academic who, for thirty years, had lived in London, in various districts south of the River: SW2 SW4 SW8 SW9 SW11, a whole narrative of slow improvement in the green flat suburbs, like a planned history, like a logical series of numbers, 2, 4, 8, 9, 11. It had always seemed as if the next number in the series would tell him what his future might hold, and now he knew that had not been the case.

An anthropologist he was, who for nearly thirty years had worked on nothing but matrilinearity in the Hindu Kush. Field trips occupied more than half his time, and he had not married. Three times he had perceived the growing irritation in a girl's letters; on each occasion (girl one, girl two, girl three) it had been a girl he had loved, and on each occasion, he had asked her to release him from his obligations, in nineteenth-century fashion. He had not married, in fact, until he had given up the idea of publishing anything more substantial than an article, and given up the idea of greatness which, when he had been twenty, had so fired his ideas, so lit up his eyes; and, giving up all his ideas of greatness, he had met Catherine.

In London he had hardly ever given a thought to his unmarried status. But, on his trips to the Hindu Kush, the universal question 'Are you married?' was quickly followed by the question 'Why not?' And perhaps they were right to express a bafflement, which, as he grew older, became more extravagant in its expressions. His training as an anthropologist made him disinclined to snub the serious and intelligent men in their drab clothes, wrapped up as if in puttees, holding their machine guns at the dinner table, who always asked him the question, and looked at him seriously, as if it were more than small talk. And perhaps it was not a case of the incompatibility of cultures; perhaps here was a question which could reasonably be asked of him even in London. Why not, indeed? So once, sitting in the grand house of a village elder thousands of metres up, trying neither to shiver nor to think about the rather lardy feast he had just forced down with all the usual expressions of overwhelmed retching gratitude, he replied that he was not married, because his wife had died. The resulting narrative improvisation, incredible as it had seemed to him, had successfully filled the increasingly cold evening; his listeners were gripped by his fictitious marriage, the hopes he and his fictitious wife (named after girl two) had held, the terrible tragedy of his wife's giving birth and killing herself and the child in the process. The village elders nodded, unsurprised, and there he was, a widower. He reminded himself that a wife dead in childbirth was not as remarkable a biographical fact among the Afghans as it was in Parson's Green, and made an academic mental note to examine the mortality rates of childbirth, infant and mother, in urban and rural Afghanistan.

Widower was an odd term. He hardly thought of it in his own context. Academically, he could place the bereaved; he could say something unsympathetic and accurate about the place a society halfway up a mountain in the Hindu Kush would find for a man whose wife had died in childbirth, and, on paper, it would be interesting and abstract and thoroughly footnoted.

So it was odd, beyond anything he had considered, when

it happened to him. Odd, when he returned from a trip and bumped into a girl he knew – she was not an anthropologist, but the dined-with cousin of someone he remembered from Cambridge, a lawyer who asked him to dinner once every eighteen months, on average. Odder when, a year later, she had no stated objection to him, nothing of sulk, nothing beyond a kindness and an interest and a respect he had never thought might form part of his relations with a woman, and they found themselves marrying; and he looked at her, and saw her happiness, and saw, in a way, his own feelings, reflected, improved upon, made perfect in her perfect eyes; and oddest beyond anything when, two years after that, Catherine was cycling down the road for some trivial purpose, no reason at all, and was hit by a car, and killed.

He met the driver of the car, who had been talking on his mobile telephone, and felt nothing towards him, watched his ugly screwed-up pained face trying to be sorry enough, and just wanted to bring the poor man's ordeal to an end. 'Who were you talking to, on the telephone?' he asked. The driver said nothing, just looked at him, having no answer, and not seeing that, if your wife had been killed, if your wife's skull had been crushed by a lump of metal under the control of another human being, if in a moment your wife, who had been a living woman, her eyes blue and her hair dark and a magical unique unforgettable superorbital ridge, a magical unique unforgettable way of raising the eyebrow, always, mysteriously, the left eyebrow, a woman with her own thoughts and her own voice and her own way, unforgettable, her own way of walking, had been turned into heavy unmoving flesh, you too would want to know why, to inquire into the circumstances and find out what you would rather be ignorant of. And then he was a widower.

He thought of his status as he had thought of previous attained and incredible states of being; just as, at eighteen, he had locked the bathroom door and gazed at his face, and mouthed an incredible sentence, I have been given a scholarship by Trinity, or, later, I am a member of the Apostles, I am an Apostle; just as he had thought of himself, with thrilled observation, as a husband, and looked forward to becoming a father. He was a widower, and that was all there was to it. Yes, he said, looking, somehow, for the right bathroom mirror to mouth into, yes, I am a widower.

'Are you sure?' his friend and colleague Conrad said. They had known each other for years. He had not got as far as Matthew had. His career had shifted restlessly from Chinese court rituals, to structures of society in American fraternity houses, to Swedish warlocks, and he had never quite established a clear reputation for anything but niceness, never quite made a mark beyond the department they both worked in. Matthew had just announced to him his intention to go and live in Suffolk.

Matthew finished his glass of wine. The bottle was not quite empty, but he would wait to be offered the last inch. He took off his spectacles, held them up to the light. 'It seems,' he said, 'like the right sort of thing to do. I feel very uncomfortable, to be honest, in London. I mean in our house. And there's nothing much to keep me here.'

'The teaching –'

'The teaching can easily be done in one day a week. I'm not going to the ends of the earth. Even in Suffolk there's a telephone, a fax, the post. I might even get on that

E-mail thing, the Net. Once you start to think, to be honest, I just wonder what I'm doing here. Why does anyone want to stay here?'

Conrad looked at him, quite soberly. They were in a slightly unexpected bar; not one near the college, not in any sense an academic bar where they might be disturbed by the sight of students, or have to nod civilly at tactful anthropologists across the way, but a chrome and green-painted bar in the West End where the transient clientele of theatre-goers, the brisk noise and the anonymous crowds of media boys awarded them an unobtrusive privacy. The wine, Matthew had noted, was half as expensive again as it was in the usual haunt just east of the Museum.

'I don't quite know,' Conrad said finally. 'I mean, I know why I stay here. I like it. Some people don't need green space – Hyde Park is about as much as I can cope with. Do you really know the country? Do you really have any idea what it's like, living outside London?'

'Of course I do,' Matthew said. 'Come on. It's not so terrifying. Going to live in Suffolk, it's not like setting off on field work, and knowing you're going to have to struggle along with your subjects for months with no one to have a laugh with. London's no good for me.'

'Well, go back to Afghanistan,' Conrad said.

'Suffolk is easier,' Matthew said.

'I don't know about that,' Conrad said.

'Easier for solitude,' Matthew went on. He wasn't going to turn this into a joke; it was what he wanted to do, and what he was going to do. 'Living in the country, it's good for solitude. And of course I know what it's like. I grew up there. It's my parents' house I'd be going to live in. I never had much of an idea what to do with the house after they died – I was going to sell it three years ago, but, you know, the state of the market – and now I might as well go and live in it.'

'But do you really think this is such a good idea?' Conrad said. 'Cutting yourself off from friends? I know, I'm just being selfish. But you and me, seeing each other, every single day. You put up a good front of coping, but what is it going to be like without – you've been through –'

'I know,' Matthew said, heavily. He looked at the crowded and crowing bar; too crowded, too loud, too full, too London. He wanted to sit in silence, and look at nothing very much. That would be good. He could not quite express the fear that he had, that the consolation his friends offered was another means of renewing the grief. 'Yes, I know. You've been good through all this. It's not far. I'll be in London every week, more, as often as you like.'

'As often as you like.'

'Thank you. And there's E-mail.'

'I love the thought of you on E-mail.'

'Yes,' Matthew said. 'I thought it was really about time. I thought the fax machine would see me out, but –'

'I know a very good man,' Conrad said briskly. 'He'll set you up, won't frighten you. He's used to dealing with terrible old Luddites like you. God, going off and living some joke Marie Antoinette existence in Norfolk or Suffolk or wherever.'

'Suffolk,' Matthew said. He smiled. 'You're right. I need to change. This is a good change.'

Conrad, supportive as he was being, would not quite assent to this, but, in any case, Matthew would go on seeing him at least once a week. The course of his life, and its value did not depend on what his friends thought of it. And there was always the Net, or E-mail, which, if you believed what people said, had opened up the world, and would bring the world even to Suffolk. The world was on E-mail, and the world had become E-mail, a great floating invisible rippling grid of individuals talking, of unknowable extent, of incomprehensible nature. There was no telling the people he would, instantaneously, be able to talk to, no imagining the voices he would be able to access, who, in turn, would seek him out and find him. His mind turned from the specific and distant – the subcontinental universities he used as his bases, his Iranian correspondents, perhaps even his Kabul informants – to the intangible, the inconceivable, the thrillingly unknown, materialising from the ether. Voices from the ether, like the first days of wireless, appearing, and talking calmly to you, just voices, just talking.

He left the professional removers to box up the books, and went to the house in Suffolk. It was not much like moving. He had no desire to replace the ancient and familiar properties of his parents' rooms with his possessions and their now unwelcome associations. Apart from removing the books, he left the London house as it was, thinking that he would decide what to do with it when his life had clarified a little, and drove out, one Tuesday morning. It was a clear April day. The roads were rather better than usual, and unconvincing as it was, it was hard to resist the banal idea that a new beginning was upon him. In the clear empty light, he drove down the clean roads, wondering what, in all correctness, he ought to feel.

The village was neither picturesquely rural nor coherently urban, and the house fell similarly between categories, neither a sombre and unique manor house nor a cottage. The notion of a cottage interested Matthew only professionally, and not much even then. There was nothing pastoral or sentimental in his character, and he responded hardly at all to the urbanite fantasies of a mushroom-squat house with a five-foot door, a rose-crawling façade and a fat rosy farmer with a herd of geese. Still, he felt, stopping outside his parents' old house, there was something unduly severe about the bleak little village. It had a sort of green, with a couple of ducks shivering by a murky pond. A group of teenagers, drunk, smacked-out or just bonelessly limp with boredom, swayed on the fence outside the less respectable of the two pubs. No doubt they came from the forty houses of the brick development at the far end of the village, which, though it had proved a trial to his father as he entered his letter-writing dotage, echoed, when viewed in purely aesthetic terms, the bleak uneyebrowed frontages of the little eighteenth-century market-place, so approved of by the gentry, behind one of which he must now begin to live.

Matthew had warned nobody that he was coming back to the village, having nobody to warn, and, as he opened the door, a cold ghostly smell damped his face, the cool and vacant smell of cement dust. He stood there for a moment, trying to summon a feeling of homecoming, of returning to the place he had begun from and a place he could set out from again, ignoring the narrative of love and marriage and bereavement which had intervened. It did not come, the feeling. He wondered why he had ever thought it would.

The shop in the village was open these days only three days a week, and it had been thirty years since there had been a market in the market-place, so Matthew had brought a big bag of food from London. He unpacked it in the cold kitchen. Bachelor food, really, he thought, as he put it into the fridge, because if there was such a thing as food appropriate to a widower, he did not care to imagine it. The fridge smelt odd; there was nothing rotting in it, but it had been kept closed and had been preserving the air and the shelves, nothing more. He unpacked, anyway, his bachelor shopping; ready-prepared dishes in white plastic tubs, things eloquent of incapacity. Chewing them, he thought of nothing.

The next day was better. Conrad's sympathetic man turned up with the computer Matthew had ordered, and connected the whole thing up. He was younger than Matthew had thought he would be, and more professional; Matthew had expected, in some vague way, a sort of workman in overalls, and hardly knew how to deal with a bright young man who talked to him with patient sympathy instead of deference. He wondered what kind of tip-off the man had been given, or if, perhaps, this particular brand of kindness was a prerequisite for the job. He stayed most of the afternoon, showing Matthew one trick after another, and bewildering him. Afterwards, Matthew found himself wanting to stroke the blank machine, looking forward to a good day exploring the recesses of the little white object and discovering for himself what the man had already shown him. Not quite a pet, something more than merely a utility, he wanted to delay the moment he sat down and really talked to it, really talked through it to the vast listening world.

The next morning, he sent a message to Conrad.

Good morning Conrad. I'm not quite sure if this is going to work, but I'll send it to you anyway. Let me know if you get this – it will give me some confidence. Your man was very helpful, so thank you for that, but I expect I'll be struggling with it for weeks to come.

Conrad replied an hour or so later.

How amusing to be talking to you like this. How is Cold Comfort Farm? Incest still the favourite occupation of the rural classes? When are you coming back – I'm sure you're beginning to miss London already. So pleased that Johnny was helpful.

They sent messages back and forth for most of the day, saying almost nothing. Before Matthew started, he had imagined that they would type for a while and then, bored of an artificial means of communication, they would simply pick up the telephone and talk. But they didn't, and after a while he began to see that this was a way of talking just like any other; a way of talking which allowed him a little space; allowed him a moment of thought, permitted him a little freedom from the pressure of people's voices, the pressure of other people's feelings. He could see the point of it; and the point, perhaps, was silence. Communication, and silence; communication, perhaps, in silence, and a virtuous solitude.

Matthew spent the afternoon going through his address book, and letting various academic contacts know that he was now on the system. In a couple of weeks, this would be ordinary. For the moment, he let his arms tingle at the idea of the ether, the magical compressor of distance, the instantaneous traveller, summoning the world to his study. He finished, and looked up; he had not quite perceived that the room had grown dark around the bright computer screen: He extracted himself from the system, switched the machine off. The house was cold; he felt an abrupt hunger.

He went for a long walk the next day. The wind was up, blowing against his face, and quickly the sense of the pointlessness of walking in Suffolk settled on him. Without hills, in a place where the walker cannot see where he is going, nor where he has been, but is just walking, as if in an empty unmarked landscape; he could see little point to it. In Suffolk, there was no companion to walk with; in Suffolk, there was no work for him to mull over, no questions of Afghan matrilinearity to sort out; in Suffolk, he started to think, there was no point to him. In the end, his planned whole morning's walk dwindled into an hour and a half. He came back, and drove to Ipswich to buy groceries. When he returned, he put them on the kitchen table. But instead of putting them away, he sat down and looked at them. He lit a cigarette; something he had never done, here, when his parents were still alive, and as he began to smoke, he felt, not as if he were claiming the house for himself, but that he was an improper and undetected intruder. He had no idea what he was doing; he had no idea what he should do in this empty place, and it came to him that it had been four days since he had spoken to another human being. It hardly mattered any more.

When he switched on the computer it winked at him. It was a moment before he understood that someone had sent him a message. He entered the box; there was no name, just a string of numbers indicating the caller.

You've been on edge. Don't be edgy. You always had too

much of an edge, a sort of sharp one, rough and hard. You cut me, you know. Do you know who this is? Can you guess where I'm speaking from, how I found you? But didn't you always know that I would always manage, somehow, to find you? Didn't you always know that?

He looked at the word edge. It was so strange, unlike an ordinary word, and he watched it behind the blinking cursor. That *d*, that *g*, banging against each other, so strange. He knew the word, he understood the expression on edge, but now he felt it as alien. There was no way of knowing when the message had been sent; it might have been waiting for him for hours, but he felt a certainty that the sender was there, at the other end, waiting for his response. He opened a file to reply, and laid his hands on the keyboard, like a relaxed alert virtuoso about to begin to play the piano. In the end he took his hand from the keyboard and placed it, flat, against the screen of the computer. He had nothing to say.

Memory was the worst thing, in the house, just as it had been on his field trips. On field trips, the memory of food, of English cheese and apples, of the tones and timbres of the voices of friends, had always had the power to bring pain into his head; once in the Hindu Kush, a taste, in a high mountainous feast for the honoured guest, had shocked him with its unmistakable school-taste of Lancashire hot-pot, and he had had to thank his Afghan hosts too effusively, afraid that he was about to start crying, and have to explain why. And here it was as if he had left everything, not as if everything that mattered had left him. He had left the London house, fearing to be reminded of Kate in an object of hers, in a corner of a room where he could see her standing, and, in this Suffolk house, a place they had infrequently visited and never lived in, she was everywhere. The silence of the dour village invited only the memory of a dear laugh; the food he made do with only summoned up the food, so different, she liked to eat. A cup of coffee; a flower; a blank wall; the white sheets and the white pillow on which no pained pale face rested; they were all filled with her, all seemed to form some tiny fragment of her giant Arcimboldo-face, within which, he began to understand, he now lived. He went from room to room, not knowing what to do, not knowing what not to do. His lack of effort; the effort they made with each other, all the time, every day. Every second a new reminder. He sat at his desk; he switched on, he switched off the computer, its hum and click like a slow rhythm, a natural rhythm insensitive to, indifferent to his existence.

There had been a party, for instance; so characteristic that now he could not remember what it was for, but only her, standing there, with her slight foot-shifting nervousness, and all the time she seemed to be holding the thing he had said to her, when they were alone, before people came; you'll be fine. He watched her, and she was fine, of course she was, because nobody could not love her, whatever this party was for: engagement, marriage, his birthday, a first anniversary, perhaps, in the course of their brief life together. She had greeted the guests, and talked to them, and made a good effort not to look at him for approval. In turn, he respected her, and made an effort not to look at her, out of his love and concern, and only once did he listen to what she was saying. 'Thank you very much, thank you very much indeed,' she was saying, 'for making the effort to come all this way', and his heart filled with her kindness, knowing that thank you was so inadequate for the gratitude she so ordinarily felt that it had to be filled out with *very much* and *very much indeed*, and they looked at each other, two hosts of a party, and shared their silent pleasure, for one moment, for just one moment.

He turned the computer on, and it was waiting for him, in the same patient kindness.

You didn't reply, the computer said. Don't worry. It doesn't really matter. I'm here for you anyway, whether you want to talk to me or not. I'm watching over you. You have a nice view there, you know. You don't know it, but you do. In one direction, you can see as far as the blue. If you look straight up, you can see the blue. The sky there, it's so big, it's enough of a view for anyone. When you go out, isn't it just like being on the top of a great big dome, doesn't it feel as if the horizon is beneath you? And no hills and no landmarks and nothing but wind, all the way to the sea? Isn't that good? And what did you go to Suffolk to look at? Did you think you might escape something? Maybe you did. But it isn't really working. I know you think about me, as much as I think about you. I'll come for you, one day, I promise. You know that, Matthew, don't you? I'm going to come for you, and I know you'll be waiting for me, and thinking about me as much as I think about you. You'll be waiting for what I've got for you. Because you know what I've got for you. You know it.

He read it, and he read it again. He reached forward to touch the screen of the computer. He was convinced that now, something extraordinary was about to happen. He felt that the surface of the screen, as he touched it, would not be cold hard glass, but something soft and warm and yielding, that a hand would mould itself around his, and take firm hold, and tug. But it was with no dread that he reached forward, and he felt only a small disappointed shock when there was nothing, after all, there, that the glass barrier remained as it was. He pulled his hand back from the cold screen, and began to type. Who are you, he tried to type, who are you. But something had happened to the computer. He pressed down each key in turn, with increasing slow deliberation, but nothing changed on the screen. The screen displayed only the message he had received, and would not register his question. Who are you, he typed again, and again, but nothing came up. Only the message he had received, and the cursor, blinking; and though he knew perfectly well that the cursor could only blink at the rate it was set at, it seemed to slow, a slow slow throb which his heart effortlessly doubled. He could send nothing; he could only wait for the next message, and he sat, looking at the screen, waiting for the machine to speak to him. Nothing came. The voice was gone, and the invisible magical net roamed through the electronic sea, and caught nothing.

The next morning Matthew got up and drove to Cambridge, very early. He got there before nine, and left his car at the railway station. He telephoned Conrad from a payphone, and explained that he was coming to London to sort out some dull things, and, if he had nothing better to do –

'Lunch?' Conrad interrupted.

'Why not,' Matthew said.

'You sound a bit strange.'

'It's a bit early, isn't it,' he said. 'I haven't –'

'Yes?'

'I mean, I haven't really been speaking to anyone much

for a few days. I've been reading nothing but Persian tracts. Perhaps I've forgotten how to. How to speak English, I mean.'

'Well, make an effort to remember by lunch.'

They arranged a place, and he went to buy a ticket. He had a segment of the train to himself. He bought the *TLS*, and a junk paperback. Reading matter; he did not want his head to be unoccupied for a moment before he saw Conrad. He did not think; he only read. That was best. He wanted not to think about the place he found himself in; he wanted not to think about the story he found himself in.

The green fields passed, the lines of rain marking the window. Matthew had been a student in Cambridge, and a doctoral student, and had held a junior research fellowship there. He had spent over ten years of his life in the town, and for most of that decade had gone either in one direction, to his parents' house, or in another, towards London. He found it inexplicable that both these routes, without his constant use, were as they had been, that the railway line still pursued the same dull slow route into East London, past the dull flat countryside with the flat-faced animals. He had changed, and the world had changed with his perception of it. But the ways of escape and entrapment were as they were, as they had always been.

He had never thought to find himself in a ghost story. He knew how ghost stories started; they started with a communication, in daylight, from a voice long thought silenced. And that had happened. If he did not know where the voice came from, from what part of the vast invisible world, that was because he did not care to look. The world was out there, the invisible world which the linking hands of the Net, like a séance of the ignorant many, had accessed for him, and now it gathered round his little computer, around his little hurting head, and tormented him. He knew how ghost stories began. He knew, too, how they ended: with the solitary widower in the solitary house, his arm chewed off, a look of inexpressible unearthly terror on his face in the locked room. He said to himself, as the train rolled over the points, don't be stupid, don't be stupid. He looked out at the land, and sitting in the empty carriage, he was only calm. There were explanations. There were always explanations. A friend might be sending them, these messages – a friend who thought he had understood quite well who it was – out of kindness, or some complicated malice. Or it could be her. Yes, he thought, looking out with a tranquillity he would never have been able to predict as he accepted the worst thing of all; it could be her, speaking to him across insubstantial space.

Unexpectedly, Conrad was there before him. It was a restaurant they had often passed, and often vaguely promised each other that they would try, in a street by the Museum. Its calm white walls and discreet waiters – and its cost – were satisfyingly unlike the usual Museum cafés, but its proximity to learning inoculated it against any fashion, against – it was a phrase, a shorthand for vulgarity and noise the two of them used – against expense-account. Conrad had ordered himself a Bloody Mary, elaborately structured with celery and a floating detritus of black pepper.

'You look well,' Matthew said. 'Am I late?'

'Not at all,' Conrad said. 'I had nothing to do this

morning and got here early out of boredom. Actually, I have nothing to do this afternoon, so I plan to get rather drunk. If you don't object.'

'Not in the slightest,' he said. 'It's been so long since –'

He stopped. In fact, it had not been long at all.

'I'll tell you,' Conrad said, sipping his drink, taking up the conversation from the awkward gap. 'I'll tell you what has been a long time. It's been years and years since I finished a book and had no idea what I was going to start working on next. It's quite a nice feeling.'

'Finished with those boring warlocks?'

'They were terrible, in the end,' Conrad agreed. 'I might come out with you to your murderers. That might be fun.'

Matthew nodded, smiling, having nothing to say to this. They looked at their menus for a while.

'It looks good, doesn't it?' Conrad said. 'What would you like?'

'I'm not sure,' Matthew said. 'But you mustn't –'

'I mustn't?'

'You mustn't buy me lunch, really.'

'I had no plan to,' Conrad said. Matthew looked up. Perhaps he had misunderstood what Conrad has meant.

'I'm sorry,' he said. 'I thought you said – I mean. I was going to buy you lunch, in fact.'

'Well,' Conrad said. 'I'd rather you didn't.'

'I'm sorry,' Matthew said, trying to get to the end of the conversation. 'I thought you said something. I thought you said, what would you like, and I thought, I thought you were saying that this one was on you. I misunderstood. I was going to buy you lunch. I mean I still am.'

'I'd rather you didn't,' Conrad said. 'Let's order.'

'What are you thinking of working on?' Matthew said, more or less at random.

'I really don't know,' Conrad said. 'There are a lot of things I feel vaguely interested by, but nothing is striking me with any enthusiasm at the moment. I might just teach for a bit and see if something comes up out of the blue.'

'Or,' Matthew said, 'you might just go back to something you've worked on before. I think – well, I've never worked on anything but my boys, you know, for nearly thirty years now, it just gets more and more fascinating.'

'Anthropologists,' Conrad said after a moment, 'they come in so many different shapes and sizes, don't they.'

The waiter came to take their order.

'How is the computer?' Conrad said when he had gone.

'Fine,' he said. 'Yes, fine. I worked out the E-mail system. Oh, you know I have. I was talking to you on it.'

'Yes, indeed,' Conrad said. 'Are you getting much use out of it?'

'Yes,' Matthew said. 'You know, something odd happened.'

'Yes?' Conrad said. 'Things often go wrong at first.'

'Yes, they do,' Matthew said. He let it drop for a moment. 'Do you – do you get messages from strangers, ever?'

'What sort of messages?'

'About you. I mean personal messages. Do you ever get anonymous messages from people who know about your life?'

'I don't remember having one,' Conrad said. He looked oddly at Matthew. 'I don't think it's as easy as all that to find someone's E-mail address. Have some more wine.'

The lunch went on. The food was quite good; perhaps not quite as excellent as they had imagined, but quite good enough, and it went on until the restaurant was almost empty. In Conrad's face was a tense expression, as if wondering why Matthew had asked him there, and, answering the questioning look, Matthew felt a need to produce a request.

'I wonder,' he said in the end. 'I wonder if I could ask you a favour.'

'Anything,' Conrad said, warmly.

'You know Kate,' Matthew said. 'I mean, you know her clothes.'

Conrad looked at him, nodding faintly.

'And you know women,' Matthew said. 'A lot more than I do, I expect. Well, I was just going through things the other day, and there are really a lot of Kate's clothes in the wardrobe still. I wondered if you knew any women who might have some use for them. Of course, I haven't given them away, don't really have anyone to give them to, or –'

He stopped. Perhaps this was a strange thing to ask someone.

'Of course,' Conrad said. 'Of course, I'll take them and give them to charity shops. Of course it isn't good for you to have them around.'

'No,' Matthew said. 'No, I wasn't saying that, I just wondered if you knew any women who would like any of them. Some of them are probably quite good, and she didn't wear them, or anything.'

'Matthew,' Conrad said. 'I'll take them to a charity shop. You wouldn't like it if you had lunch with the librarian and she was wearing an old dress of Kate's.

Don't worry. I know what to do. I'll arrange the whole thing.'

He nodded, knowing from the tone of Conrad's voice that he was right. He put his coffee spoon down in the saucer. 'I am a widower,' he said. 'My wife died.' He looked at Conrad. Oddly, it was not the first time he had declared himself a widower.

'I'm sorry,' Conrad said, and there was feeling, unfeigned in his eyes. Matthew nodded.

'You knew that, though,' he said.

'Yes,' Conrad said. 'Of course I knew.'

'I just thought,' Matthew said. He gulped. Here in this restaurant, this unfamiliar good restaurant, something was sticking in his throat. It was not emotion, but only, he was sure, food. He wanted to say something, and could only say what everyone knew. He wanted to say something truthful, and food, surely, was getting in the way, some lump of bread, some fishbone.

'Are you all right?' Conrad said.

'Yes,' Matthew said. 'It was nothing. I can't remember what I was going to say.'

'No one's sending you messages, are they?' Conrad said. 'Offensive messages?'

'No,' Matthew said. 'No, nobody. It doesn't matter.' Sometimes you understand events as they happen; sometimes you understand too late to respond to them and have to live with your understanding. Lunch was over. They got up.

The Persians sewed mirrors into their hunting nets, and caught small birds with their own reflections. And this Net too, was mirrored. He had thought that he was looking at the world, and beyond this world, and all the time, like a trapped and fluttering lark, he had only seen himself, and the fluttering and brilliant sudden movements which had appeared to him were only his own last movements, bringing not freedom, nothing new, no change, but the last desperate gestures of one confined and caught.

He made his way back to Suffolk. He took a taxi to the station, making no communication with the driver. He got on the train to Cambridge, and noticed only that it was full at the beginning and emptied slowly at each stop, like a full stage gradually revealing the protagonist of the drama. He got in his car, at Cambridge, and drove. The whole journey took three hours. He stopped his car outside the blank house, and got out. The sky was blackening with clouds, black and weighted as zinc. He stood there for a moment. The house was empty, and night was coming on, and, as he stood, a light in an upstairs room flicked on. It was the timer switch, but it made him jump. The house, empty, had its own life now. It would continue with its on and off, indifferent to human presence or absence. He went towards the front door, having nowhere else to go, and as he put his hand on the doorknob, there was a thunderous certainty in him that here was no ghost, here was no torturing outside presence, but only himself. In his house, and in his head. No ghost, nothing but the great mirrored Net, seeming to offer him the thought of possibilities, of other torments which might have been spared him, and showing him only himself. In his head and his house, there would always be the pain, the grief, the truth, and he contemplated the consolation of a ghost with the unarguable knowledge that there was nothing as good and kind as that here; the unarguable familiarity with the unnameable thing which could search the great invisible universe, and, in less than a second, infallibly find him.

GOD

When I got halfway down the stairs I realised I had the shoes on the wrong feet. Then I stopped and I sat down and I took them off and I put them on the right feet.

Then I realised that I not only had the shoes on the wrong feet, but I had the wrong shoes on the wrong feet. These were shoes I had never seen before. These were ankle boots which had been covered with silver glitter. They were decidedly the wrong shoes. They were someone else's shoes.

This seemed to be happening to me more and more often lately. I took the unmorning-like shoes off and left them on the unfamiliar staircase.

When I came back into the room in which I had been sleeping, I opened my eyes for the first time, properly, and sustainedly. I noticed that the room had something of the smell of a wet camel. Oh, I thought. It was a room I do not think I had seen before, and it got me thinking of all those rooms I had recently been sleeping in without recognising them when I finally woke.

It was a red room. It had been painted red. The ceiling was low and the walls were hung with pictures. Whoever had painted the room had not been a professional painter, I hope, since against the ceiling – the ceiling was white, or intended to be white – there were odd splashes of red as the enthusiastic roller or brush had worked its way up and soiled, ruined everything. The paintings were Indian or Eastern anyway miniatures. I knew nothing about them. I admired them, slightly painfully.

After a while standing in someone else's underpants looking at these things – too loose, the underpants, I had the waistband round my fist to keep the things up – looking at this ugly room I realised two things. One was that the pain in my head was coming from the fierce orange afternoon light outside the mauve curtains.

Then I wondered what I was doing in my underpants and trying to put shoes on anyway.

The second was that there was a boy in the bed in which I had slept. He was unmoving. More than that; he was far from moving. He did not seem to be breathing or moving or anything. Just pale and blond and face down and still. This had not happened to me before. When I woke up after these nights, I was in general alone. And in general I was alone without a woman.

If you see what I mean. I thought of Angela.

I shrugged in a solitary way, as if trying out the manoeuvre for the first time, and I rubbed the back of my head. There was something crusty on the back of my head. I had the feeling it was the same crusty stuff which now was brown and vile on the pillow which the blond boy wasn't sleeping on. I think that's right; I think it was blood.

My head hurt; God it hurt; the thwacking with clubs of great invisible dwarfs. And my dick. I was suddenly aware; sore as anything. I preferred not to think of that. The blood came off like the crusting of crustaceans; a phrase that came to mind. Still the boy didn't move, thank heavens, and I did not know where I was.

The room was bigger and more elegant than many rooms I had been in in similar circumstances in recent months. The bed, I suddenly saw, was quite a good one. None of your MFI. It was walnut or cork or that tree in Africa which grows upside down, but carved beyond the call of duty with cupids and cherries and so on. I did not know what I had been doing falling asleep in such a bed. I stood and looked at it. There was a telephone next to it; a white one.

It made me recall a conversation I had had once with Angela. I mentioned her I think.

'In the nineteen-thirties,' she said, as we were walking down the vertically carpeted corridors of some cinema as the crackly trumpets of credits sounded reproachfully after us, 'the Italian film industry made a great deal of money producing films about the rich for the benefit of the poor. They were all about how wonderful these glamorous women were, and how beautiful the flats they lived in were. But they made them for poor people living in provincial towns just to keep them quiet and to make them happy because there were people who lived beautiful lives.'

'Mm hmm,' I said. Angela knew things; it was as well not to interrupt her in flow.

'Anyway, they have this very good phrase for them, these films, in Italian. They call them white telephone movies. Because there's always a scene where the woman answers the telephone in her dressing gown, and it's white, a white telephone. Most of the people who saw these movies wouldn't have had a telephone or knew anyone who had one, and when they saw one, it would have been black. So a white telephone is like the ultimate symbol of glamour and difference and aspiration.'

'There was a white telephone in that film we saw on Friday,' I said.

'Yes,' she said patiently, 'although that was an American film made this year. I think it's different.'

'And my telephone is white,' I said.

'But I don't suppose anyone is going to make a film about your life and pretend it's glamorous,' she said. She could have saved me; but even I knew that she could not save me now. Here I was in a room I had never seen before with a white telephone by the bed. It reminded me for some reason that I had a job which I ought to go to. Then I felt again the crusty stuff encrusted in my hair and I realised there was no point in even trying.

But I felt I ought to try to telephone them, the office I worked in, and out of nowhere came the number. Two one nine five seven six six. I picked up the phone and dialled it. There was a long strange silence and a quick strange noise, and then a voice spoke.

The thing was, that I couldn't understand what the voice was saying. It wasn't a voice I recognised. It was speaking to me but it made no sense. The noises it made I could not reconcile into words.

'Hello,' I said, but my tongue too was strange and heavy in my mouth. And then I went on speaking, saying I couldn't come in, that I was ill. The voice went on back at me.

Something very strange had happened to me. I could not understand. I could hardly speak. Everything had gone. I closed my eyes against the voice, jabbering, and it was into the room behind me that I felt as if I were falling. I tried to say again that I was ill, that I couldn't come to the office, but a strange climax in the voice on the telephone came, a climax I could not understand. There was a heavy click and then the buzz of having been hung up on. I held the receiver for a moment, shaking, and with the other hand I felt the wound behind me. It was worse than I thought. Everything was worse. Nothing made sense. I did not know where I was or how I got here and I could not comprehend the words that were spoken to me. I felt my left hand with my right, and then the right with the left. They seemed all right. The word *stroke* came to me. I was thirty-four.

Shaking, I got up. Opening the windows was too much; the shadow of light that was cast on the heavy curtains from outside was already too much. I wondered briefly, but without concern, whether the boy still had life in him.

The boy puzzled me. This had not happened before. I looked for a second at him; the face-down rump of him, the curve of his down-sprinkled back, his unmoving side and the scrub of blond hair, so quiet in the room with me. The strange thing was that there were no clothes in the room, none cast off, or only a few fragments of mine. There were no clothes which might belong to him, apart from the grey underpants I wore and the spangled boots I had cast off; just the pile of my suit and my briefcase.

I sat down again on the bed and took my briefcase. That

would help; I kept things in it. I opened it with its familiar click, and looked at the unfamiliar contents. It was full of money.

When I say full I mean full. There were neat piles of twenty-pound notes, I don't know how many. The thick bricks of bright dyed paper meaning so much and so thick and damp in the hand. I sat for a long time, thinking and thinking and thinking.

Then I stopped thinking and I emptied my briefcase of all this money. When it was in a pile on the floor, I sorted it, and I began to count the bricks. There were forty of them. Then I took a single brick and I undid the rubber band around it, and I counted the notes which were in that single pile. There were one hundred of them exactly. I sat and looked and tried to think. God was it difficult. You can work it out.

There was an immense noise like a dugong surfacing.

'I thought,' the boy said, raising himself, eyes closed, from his unstained pillow, 'when were you going to get up. I was really thinking about it.'

'I can't remember,' I said, and stopped.

'You do not surprise me,' he said. 'I can.'

'Tell me something,' I said. It suddenly struck me that his accent was French, the seducer or the waiter in a bad farce. I had no idea where I had found him, or why.

'Oh, not now,' he said. 'That's just what you wouldn't stop saying, all yesterday, all last night, and all night. I don't know what I'm doing talking to you.'

'No,' I said. 'In your place I wouldn't either.'

Conversation lapsed for a while. Everything was hurting and bright.

'Tell me something.'

'No,' he said. 'You tell me something. I want to sleep some more.'

'Did we –'

'Yes,' he said. 'You, you love God too much.'

'I love God too much?'

'You know God.'

'I think so.'

'I don't know why you have God with you. You want only God, last night. All night. Terrible.'

'God?'

'You don't understand,' the boy said. '*Godes, godes, godes*. Here is *gode*.' He reached beneath the bed, and pulled out a black rubber phallus of terrifying size and dimensions. I closed my eyes; I could hardly look at a tool which I could not remember, but as I closed my eyes, my body remembered it for me with a splendid burst of suffering and shivering thrill.

'Too much,' he said, collapsing back on to the bed. 'Has Jack been here?'

'No,' I said.

'I think he kills you when he comes here,' the boy said. 'I don't know why you're still here. Why are you still here?'

'Where am I?'

'Istanbul,' he said.

I took this in for a while. I live in Ealing.

'What's your name?' I said.

'What's yours?'

At that point a noise began I needed no help to identify, the horrible ordinary noise of someone banging on the door to the house I was in, wherever I was, and shouting in fuck knows what language. I gathered up the flaring grey underpants of someone else, and went downstairs to face the afternoon and what I knew, what I later discovered to be waiting outside the door, the worst thing imaginable, the worst thing in the world.

ACKNOWLEDGEMENTS

The following editors commissioned and worked on individual stories with unfailing and exemplary sympathy: A.S. Byatt, Tibor Fischer, Simon Frith, Alan Hollinghurst, Christopher Hope, Ian Jack, Duncan Minshull, Lawrence Norfolk, Rowan Pelling, Peter Porter, Alan Ross and Sarah Spankie.

A number of the stories in this book have already appeared elsewhere: 'White Goods' *Vintage New Writing 5* and *The London Magazine*; 'To Feed the Night' *Granta*; 'A Housekeeper' *Critical Quarterly, Telling Stories 4* and *BBC Radio*; 'A Geographer' *Vintage New Writing 4*; 'Quiet Enjoyment' *The Independent*; 'A Chartist' *Sex, Drugs and Rock and Roll*; 'Elektra' *Vintage New Writing 8*; 'Work' *Granta* and *Mail on Sunday*; 'Dead Languages' *Vintage New Writing 6* and *The Oxford Book of English Short Stories*; 'God' *The Erotic Review*.